KRYSTAL

Also by Michael R. Davidson

Harry's Rules

Incubus

The Incubus Vendetta

Caliphate – The Inquisitor and the Maiden

Caliphate - Retribution

To the reader:

This is a work of fiction and the situations described, as well as the characters and their actions are totally imaginary.

As a former intelligence officer the author was required to submit the manuscript of this novel to the Central Intelligence Agency for review prior to publication. Having reviewed the manuscript, as required by law, the CIA instructs that the following statement be made:

"All statements of act, opinion, or analysis expressed are those of the author and do not reflect the official positions or views of the CIA or any other U.S. Government agency. Nothing in the contents should be construed as asserting or implying U.S. Government authentication of information or Agency endorsement of the author's views. This material has been reviewed by the CIA to prevent the disclosure of classified information."

KRYSTAL

Copyright © 2014 by Michael R. Davidson.

MRD Enterprises, Inc.
PO BOX 1000
Mount Jackson, VA 22842-1000
mrdenter@shentel.net

Library of Congress Control Number: pending

ISBN-13: 978-0-692-27471-2
ISBN-10: 0692274715

Front cover illustration from Can Stock Photo, Inc.
Back cover illustration: Arlington County Police badge
Cover design by Michael R. Davidson

Printed and bound in the United States of America.

First printing 2014

PROLOGUE

Ramon Gutierrez was impressed and embarrassed at the same time. His loose cotton slacks, sandals, and loud Hawaiian shirt clashed with the richly refined décor of the law office. It was an alien environment, all mahogany and leather, rich carpeting, soft lighting, individually illuminated paintings on the walls. He sat nervously in a comfortable leather chair directly across from the reception desk behind which sat one of the foxiest blondes he'd seen in a long time. For most of the ten minutes since his arrival he'd alternated between nervously tapping his foot against the floor and surreptitiously admiring the receptionist's sun-kissed skin, imagining tan lines surrounding areas of unblemished white beneath her peach-colored Dolce & Gabanna suit.

The intercom on her desk buzzed, and the receptionist gave him a professional smile and told him that Mr. Cottrell would see him now.

Brian Cottrell was one of the most well-known criminal attorneys and political movers and shakers in Dade County, as the luxurious office suite high in one of Brickell Avenue's tall, shiny glass buildings attested. The reason he was here remained a mystery to Ramon. His boss had simply instructed him to appear at the office, and Ramon was accustomed to taking orders. So here he was.

He knew the attorney. Cottrell had defended him successfully against an assault with intent charge, but this was his first visit to the office. Ramon could never have afforded Cottrell's fee, but that had been handled by his employer, the head of South Florida's most prosperous drug distribution ring. Ramon was an enforcer, not a high-ranking one, but he had proven effective, and his boss took care of his men. His boss was one of Cottrell's best clients.

The door to the attorney's office opened, and the great man himself appeared to usher him inside, silently closing the door after them.

Cottrell's appearance matched the sumptuousness of his office. He was one of those vigorous older men who emanate prosperity, from his handmade shoes to the top of a tanned scalp that was surrounded by a carefully trimmed fringe of white hair. He was in his shirtsleeves with French cuffs folded up to display the gold Rolex on his wrist. Ramon estimated his age at mid-60's, and his generous mid-section hinted strongly at love of the good life. He wondered idly if the lawyer was banging the blond receptionist.

"Have a seat, Ramon." Cottrell indicated a chair, one of a matched leather pair that sat before an ornate mahogany desk with a surface that rivaled an aircraft carrier. The huge expanse of smoked glass behind the desk overlooked a panorama of the Port of Miami to the east and the Atlantic beyond, a very expensive view.

"Would you care for a cigar?"

Ramon blinked away from the view out the window to find Brian Cottrell solicitously leaning over him with an open box of what looked like genuine Cuban Montecristo No. 2 cigars extended in his direction. Ramon cautiously removed one of the fat sticks from the yellow and red box and rolled it between his fingers, appreciatively noting the suppleness of the oily leaf.

Cottrell indicated a silver clipper and butane lighter on the desk and selected a cigar for himself before settling his bulk into the throne-like executive chair behind the desk. With the light streaming through the window behind him, he could have been a god on Mount Olympus, his head surrounded by a nimbus of fragrant smoke. "Would you care for something to drink with that," he said. "Coffee, tea? There's also some fine Flor de Caña rum from

Nicaragua in the bar over there. Anything you'd like, really."

Ramon was desperately struggling to process what was happening. He was unaccustomed to deferential treatment from powerful men. In his narrow world, such men gave orders, and he carried them out. Ramon Gutierrez knew his place. Was he in some kind of trouble, or did this lawyer want something? These were the only reasons people like Brian Cottrell ever spoke to anyone like Ramon Gutierrez. Uncertain of the protocol, he decided he should probably take advantage of the situation. It was the agreeable thing to do. "Sure, could I have a Cuba Libre?"

Cottrell studied him for a moment from beneath clipped eyebrows before rising from behind the desk to amble over to the marble-topped wet bar where he found the aforementioned bottle of rum and mixed it in a tall, cut crystal glass with ice and coke. The lawyer carried the drink to Ramon and pointedly placed a square glass coaster on the desk in front of him, precisely aligning it with the edge of the desktop, before returning to his throne. "I have a proposition for you," he intoned, "a proposition that could allow you to earn a considerable amount of money. Would you be interested?"

The only propositions that promised a lot of money in Ramon's experience involved some sort of illegal activity. The conversation was becoming interesting. Apparently, he was not in trouble. He cautiously sucked down some of the Cuba Libre before answering. It tasted good. Faced with the conundrum of an unlit cigar in one hand and a drink in the other, he slipped the cigar into his shirt pocket, eliciting a Mona Lisa smile from the attorney.

"Sure, Mr. Cottrell. Anything you say."

"Anything?"

The single-word question confirmed that whatever the prosperous *abogado* had in mind, it must be illegal. This time Ramon took a long draught of the rum and coke and let the cool sweetness slide down his throat before answering. "Sure."

"Good." The attorney squinted at him for a second and his initial solicitousness was replaced by a serious mien. "I want you to kill someone for me."

Ramon sucked in some air, almost choking on the rum and coke. Could this be a trap of some kind? No, of course not. There was no reason he could think of. This was a serious proposal, and, more importantly, it represented a big step up. His boss used him as an enforcer, but so far he'd not "made his bones." He only roughed up people who could not or would not pay what they owed to his boss. Yes, this was an opportunity. Images of himself as a feared and respected member of the underworld shouldered caution out of his brain. He could be smoking Cuban cigars all the time.

"*Si, Señor.*" In his excitement he responded in the language of his native Puerto Rico.

Cottrell settled back into his chair with a satisfied grunt. "I'll pay you twenty thousand dollars for the job, ten now and the rest when it's completed."

Ramon was impressed. This was four times the going rate for murder in Miami.

Michael R. Davidson

All that remained was to learn the identity of the intended victim.

CHAPTER 1

She had never physically harmed another person in her life, let alone killed anyone, although in a perverse way she had imagined it – wondered what it would be like to take another's life. Now she would find out. She had been left with no choice.

How it would feel afterwards? There was no doubt she would pull the trigger, but she wondered if she would be overcome by guilt. In the end, however, it had been curiously anticlimactic. The only emotion she experienced was relief at the elimination of a threat.

She knew the venue well, and she'd planned carefully. *Keep your face down away from the cameras. Hide from the cameras.*

The litany repeated itself over and over like some inane jingle from a television commercial that you can't get out of your head. She made her way through the corridor to the bank of elevators, head down, shielding herself from observation.

Don't run. Don't draw attention.

She got off on the second floor and took the stairs the rest of the way down to the ground floor, then flitted over the same route she had used to enter the hotel to a side entrance. The late spring night sky was clear, and the blooms on the dogwoods planted at intervals along the hotel perimeter glowed dimly in the moonlight. This was a night meant for lovers, not murder. Keeping to the shadows she quickly covered the five blocks to where she had left her car.

Her heart still beat a staccato tattoo against her ribs when she finally settled behind the steering wheel, but she was filled with a sense of exhilaration. She let down a window and sat for several minutes, immobile, breathing the sweet evening air in and out through her mouth like a long-distance runner after a marathon until she achieved a modicum of calmness.

The look on his face!

She had rehearsed what she would do once inside his room. It had to be fast with no warning, no words. Nothing he could have said would have made a difference anyway. Make sure she was too close to miss, draw the revolver from the large bag she carried, aim, and fire. *Get out quickly in case the shot attracts attention.*

Her aim had been surprisingly perfect, placing the bullet squarely in the middle of his forehead. He had been standing only a few steps in front of her and had started backwards when she pushed the gun toward his face. When she'd stretched out her arm the muzzle of the pistol had been only a few feet from him.

She'd feared the old gun might not be up to the job. It was small caliber, and she had no idea when the bullets had been purchased, but it was all she had, and she was certain it could not be traced. That was important. It had been her grandfather's "varmint gun," a Harrington and Richardson 626, six-shot .22 caliber revolver, manufactured in Gardner, Massachusetts in 1979. The company had ceased to exist in its original form in 1986. The gun was untraceable.

She'd expected him to fall immediately, but he hadn't. He had stood there teetering with the neat, round hole in his forehead beginning to ooze crimson for what seemed an eternity, a look of confusion and surprise frozen on his face. She imagined the bullet bouncing around inside his skull turning brain cells to mush destroying delicate neuro-circuitry. He'd actually reached up to find the hole in his forehead and then stretched his right arm out toward her like a blind man groping for support, an act that had horrified her so much she almost had fired a second time. But then his eyes had rolled up until only the whites were showing, and he had teetered backwards onto the floor, his robe flying open to reveal his repulsive nakedness. There was surprisingly little blood. The body twitched and jerked from stray electrical impulses transmitted along his nerves by his dying cerebral cortex before finally going still. She'd feared for a moment that he wasn't dead, but the single shot had done its job.

She recalled standing there staring down at the body of the person who had been capable of doing so much damage to her, who had made her life a nightmare of recalled revulsion and degradation. The man was a pig, and he'd deserved to die like a pig in a slaughterhouse with a piece of metal penetrating his skull.

She'd been in the room only a few minutes and had touched nothing. There would be no trace of her, no DNA, no fingerprints.

Nerves now under control she started the car and drove away, joining the Friday evening traffic. It was shortly after 8:30 PM, and the streets were busy. No one noticed her.

Chapter 2

The room was generously proportioned with a king-size bed, a 42-inch flat screen TV encased in a *faux* walnut wall unit, a desk, and a space occupied by a small table and chairs by the window. The overall effect was impersonal rather than cozy, with anonymous abstract paintings on the walls, imprecise splotches of color calculated to offend no one because they imparted no meaning. The carpet was beige.

In fact, everything in this hotel, from Reception to the rooms, was in tones of brown and beige, yellow and ochre, as though the decorator's palette had been devoid of other colors. Arlington County detective lieutenant Krystal Murphy suspected the choice had something to do with a promise of anonymity. No color is more anonymous than beige, and hotel guests often have reasons for seeking anonymity.

The most prominent feature of this particular room on this night, however, was the dead man on the floor.

She was embarrassed for the corpse.

The detective she had become had long ago shed the natural human revulsion at the sight of mayhem. The blood, the mess, no longer shocked her. But the remains of murder victims suffer indignities the departed souls would abhor. Violent death is an obscenity and the ultimate indignity.

The dead man lay face up on the floor at the foot of the bed in an expensive room at the Crowne Plaza Hotel just a few miles from Ronald Reagan Washington National Airport. The face was that of an older man who had once probably been quite handsome and still retained a certain mature attractiveness. The face held what might be described as an eyes wide open surprised look, possibly due to the hole in the middle of his forehead surrounded by a circle of black, coagulated blood.

The victim wore a thick terry cloth robe furnished by the hotel and nothing else. The robe had flopped open providing a full frontal view of a well-maintained body going soft with age with graying body and pubic hair. The skin was pallid because without the heart to keep it circulating the blood had settled toward the floor and found its level. The bullet had not exited through the back of the victim's head, and

the hotel undoubtedly would be pleased to find no blood soaked into the beige carpet.

Jeff Headley from the Forensic Unit in a pea green disposable sterile jumpsuit and purple nitrile gloves that oddly complemented his thinning ginger hair was kneeling beside the body when she entered the room. A uniformed cop stood guard outside the door.

Headley looked up to greet her and did a double-take worthy of Rodney Dangerfield. He started to say something, and then interrupted himself. "Murphy ... wow!"

The reason for the goofy reception was her iridescent blue, clingy Victor Costa knock-off of a dress some movie star had worn to some glitzy event; her auburn hair was down, and her grandmother's pearls were around her neck. The Tory Burch heels for which she had impulsively paid $275 on sale at Nordstrom were covered by sterile booties she'd put on before entering, but the overall effect evidently was mesmerizing for Headley.

Her colleagues normally saw her in blue-jeans, an Arlington County Police Department polo shirt, sneakers, and a Beretta Px4 Storm .45 caliber pistol on her hip. But tonight she had been called to the scene from what she had planned to be a special evening with a man whose company she was beginning to enjoy. A month earlier her closest friends, Robert and Amy Strachey, had introduced her to Thomas Stewart, a former colleague of Robert when he still worked at CIA. Krystal had resisted at first but finally surrendered to Amy's insistence and found herself pleasantly surprised by her reaction to Thomas. Tonight she had intended to invite him up to her apartment, a momentous decision for her. She hadn't had a serious boyfriend since college. There had been a marriage proposal then, from an earnest young man whom she judged to have been motivated more by infatuation than common sense. She had already seen the wider world during her military service and believed herself to be more mature than the majority of college students. She was preparing a future for herself in law enforcement that would require her full attention.

She kept relationships strictly within her own comfort zone. If things seemed on the verge of becoming "serious," she broke them off. She never dated cops, and since coming to work for the Arlington police her social life had come nearly to a standstill. To her surprise, she was finding the company of Thomas Stewart increasingly pleasant.

The call to report to the crime scene spoiled the plans for this evening. Her position as senior detective in the Homicide/Robbery Unit of the Arlington County Police guaranteed that she would be the one called. All of this conspired to put Krystal Murphy in a bad mood.

It was Saturday night and they had just concluded an intimacy-enhancing meal in a booth at the Palm Restaurant on 19th Street when her cell phone vibrated with the incoming call. Thomas drove her across the 14th Street Bridge and down the GW Parkway to the Crowne Plaza and offered to wait, but she knew from experience that it would be a long night. She'd kissed him lightly and told him to go home. She'd get a ride later in a cop car.

She bent to take a closer look at the corpse and caught a face-full of cologne. The fact that there was no exit wound suggested a low power, low caliber weapon. The shooter had been close, but there was no stippling around the wound. She noted, however, a pattern of small powder burns on the face. The man had been shot point blank from no more than a few feet. The burns were slightly denser on the lower part of the face indicating that the shot had been fired at an upward angle. The shooter had been shorter than the victim.

She turned from the corpse to Jeff Headley. "What's the story?"

Headley waved an arm over the body like a conjurer about to perform a levitation trick, but the dead man remained firmly anchored to the floor. "Krystal, meet Judge Fernando Fernandez, according to the papers in his wallet. He's from Miami." He jerked his head toward the other side of the room. "The wallet and other personal items are over there on the breakfast table. The ID matches the name on the hotel register."

Krystal groaned inwardly. The murder of a judge would bring the press, and the press could muddy up an investigation.

She looked down at the dead face again and thought it looked vaguely familiar. "How long has he been dead?"

Headley raised the dead man's arm which refused to flex and let it drop back to the floor.

"He's in full rigor, and the body's cold. That means he died at least eight hours ago, but it's probably been longer. The air conditioning's cranked. The liver temperature was pretty low, though, so if I had to guess right now, I'd say he's been dead between 18 and 24 hours."

"Since last night, then."

"Yeah."

"Looks like he was killed with a small caliber pistol."

"You're probably right. The bullet didn't blow the back of his head off. It probably bounced around inside his skull and scrambled his judicial brains."

She had a fleeting vision of a brain in a Mix Master. "Who found him?"

"The maid. The room hadn't been tended for over 24 hours so she came in despite the Do Not Disturb sign on the doorknob. People forget to remove them all the time."

Anything in the room that catches your eye?"

"I already dusted for prints and we'll have to compare them with hotel staff. We might get lucky. There's an open bottle of champagne on the table over there and two champagne flutes, both of them filled, but only the judge's prints on them. I checked. You can poke around if you want. He reached into a bag at his side and held out a pair of gloves.

Pulling on the purple nitrile, she went to the table where flat, slightly yellowish liquid sat listlessly in the glasses as devoid of life as was the corpse on the floor. Beside the tray with the wine was an expensive laptop computer, a wallet and a gold Rolex watch. The champagne was Moët et Chandon.

She could feel Headley's eyes following her across the room, trying to read her mind, and probably studying her ass. "Expensive taste," he said, "He was expecting someone, all right."

Krystal's knowledge of champagne vintages was practically nil, despite her name.

Hedley snorted and said, "From the looks of it he was expecting a woman and an evening that did not require a lot of clothing."

She considered this. It was a fair read of the crime scene. "Let's hope we get lucky with the prints, and I'll make sure we get the footage from the hotel security cameras."

She made a final circuit of the room, poking into drawers, closets, the bathroom, but found nothing of interest. There was a bottle of Channel *"Egoiste"* cologne on the counter.

She had a premonition that luck would be an elusive ally.

Michael R. Davidson

CHAPTER 3

By the time she left the Crowne Plaza it was well after midnight. Hotel management had been cooperative and agreed to hand over the disks from the surveillance cameras without a fuss. They would be waiting for her to review as soon as she got into the office. She debated going in tonight, but decided instead to grab a few hours' sleep. Fatigue was unhelpful to investigations.

Krystal had worked hard to cultivate a tough image at work, so hard that she knew there were rumors she was a lesbian, fortified by her steadfast refusal of invitations to go out with fellow officers.

Judging from the sly sidelong glances from the uniformed cop who drove her to her apartment on North Barton Street the image was crumbling fast. She pointedly tugged at the hem of her dress, gritted her teeth, and ignored him as she concentrated on next steps.

The following day she walked through the big, glass doors into the lobby of Arlington Police Headquarters at six A.M. It was Sunday and by this time the drunks from the previous night had been booked and placed in holding cells. The lobby was deserted except for the duty sergeant.

She'd grabbed a large coffee at the Starbucks on North Clarendon Boulevard, a stop that had become a daily ritual, on the way in and carried it to the elevator for the ride to her third floor office. The former head of the Homicide/Robbery Unit, Marty Jefferson, had been promoted to Deputy Chief and moved to head up the entire Criminal Investigation Division, which meant he was still her boss. In an unusual burst of politically correct zeal, the powers that be had promoted Krystal to Lieutenant and put her in charge of Homicide/Robbery. She now occupied Jefferson's former office with its glass wall overlooking the common area bull pen with its array of gray, metal desks. She kept her wall blinds closed most of the time. It was sort of a shield to deflect the resentment emanating from the detectives she had been promoted over. Glaring over their desk tops, they reminded her of malevolent frogs on gray lily pads. But it was her pond now.

Thankfully, the place was empty today.

She generally ignored the resentment. There were only thirty detectives in the entire department, and she didn't give a damn about whether political correctness might have accounted a tad toward her promotion. She deserved the job and was glad it was hers.

She had paid her dues with three years' active duty as an Army MP in Germany and another six months with the Reserves in Iraq. She'd earned a degree in criminology thanks to the GI Bill and had been on the Arlington force for almost ten years, the last three as a detective. Her successful resolution of the two highest profile murder cases in Arlington living memory also had boosted her profile with the bosses and the public.

There were aspects of those cases that had involved the FBI and the CIA that even the bosses knew nothing about and never would. The FBI had twice tried to recruit her away from the police, even offering to pay for her to get a law degree so she could qualify as an agent. But she didn't want to start over. She'd worked with the FBI and the CIA in the past, and they brought enviable resources to the table. But she could never be one of them. She'd glimpsed the peculiar secret parallel universe in which they worked and lived and didn't like it. She was suspicious of people who couldn't say what they did. Deceit was not built into her DNA. The CIA's motto might be "Ye shall

know the truth, and the truth shall make you free."
But truth in their world was a subjective commodity.

The security camera disks from the Crowne
Plaza awaited her in a brown manila envelope in the
middle of her desk. She'd asked the hotel to mark the
one containing footage of the hallway outside
Fernando Fernandez's room and slipped it into the slot
on her computer. The video viewer popped up on her
screen, but she didn't push the 'play' button
immediately.

The interrupted plans for the previous evening
came unbidden to her thoughts, and not for the first
time she reflected that cops shouldn't have personal
lives. She'd seen too many ruined marriages and
alcoholic rejects in the Department. The job required
total dedication, a perfect melding of desire and
performance. Few could meet those requirements, but
Krystal knew that she was one who could. She'd
swum against the current of misogyny in the Arlington
County Police Department to get where she was today.

So what was she thinking when it came to
Thomas Stewart? Was she being fair to him or using
him? She'd been ready to make the transition from
friendship to sex, and she knew he wanted it too. But
this would bring with it a sense of commitment that
would leave her torn between duty and pursuing a
meaningful relationship. Those two words had
connotations that frightened and repelled her. She
sensed that Thomas wanted more than mere physical
intimacy from her, that he was seeking a life partner.
Danger signal!

Her entire life to this point had been one of

commitment to career. She didn't understand where the drive came from. Her childhood in Indiana in no way augured what she was to become. But she'd been restless and couldn't wait to escape the endless flat fields of corn, soy beans, and milo stretching toward the Wabash to find something else, and the Army had promised to take her somewhere else. The more barriers she encountered to advancement, the harder she persevered, the more determined she became.

And now here she was. But was she happy? Did she even want to be? Even the possibility of personal commitment outside her career already was right now distracting her from the job at hand. She shook her head to clear away the stray thoughts and punched the 'play' button so hard that the keyboard jumped.

She arbitrarily chose six PM Friday as the starting point to begin watching the videos and sat back with her coffee to watch hotel guests enter and leave the corridor. There was only one camera covering the area, but the Judge's room was at the end of the corridor giving her a clear view of his door. An hour passed, interrupted only when she switched off the recording to give her eyes a rest and brew a fresh pot of coffee, before anything of interest appeared on the screen.

Judge Fernandez exited the elevator and entered his room shortly after seven PM. In life, he had been a handsome man. He wore a dark suit, and his abundant silver hair was brushed back in a pompadour. He obviously cared for his appearance. There was a smile on his face. Was it anticipation?

Thirty minutes later a hotel waiter appeared pushing a cart containing an ice bucket, glasses, and the bottle of Moët et Chandon that Jeff Headley had pegged as an expensive choice. When the Judge opened the door for the waiter he had removed his jacket and tie. The waiter left the room pushing the empty cart after a few moments stuffing some folded bills into his pocket with a satisfied smile. Fernandez had been a generous tipper.

When the time stamp on the image showed ten past eight a blond woman exited the elevator. Her face was away from the camera and she looked down into the large handbag she carried, her hand rummaging inside for something. She straightened and walked to the Judge's door and knocked. The woman was shapely and well-dressed, and she offered the sort of rear view that would command men's eyes to follow her progress as she crossed rooms.

Krystal was instantly alert and squinted at the screen as the door opened. Fernandez greeted the woman with a broad grin, looking her up and down with obvious approval before standing aside to let her pass into the room. He clapped a splay-fingered hand on her derriere as he closed the door. He was wearing the white terry-cloth robe in which he'd died.

The recording continued, showing the closed door. The woman could be the killer, but it was still early in the evening and at the outside limits of what Jeff Headley had estimated as the time of death.

A few minutes after she'd entered, the blonde came out of the room. She literally backed into the corridor, then ducked her head and walked quickly to the bank of elevators where she turned her back on the camera again as she waited. The doors slid open, and she was gone.

The time stamp showed 8:16 PM.

Krystal rummaged through the surveillance disks until she found the one for the Crown Plaza lobby and slid it into the computer. Two hours later she had established that the woman had entered the hotel via a side door and had at all times kept her face away from the cameras as she pretended to search for something in her handbag.

She would still have to review all the disks, but Krystal was convinced she'd found the judge's murderer.

CHAPTER 4

The sun was touching the horizon by the time she returned to the small apartment on North Barton Street. Krystal remained in the car for a moment scanning the parking lot for anomalies before she opened the door. The previous year she'd been ambushed and knocked unconscious by a serial killer in this very spot, and she vowed never to let her guard down again just because the surroundings were familiar or she was in a hurry.[1]

---

[1] "THE INCUBUS VENDETTA," Michael R. Davidson, 2013

Her eyes hurt and her back was stiff from the marathon review of all the disks from the Crowne Plaza, including the parking garage. The blond woman had not brought a car to the hotel. Crystal City was a long humorless strip of high rises bordering both sides of Jefferson Davis Highway that led south to Alexandria and Reagan National Airport. The suspect probably had parked on one of the side streets well away from the hotel to avoid detection. This had been no crime of passion. It had been meticulously planned and carried out. The killer had likely left no physical clues and had been in and out of the Judge's room in ten minutes. She had known what she was going to do before she went in. A professional hit, maybe? The crime scene gave no indication that it might have been a crime of passion.

Judge Fernandez had greeted the woman with a broad, salacious grin. All that was missing was a dribble of drool from the side of his mouth. He'd obviously been expecting her and had ordered up the bottle of champagne and two glasses in preparation. Had he known his killer? He'd worn only the robe, and the pat on the ass strongly suggested the judge was anticipating an amorous encounter. Was the woman a prostitute? If so, the fact that nothing had been taken from the room was as unusual as the murder. Nevertheless, a discrete check with known escort services would be wise.

The suspect had gone there intending to kill, and that meant there was a motive, which likely meant a previous connection with the victim. The place to start would be the judge's recent movements and his personal life, work backwards until she found something significant. According to his documents he was from Miami. What was he doing in Washington?

Krystal entered her one bedroom apartment and switched on the light. She unclipped the holstered pistol and spare magazines from her belt and laid them on the table beside the door before retrieving a half-full bottle of Laphroaig from under the kitchen counter, a peaty single malt scotch her friend Robert Strachey had recommended highly, describing it nebulously as "the modest man's Lagavulin." She splashed herself a generous dollop and flopped onto the sofa where she leaned back and closed her eyes.

Drinking alone? She considered the glass in her hand and decided it meant she must be a real cop. A job that exposed a person daily to the worst side of human nature demanded some relief.

Belatedly she noticed the message light flashing on the phone and punched the message button. The recording said the first call had come at noon, and the voice was that of Thomas Stewart. He'd left three messages in all, the latest about an hour before she had left the office, and his voice betrayed increasing frustration mixed with disappointment with each call. She should have given him her cell phone number, but she liked to keep that for official business, another manifestation of the separation between her private and professional lives. Who was she kidding? She hadn't had a private life for a long while now.

She should call Thomas, but she couldn't think of anything to say. He would want to see her again, and she wasn't certain she had the time or inclination for it now despite the ambitious plans she had had the night before. Maybe it had been a bad idea and the call to the crime scene had saved her from a mistake.

Her cell phone rang.

The caller i.d. told her it was Sara Hampton, the Arlington County Commonwealth Attorney, the person responsible for prosecuting crimes in County. She been elected to a four-year term two years ago and headed an office comprised of over thirty attorneys, victim specialists, and others.

Krystal sighed. She'd hoped to put off dealing with the Commonwealth Attorney's office until tomorrow when she could present a coherent picture of the crime, as far as she could piece it together. At the moment, after watching hour after hour of security footage since six AM, she wasn't sure she could carry on a coherent conversation with anybody.

Sara would understand if she wanted to put off the formalities until tomorrow. She answered the call.

"Hi, Sara."

"Hi, Krystal. You sound tired, honey." Sara's voice was throaty with the hint of a Southern drawl. She was often mistaken for a man on the phone.

"Another astute observation from our esteemed Commonwealth Attorney." Krystal leaned back into the soft comfort of the sofa and took a sip of the scotch. "Are you calling about the Crowne Plaza thing?"

"You know it. What can you tell me?"

"I'd really rather wait until tomorrow morning, if that's ok. I just got in from the office. All I've been able to do so far is review the security camera footage from the hotel, and that took all day today. Other than providing the CCTV disks, the hotel staff wasn't much help. No one saw anything. I'll need some more time to develop a real theory. I need more time to think."

Sara didn't take the hint. "What does the security footage show?"

"Really, can't this wait 'til tomorrow?"

"No. There's more to this case than you might suspect."

"What does that mean?"

"It's best I tell you face to face, but the victim was a speaker at a conference I attended Friday afternoon. Now he turns up murdered *on my turf*, at the worst time possible, and I'm pissed off. But I still want to know what the security footage shows. Can you identify the killer?"

"The 'worst time possible'?"

"You know what I mean – politics."

Krystal knew what she meant. The Commonwealth Attorney had ambitions beyond her current office. The vic was a prominent personality. *Publicity.*

"Yeah, I know what you mean, Sara. For the time being I can tell you that the murderer is a woman. There was no one else in or out of the vic's room after the last sighting of him alive."

"Is there an identifiable image?"

"Nothing of her face. She was real careful to keep it hidden. She knew where the security cameras are positioned. I don't think the murder was a spontaneous event. She had it planned. But really, can't we leave this until tomorrow?"

Sara relented. "OK, but come see me first thing. I'll keep a half-hour open for you."

"I still won't have any more for you than I have now. I'd like to do some research on the victim first. And we're still waiting for a complete read-out of prints from the scene."

"That's why I need to see you first thing. I want to give you some important background before you get much farther along." *Pregnant pause.* "There are certain, ah, sensitivities you need to know about."

Crap. Was Sara talking about her own 'sensitivities' or some else's? Murphy had learned to be wary of political "sensitivities," something not so simple in and around Washington, D.C. The two biggest cases in her career had had international political implications and had darn near gotten her killed.

Murder was murder whether the motive was sex, politics, or passion. Someone ended up dead, and it was her job to bring the guilty to justice regardless of how it might affect some shit for brains politician's career. Living in a black or white world was a luxury she permitted herself.

"OK, Sara, I'll see you first thing tomorrow."

She sat there in semi-darkness sipping the scotch until the glass was empty, and then dragged tired bones to the bathroom to brush her teeth and change for bed. It was only eight PM, but she was exhausted. The week-end had been a complete bust.

CHAPTER 5

At eight the next morning Krystal rode the elevator two flights up from her own office to the Commonwealth Attorney's suite on the fifth floor. On the floor above was the 17th Judicial Court where Sara Hampton argued her cases.

Sara, resplendent in a Lafayette 148 suit and Stuart Weitzman pumps, rose from her desk and ushered her to a settee at the other end of the office. A silver carafe of fresh coffee and two fine bone china cups and saucers had been laid out for them on the polished coffee table.

Sara's maiden name was Villeneuve, and her middle name was Marie. Her dark good looks betrayed her Mediterranean origins. She had once commented sardonically that if she had had a name like Murphy she would have retained it when she married. Sara was a political animal, and she believed her husband's solidly English name would find greater acceptance among voters than a moniker as suspiciously foreign and difficult for the American tongue as Villeneuve.

A *summa cum laude* graduate of Georgetown Law fifteen years earlier, Sara had worked her way diligently up through the local Democrat Party ranks and the Commonwealth Attorney's office until two years ago she won election to a four-year term as Arlington County Commonwealth Attorney. You didn't do anything in Arlington and you certainly never won an election there if you weren't a Democrat. She had her eye on higher political office, and had confided that her next goal was either a political appointment at the Federal level or a run at the Virginia Senate. She wouldn't turn down a judgeship either.

Krystal felt a kinship with Sara despite the fact that the two could not have been more different. The Commonwealth Attorney was sophisticated and worldly compared to Krystal's secret view of herself as a country mouse. The level of ambition was intense in both, but it had taken them on different trajectories, and perhaps this was why they had become friendly – neither saw a rival in the other. They had worked together successfully, and Sara appreciated the detective's diligence in collecting the evidence required for the convictions that moved her up the ladder.

Sara poured the coffee. "OK, what do you have so far?"

Krystal accepted the fragile cup and saucer carefully and took a sip. She preferred the sturdy mugs in the squad room or a large paper cup from Starbucks. With Sara's bone china in her hand, all she could think about was not dropping it. "Like I said last night, everything points to this unidentified woman as the culprit. But all I can say right now for sure is that she's blond and clever. She apparently entered the hotel via a side entrance and left the same way, on foot. Probably had a car parked some distance from the hotel in Crystal City. And as far as I know she left no trace of herself."

She described the murder scene.

Sara frowned. "You mentioned last night it looked like a premeditated murder. That's unusual for a woman. You think it was personal?"

"Can't say for sure yet. But the motive wasn't robbery. The next step is to research the vic's background and activities. He was a judge, and judges make enemies. CSU ran a quick check last night but couldn't find any family locally. He was from Miami."

"Yes," said Sara, the frown again creasing her brow, "that's right. I think I can help you get started. I gather you don't know who Fernando Fernandez was."

"Like I said, I haven't had a chance to do a detailed background check yet. I wanted to see the videos first."

"Fernando 'Ferny' Fernandez was Circuit Court judge in Miami, and there were rumors that he was up for appointment to the Third District Court of Appeals. He was a controversial figure throughout his career and rendered a number of unpopular decisions. He was staunchly liberal, excessively so in the opinion of many, and he made a lot of enemies. One of his cases reached national prominence a few years ago. He freed a sex offender, a pedophile, from custody and less than a week later the man kidnapped, sexually molested, and murdered an eleven-year-old girl."

A bell sounded somewhere in the back of Krystal's mind, and she dispatched a search party of neurons to find its source. So that's why Fernandez's face had looked familiar. "The Melissa Tandy case," she finally ventured.

Sara smiled and nodded. "Correct. The Melissa Tandy case. Although Judge Fernandez cited sound legal reasons for releasing a known pedophile, Fred Cummings, on his own recognizance, he was widely excoriated in the Right Wing media, especially Talk Radio, for the decision. There was an ultimately unsuccessful campaign to remove him from the bench. Melissa Tandy's grieving parents were on television a lot, and quite a lot of hostility was directed at the Judge. He was even given police protection for a while. More recently his potential ascension to the Third District raised a lot of hackles, and the Tandy case was dragged through the media again."

"I remember the case now. It was horrible, and I thank Heaven that I've never had to handle one like it here. What you're saying is that we might find a motive there? There could be a political angle?"

"Correct. There's more, of course, in Judge Fernandez's professional record that would enrage the Right. Give the increasing polarization in this country and the rise of Right Wing hysteria it's possible we have a politically inspired murder on our hands."

"It would make for a large pool of suspects if you think the Tea Party killed him."

"I'm not saying that, but it's not beyond the realm of reasonable speculation. Right now, aside from your description of the mystery woman in the security videos, we have no idea who killed the Judge or why. The history suggests it could be a member of the Tandy family or someone close to them. That's why you need to give the case priority over anything else you're doing and narrow down the list of suspects. We can't allow generalized accusations that would enflame public sentiment to surface. The press is going to have a field day with this, and I want to stay at least one step ahead of them."

Sara gave her an encouraging smile.

"You're the best we have, Krystal, and I want us to work on this closely together. We need to resolve it and get it behind us."

Flattery was not an especially effective motivator for Krystal, but she appreciated it coming from the Commonwealth Attorney. "What you've told me just makes it more complicated. What was he doing up here? You mentioned last night that he spoke at some conference?"

Sara placed her cup and saucer on the coffee table, stood and walked to her desk from which she plucked a glossy folder. She displayed the cover as she returned to the settee. "This is why he was in town. I heard to him speak there Friday afternoon."

The cover of the folder showed the logo of the American Civil Liberties Union and announced a conference at the Washington Hilton on "Modernity and the Evolving Constitution."

Krystal shuddered inwardly at the term "evolving Constitution." New interpretations of old principles, in her view, undermined the system and tilted it in unexpected directions like the shifting foundations of that leaning tower in Italy. Enough shifts, and eventually it would topple. A mid-western upbringing had produced in her a black and white view of the world, but the legal system in which she now worked was a labyrinth of unexpected twists and turns. In any event the ACLU was not the favorite organization of cops.

"This was the conference you attended?"

Sara gave her a lopsided smile. "One of the costs of admission to the club. I have to pay my dues."

"Mmm. Did you see anything relevant to the case? Any odd behavior?"

Sara glanced at her watch to signal that the time allotted for their *tete-a-tete* was coming to an end. "There was a cocktail mixer after the speeches. Fernandez spoke to a number of people. He was a well-known personality and he was on the make for support to move up to the Court of Appeals. He acted normally enough as far as I could tell. He wasn't even supposed to be making a presentation, but there was a last minute cancellation and the organizing committee asked him to step in. You won't find him listed in the brochure as a speaker."

"He didn't get into an argument with anyone? Should I talk to any attendees?"

"Everything looked amiable to me. I doubt you'll find anything useful along those lines. He was in his element with that group, but I can make some inquiries, if you like. They're more likely to talk to me than to you, and it'll give you more time to pursue more likely avenues of inquiry."

Krystal had no desire to question members of the ACLU. "That sounds good to me."

CHAPTER 6

Frank Tandy leaned rigidly forward in his chair and stared intensely at the screen of the 10-year-old television for a full minute in concentrated silence as he processed the information that had been breathlessly announced on the Channel 7 News. It was Sunday morning in Miami, and a dark suit hung loosely from his spare frame, augmented by a threadbare white shirt, and a narrow black tie – the only one he owned. His wife, Charlotte, was still in the bedroom of their mobile home getting ready for church.

They were regular attendees of services at the Wayside Baptist Church on Southwest 98th Street where Charlotte sang in the choir. But the emotions that now flooded Frank and electrified his nerves were anything but Christian.

"Charley!" he shouted, his voice hoarse with excitement. "Someone shot the bastard! He's dead!"

Charlotte stepped out of the bedroom, still clipping on her earrings. "What did you say?"

Frank sprang from the chair to face her, shaking with repressed emotion.

"It's Fernandez. Someone shot him dead in Washington."

Charlotte gripped his arm, letting one earring drop unnoticed to the floor. "Oh, my Lord! Who did it?"

"They don't know, but the sonuvabitch finally got what he deserved."

"Frank, don't talk like that. You know you shouldn't." Fat tears began to roll down her cheeks leaving tracks in her freshly applied make-up. "It won't bring Melissa back."

Frank stood and wrapped his arms around his wife's ample shoulders. "The Lord works in mysterious ways. I can't feel any regret for Fernandez, and the Bible says 'a tooth for a tooth and an eye for an eye.'"

"That was the Old Testament, Frank. We're New Testament folk."

"I can't help the way I feel."

Frank's eyes were drawn to the large photograph in a silver frame that stood on an occasional table near a window. The picture had been taken five years before, when Melissa was eleven and Dawn, their older daughter was fifteen.   Frank remembered taking the photo. It had been just after Melissa's team had won a soccer game, and Dawn was hugging her sister as the two grinned happily into the camera.

The two had been very much alike, and anyone could tell at a glance that they were sisters. Both had inherited their mother's blond good looks. Charlotte had once been slender and beautiful like the girls in the photo.

Melissa's kidnapping and brutal murder had aged them both beyond their years, and the pounds had piled up on Charlotte to make manifest the weight of her grief. The Tandy's were only in their early 50's, but each looked a decade older. What had happened to Melissa had changed everything.

They'd been living in a small house in Coconut Grove at the time. Fred Cummings lived two houses away, and no one in the neighborhood had been aware of his history of child molestation. There had been no warning from the authorities. And then one warm day in September Melissa had disappeared. The police, better informed than the Tandy's and their neighbors, had arrested Cummings within just a couple of days, but it was another ten days before their daughter's decomposing body had been discovered buried in a shallow grave in a public park near Coral Gables. Frank would never forget the ordeal of identifying Melissa's body. He had insisted on seeing it, but only the dirt-encrusted clothes and the silver bracelet she had won at the Bible Bowl for memorizing Bible verses were recognizable. The sight of his young daughter's skeletonized remains still haunted Frank's sleep every night.

Cummings confessed he had lured Melissa into his house where he had raped and strangled her. The fact that only a few days earlier he had been in custody on a charge of attempted child molestation and had even served time for a similar offense in another state but was still set free on his own recognizance by Judge Ferny Fernandez had caused a stir of indignation in the community. The judge had determined that Cummings's behavior did "not rise to the level of conduct which would make him a menace to the health and safety of others" and released him on a mere ten thousand dollar bond.

Cummings had been sentenced to death for Melissa's murder but still waited on Florida's Death Row as his appeals ran out.

Frank Tandy launched a personal crusade with the help of a popular local conservative talk show host. Although ultimately unsuccessful in disbarring the Judge, the campaign did achieve national prominence, and occasionally Frank was still asked to speak at rallies. He'd been active in supporting the passage of the Jessica Lunsford Act in Florida. He had never minced words in voicing his opinion of liberal judges and Judge Ferny Fernandez in particular.

CHAPTER 7

Frank Tandy was not a physically imposing person. He was thin and the deep lines carved into his leathery face bespoke a life of hard labor out of doors. That he was not well-off or sophisticated was immediately evident from his pure Florida cracker accent and the cheap, ill-fitting suit. But his fierce emotions flared like supernovas from his eyes as he denounced Ferny Fernandez and declared that even now he could not find it in his heart to forgive the Judge.

Krystal Murphy had no sooner returned from the meeting with Sara Hampton than Tandy's appearance had been announced on CNN. Murphy was certain that Sara was glued to the television in her office upstairs, as well. The murder already was receiving national attention.

The TV reporter asked, "Don't you have any regrets, Mr. Tandy, that the hatred your campaign aroused around the country against Judge Fernandez might well have inspired his killer?"

Tandy was being interviewed outside his mobile home in a Miami trailer park. The sun cast bright, dusty rays through the branches of the cypress trees in the background as he averred to the reporter that Ferny Fernandez had surely been turned away from the Pearly Gates and directed into the fires of eternal damnation. "I have no more regret," he concluded, "than I will when they stick the needle into Cummings's arm."

She switched off the set. That was the kind of deep-seated hatred nurtured by grief that could drive one person to kill another. But if Frank Tandy was involved, why had he waited so long, and why do it so far from familiar territory? And who was the woman in the security footage?

She sighed deeply. The Tandy family had suffered a terrible loss at the hands of a heinous murderer. They were victims, yes, but she had to put them at top of her suspect list for possible involvement, if not the murder itself. Frank Tandy could have had help. Florida was home to a disproportionate number of radical armed anti-government groups of every stripe and color, and she wondered if he belonged to one. Profiling might be frowned upon, but he fit the stereotype.

She would need the assistance of the Miami-Dade Police Department.

Miami-Dade had a large criminal investigations division that included a Homicide Bureau and a Sexual Crimes Section. They would have extensive information on file regarding the Melissa Tandy case and the Tandy family. The Fernandez case had begun in Miami, and it might well end there, but the murder had occurred in Arlington, and it was up to Murphy to request Miami-Dade's assistance.

A call to Miami put her in touch with a cooperative employee of the Florida Homicide Clearing House, a sub-division of Miami-Dade's Homicide Bureau, and she secured a promise that all files relating to the Tandy case would be forwarded to her in Arlington.

She was then put in touch with Detective Ray Velazquez of the MDPD's Specialized Investigations Squad who proved anxious to learn the details of the case. When she told him the murderer had been a woman, Velazquez said, "That's hardly surprising."

"What do you mean?"

"Old Ferny had a reputation with the ladies. His favorite sport was grab-ass, if you'll pardon the expression."

Krystal recalled the video image of the Judge's hand groping the derriere of the woman as she entered his hotel room. Velazquez's comment opened a second line of speculation that could prove fertile.

"You think one of his 'ladies' might have done him in? Anyone special you can think of?"

"As far as I know Ferny didn't make enemies of the ladies. He was a pretty generous guy. He liked 'em too much, and there's never been a dust-up as far as I know. Except, of course, for his divorce, but that was years ago."

She explained her speculation that Frank Tandy might be associated with an extremist group of some sort that had helped him avenge his daughter's death.

Velazquez barked a laugh that contained little in the way of humor. "Well, Florida's the right place for it, unfortunately. The state usually comes out first or second on anybody's list of states with the most hate groups. At last count there were forty-three of them spanning the gamut from extreme Left to extreme Right. And terrorism seems to be an equal opportunity pastime. We'll look into it. And you might be getting a call from the State authorities."

As she had anticipated, with Fernandez being such a well-known figure in Miami, the MDPD was more than willing to cooperate. Velazquez promised to set an investigation in motion right away.

She called Sara Hampton and filled her in.

"Your idea about a hate group of some kind is a good one, Krystal. They do have affiliations across state lines. I hadn't thought of that angle, probably because the killer was a woman. Most of the groups in Virginia are extreme right wing racists. There is the fact that Judge Fernandez was a Latino."

"Yeah, that's true. Maybe there's some sort of link-up between a group here in Virginia and one in

Florida." A thought occurred to her. "Sara that would be an inter-state conspiracy and that would bring in the FBI."

There was a pause before Sara said, "Let's not jump to conclusions and invoke the RICO statutes just yet. If there was a conspiracy that crossed state lines the Feds would come in, but Fernandez sat on a state bench, so they have no role unless we uncover hard evidence of a conspiracy. We can bring them in later if we have to. Let's not make this more complicated than it has to be. Just keep doing what you're doing and let me know what turns up."

Krystal had to smile despite herself. Sara Hampton's hesitation about bringing in the Feds was due to the high profile nature of the Fernandez case and what it would mean to her politically if she could carry out a successful prosecution. Sara didn't want to hand anything over to the Feds if she didn't have to.

"There's something I forgot to mention," said Sara.

"I'm listening."

"There was a small group of demonstrators outside the hotel at the ACLU conference. Not unusual, but you never know."

"I'll check with the Metropolitan PD to see if they had the event covered."

CHAPTER 8

Krystal placed a call to Marty Jefferson. She resigned herself to this being a day consigned to phone calls, official requests, and reading files. This was not a list of her favorite things.

Jefferson answered after the first ring. His well-oiled voice slid down the line to fill her ear.

"Lieutenant Krystal Murphy! Congratulations on the promotion."

"I owe it all to my previous boss," she said and almost meant it. She didn't doubt that Jefferson had recommended her for the job. He was almost as adept at advancing others as he was at advancing himself.

He could be generous that way, so long as there was something in it for him. The cases she had solved while working for him hadn't exactly hurt his career, and promoting a female had enhanced his PC credentials.

Jefferson laughed. "You're too modest, Krystal. It's not a particularly good trait for someone who wants to get ahead."

"Right now I just want to get ahead on this case, Marty. I need some help from the Metro cops."

She could almost see Jefferson shaking his head smiling to himself like a man who possessed all the secrets in the world, a guru in a cave in a Tibetan mountainside. "Straight to the point, as usual. Go ahead and call them. If you need to back up your request, let me know."

Her next call was to Sam Becker, her contact in D.C.'s Metropolitan Police Department.

"There was an ACLU conference at the Washington Hilton a couple of days ago. You've undoubtedly heard about the homicide at the airport Crowne Plaza Saturday night. Our victim was at that conference. Were you guys covering it?"

The DC cops had a lot of practice covering demonstrations. People might not like the idea that the authorities could take their photos and put them on file for simply exercising their basic rights, but they were on public property and thus exposed to quite legal official observation.

Becker said, "I'll check it out for you. Odds are the public safety guys did cover the event. These days every demonstration is a homeland security matter.

There might even be some video." He promised to get back to her as soon as he had anything.

She'd just begun a Google search of Judge Fernandez that brought up page after page of old media stories, mostly relating to the Melissa Tandy case, when the phone on her desk rang. A glance at the Caller I.D. told her it was Thomas Stewart who by now must have given up calling her home number.

Her hand wavered over the receiver as yesterday's misgivings bubbled again to the surface. But she could not just continue ignoring him. There were not only his feelings to consider, but also those of her friends, the Stracheys. Besides, maybe she really did not want to ignore him. She lifted the receiver from its cradle and put it to her ear. It was only when she heard Thomas's voice that she realized she had remained silent, still lost in her thoughts.

"Krystal? Krystal, is that you?"

"Hi, Thomas. Yes, it's me. I'm sorry I haven't gotten back to you since Friday night. The entire week-end sort of went up in flames."

"I read about it. Is this one of those things that will take you off the grid until it's finished, or is there a chance I can see you sometime soon?"

"I have a feeling it'll be a while before I can take any time off."

"I see." His voice dropped a scale. "That's not good. I'm leaving on a temporary assignment the day after tomorrow and hoped we might get together before then."

She felt a twinge of anxiety at this. "Where are you going?"

"Can't say."

"Typical CIA," she said and wondered what it would be like to live with someone who could never tell you what he was doing? It seemed like a recipe for disaster.

"C'mon, Krystal, be fair. You can't always say what the cops are up to either. I want to see you again before I leave."

She found herself unable to disappoint him again. He deserved anything but a cold shoulder. "OK, sure."

They set a time to meet for drinks that evening, and when she hung up the phone Krystal silently berated herself for being such a pussy. Why did she feel all girly whenever she talked to this guy?

The records from Florida began to arrive via LEO in the early afternoon - Law Enforcement Online, a secure Internet communications system provided to Law Enforcement by the FBI for "sensitive but unclassified" communications.

Krystal didn't expect the info from DC before tomorrow and was glad to be able to get to work right away. The chances of solving a case diminished in direct proportion to the passage of time, and the magic first 48 hours already had expired.

The MDPD was a big-time operation compared with Arlington, but then Miami's crime problem was a bigger and nastier one, too. The Florida Homicide Clearing House had done a good job organizing the files. Everything from crime scene photos to cops' notebook entries and court records had been reduced to digital media, and there were even mpegs of televised interviews.

The man responsible for the little girl's death, Fred Cummings, had been taken into police custody two days after the disappearance, and it was another ten days before he finally led police to the park where he'd buried the body.

Local and national television had kept the story alive for over a month. The first televised interviews were sadly typical. The grief-stricken, panicked parents could not understand how this had happened. The mother made distraught appeals, almost incomprehensible through her sobs, for their daughter to be returned safely while Frank Tandy stood mutely beside her with his eyes downcast. Prayer vigils were organized at their church.

The pictures broadcast by the media showed that Melissa Tandy had been a pretty little girl with long blond hair and blue eyes. She reminded Murphy of a young Jodie Foster. There was a picture of a gangly Melissa in her soccer uniform grinning into the camera, a happy, spunky girl with her whole life before her. There were family photos, too. The Tandy's two daughters were both blond and beautiful, youthful reflections of what their mother must once have looked like.

Dawn Tandy was five years older than Melissa, which would make her twenty-one now. The promise of real beauty in her teen-age features would by now have blossomed into reality.

Things heated up in the media when Cummings was detained for questioning and his previous release by Judge Fernandez became public knowledge. And all hell broke loose when Melissa's body was found. Both Cummings's confession and forensics made it clear that she had been raped and then strangled to death.

It was at this point that Frank Tandy found his voice, and his charge that Judge Fernandez was as guilty of his daughter's murder as Cummings resonated with and was amplified by the right-leaning media. Animosity toward Fernandez was whipped to such a fury that the Judge required police protection.

The confession guaranteed a foregone conclusion to Cummings's trial, but he still languished today on Florida's death row as the standard appeals process ran its course. Because of the near hysteria of the public outcry the ACLU provided his defense *pro-bono* claiming he could not have received a fair trial in Miami.

CHAPTER 9

She'd agreed to meet Thomas Stewart at 7:00 PM in the bar at The Four Seasons in Georgetown. The CIA man liked upscale locales, maybe because he was trying to impress her, maybe because he had a James Bond fetish. In any event Krystal knew she would be late as she ransacked her meager evening wardrobe for something appropriate to wear, finally settling on a plain black sleeveless dress.

The outfit provided no space to conceal her service pistol so she dropped her back-up weapon, a conveniently sized S&W Bodyguard .380, into the small handbag she'd selected and rushed out of the apartment.

Forty-five minutes later she placed an "official police business sign" in the windshield of her Ford, and left the unmarked police car parked illegally on M Street to hoof it a half-block to The Four Seasons. The hotel had an excellent valet service, but she wasn't going to let them mess with a cop car.

The Four Seasons is a venue preferred by celebrities, and she'd never been inside a room here. The outside was nothing special, but judging by the hotel's reputation, the rooms must be sumptuous. The vast, marbled lobby was a beehive of activity, but failed to impress her as anything but utilitarian. The bar was in a raised area at the rear of the lobby, where she found Thomas at a table in a corner. He stood when he saw her, his perfect teeth displayed in a pleased grin, and pulled out a chair for her like the perfect gentleman. He was handsome by anyone's definition, a shade over six feet, an unruly mop of thick, brown hair that had been bleached by the sun, and broad shoulders that tapered to a narrow waist. His skin was tanned to a Hollywood perfection that was not artificial. She suspected he was spending a lot time somewhere the sun shone a lot.

They embraced lightly before she sat, and he brushed her cheek with his lips. Murphy felt a flush of pleasure rising up her neck that embarrassed her.

"Sorry I'm late. Work."

"I've been reading about it. The story in the Post even mentioned that you were heading the investigation. You're famous. How's it going?"

"Still looking for evidence. There's a lot of information about the victim, but nothing that would identify his murderer." This was not entirely true, but no one but she and Sara knew about the video.

They ordered drinks. Murphy was amused that he ordered a dry martini straight up with olives. Maybe he really did have a James Bond fetish. She asked for a Heineken.

"So, you're leaving again?"

"'Fraid so."

He'd disappeared on such trips twice before during the month they had known one another, but was never away for more than a few days. She had the impression his absences were connected with something he'd been involved with a long time before they met.

"Still can't say where you're going?"

He looked ruefully into his drink, as though his 'need to know' credo embarrassed him. "'Fraid not. Sorry."

"You don't have to be sorry. Creepy secrecy is part of the spook trade, isn't it?"

"It's our stock in trade," he said with a sudden boyish grin, "It makes us mysterious and irresistible to young women."

Murphy raised an eyebrow at him, but said nothing. She was too tired to engage in meaningless banter.

He studied her face for a moment. "You don't like the secrecy, do you?"

"It can be annoying."

"Sorry. Can't be helped."

"I know," she sighed, beginning to think it had not been a good idea to meet him, after all.

"Do you know what the motto of the Mossad is, the Israeli secret service?"

"No."

"'By deception thou shalt make war.' The CIA's motto is 'Thou shalt know the truth, and the truth shall make you free.' Do you think the concepts are incompatible?"

"I don't like deception. It's what criminals do to escape justice."

"Justice can be very subjective. I suspect that's especially true for the Israelis."

"But not in my business. There's right and there's wrong. People with things to hide are usually on the wrong side of the law."

"Different set of conditions altogether."

"There's right and there's wrong," she repeated. They'd had this discussion before, and she didn't feel like having it again. She was tired and preoccupied. She thought again that she shouldn't have agreed to see him tonight.

"That's an absolutist point of view. Outside the laws of physics there are few absolutes in the world. For example, here in the United States I would never consider breaking the law you are sworn to uphold. I'm an American, and so far as my own country is concerned I see right and wrong exactly the same as you. But part of my job is to steal the secrets of other countries. In a way you could say that every second I'm overseas I'm engaged in criminal activity."

"I know." Thomas was trying hard to convince her to see things his way. Perhaps she was too one-dimensional. Was the world really a jungle as these CIA men saw it? Did she have to accept Thomas's cynical world view to love him?

Had that thought really just crossed her mind? Why did it frighten her so? She knew the answer, of course. She didn't mind being alone. She was independent, both by choice and the circumstances of her career. And she treasured the freedom that condition bestowed upon her. She'd received no special considerations in her life and had made of it what she wanted. The compromise of independence implicit in a serious relationship frightened her. And Thomas was not the sort of man who would sacrifice himself and his career to become an accessory to her own, the way Fred Hampton had done for Sara.

"Can we change the subject, please, Thomas? My mind is engaged in trying to solve a murder, and I'm not sure there's room for philosophical debate right now."

He frowned and leaned back in his chair, his eyes searching for a hint of her thoughts. She wondered what he saw when he looked at her – a potential conquest, a possible mate for life, children and a sunny garden?

"This isn't what I wanted to talk about, either," he said, and placed his hand over hers on the table. She didn't draw it away. "It was important to me that I saw you before I left."

How should she respond to this? If she asked why it was important to him he might say something she was not ready to hear, ask a question she was unprepared to answer. She softened her tone and steered a neutral course.

"I'm glad you called. I wanted to see you, too."

"So," he said, relaxing, "the Colts haven't done much since Manning left." Perhaps he read her mood better than she realized and decided to lighten the conversation, put off more serious things, relationship things, to a more propitious moment.

Murphy was a dyed in the wool Indianapolis Colts fan, and their star quarterback had been traded a couple of years earlier after a season on the bench with injuries.

She snorted. "And now just look at Denver."

The tension dissolved, and they spent the next hour avoiding serious subjects, although Thomas's eyes retained the look of a man seeking something he feared might not be there, trying to peer into her soul.

Suddenly regretting the way she was treating this good man, she considered inviting him back to her apartment for that frolic she had planned for Friday night. But it was not to be.

He looked at his watch, a rugged, battered stainless steel Rolex GMT Master, and shook his head. "Sorry, Krystal, but I have to go. I fly out of Andrews at midnight."

Andrews Air Force Base in near-by Maryland. He wasn't flying commercial.

He walked her back to her car and stood on the curb as she drove away. He'd kissed her passionately, and the vision of the pensive look on his face stayed with her all the way home.

CHAPTER 10

By nine A.M. Tuesday morning Murphy was on her third cup of coffee, having already fielded a call from the Chief of Police who had interrogated her for ten minutes about progress in the Fernandez case as though he suspected she might have solved it and not told him. TV cops always solve all their cases and solve them quickly between commercial interruptions. Reality was much less efficient. Arlington had seventeen cold case murders going back to 1970, and the crime resolution rate was around 40%. In fact, this was well above the national average. Which meant, of course, that the criminals won 60% of the time.

Dustin Smiley from the Media Relations office called to let her know the media was hounding him for information. She was amazed and gratified that three full days after the murder the fact that the police had a video that showed the most likely killer entering the Judge's room had not been leaked to the press. She told Smiley to hold the line.

There was a knock at her door and she looked up to see a cop in a Metropolitan police uniform standing there.

"Lieutenant Murphy?" he said.

She waved him in. He laid a thin manila envelope in front of her and grinned. "Courtesy of the Metropolitan Police. Better you than us."

The envelope contained a single computer disk and a couple of sheets of paper, copies of MPD incident reports.

"Tell your boss I appreciate the courtesy." Metro was giving her first class treatment having the materials hand-delivered. The cop gave her a casual wave of the hand and left.

The written report was concise and noted only that the demonstration outside the Washington Hilton had been small and orderly. The protestors complied with police instructions, and there had been no incidents. No arrests had been made, no names had been taken.

The video showed there had been only a handful of demonstrators, all of them well-dressed, carrying placards denouncing what they described as the ACLU's "assault on American values."

There was one scene that Murphy played over and over that focused on several younger people among the mostly middle-aged demonstrators. One of these in particular caught her attention. The image was clear – a young, slim-figured woman in her twenties with blond hair and features remarkably like those of Dawn Tandy.

The pieces fell into place with an almost audible clang that jangled Krystal's nerves. She would have to ask the MDPD to determine where she could find Dawn Tandy. She was all grown up now, and she certainly had a motive. It was possible Krystal was mistaken -- that Dawn had been nowhere near Washington last Friday, but her gut told her otherwise.

She called Ray Velazquez in Miami and asked him to keep the inquiry as quiet as possible. She didn't tell him about the video. The Fernandez murder was drawing considerable local media attention, both in the Washington metropolitan area and Miami, and she didn't want to fan the flames with premature speculation that would re-focus the public away from the Fernandez murder and onto the Tandy family tragedy.

She sensed that Velazquez was unhappy with the request, and she sympathized with his predicament. If, or more likely when the story broke it would be the MDPD as well as the Arlington Police that would receive the opprobrium for "going after the victim."

"Sorry, Ray. Maybe it wasn't her in Washington, after all, and that'll be the end of it."

Her gut told her that this was unlikely.

"I'm going to have to interview the Tandy's. Care to guess what Frank's reaction with be?"

"I know. Just tell him we're eliminating possibilities."

"Just like they always tell the prime suspects on TV."

"It's a crappy job, Velazquez."

"Yeah, I know, but somebody's gotta do it. I sure hope your case doesn't bleed all over us. It was a regular shit storm five years ago."

"I've been reading about it. Were you on the case then?"

"I was, and I don't want to go through it again. Pray you never have to interview Frank Tandy. I can check out whether he's a member of some extremist group without his knowledge, and I'm still working on that, but now you're asking me to talk to the guy and suggest we suspect his only remaining child of murder."

"Like I said, it's a crappy job."

"There are really no other suspects?"

"You know everything I know, and the video is pretty conclusive that we're looking for a blond woman. By the way, see if you can get a recent photo of Dawn. I'm still working to find other leads, but you know as well as I that the Tandy family has to be at the top of the list."

Velazquez was defeated, and his voice was suddenly resigned. "I can't argue with that, Lieutenant. I'll get back to you."

Krystal replaced the receiver and settled back in her chair. Poor Velazquez. She hoped she would not have to travel to Florida, but she could see palm trees in her future. She decided to call Sara Hampton with the news.

"You're kidding!" Sara sounded flabbergasted.

"It's a real stroke of luck."

"If it really is Dawn Tandy in that video."

"In a way I hope it isn't. That family has gone through enough."

"We'll have to let the facts speak for themselves. At least we stand a chance of wrapping up the case sooner rather than later." Sara sounded happy.

Krystal spent the rest of the afternoon catching up on paperwork and wondering how Velazquez was doing in Miami. He called shortly after four. Frank Tandy and his wife had refused even to let him inside their trailer when he'd asked about Dawn.

"He howled like a banshee when I asked for a picture. I think he might have come through the door at me if his wife hadn't had a grip on his arm. Frank is worse than I remember. He's gone a little loco, I think."

"Can you get a warrant for a picture?"

"Looks like you have probable cause. If you can send me a copy of that video it would help with the judge."

"Sure. I'll get it to you through LEO right away. Did you question any of the Tandy's neighbors?"

"Sure did. Talked to 'em before I approached the Tandy's. Guess where Dawn is supposed to be."

A *frisson* of anticipation ran up Murphy's spine. "Just tell me."

"She's a junior at George Mason University. I looked it up. The campus is not far from Arlington, isn't it?"

Velazquez seemed pleased to share the wealth: Murphy had her very own Tandy to go after locally.

"Correct."

"Full boat soccer scholarship."

Getting a recent photo of Dawn Tandy would not be so important if Murphy could interview her in the flesh. The main George Mason campus was located to the west of D.C. in Fairfax County, just outside the Beltway. The Law School was actually in Arlington. The palm trees disappeared from Krystal's imagination – poof – to be replaced by visions of quickly solving the case. She might just be able to wrap the whole thing up without leaving the Metro area. There were so many extraordinarily unpleasant aspects to this case that she would be more than usually happy to get it behind her.

The university more than likely would not provide information on Dawn Tandy without a court order, privacy laws being what they were these days, so Murphy took a shortcut. The girl was probably still an under-graduate which would mean she attended classes at the main campus. She had to live somewhere, and she probably had a telephone.

A check of the university's website revealed that it provided a handy "people finder" through which faculty and students could be contacted. She typed Dawn Tandy's name in the space provided and was rewarded with a page showing the girl's name, a link through which an e-mail message could be sent to her, and the fact that she was a third year "Criminology: Law and Society" major. The website did not provide a personal address, but the Fairfax County phone book did.

An hour later following a tedious drive through the Metro area's almost constant rush hour traffic during which she miraculously avoided a series of maneuvers by other drivers designed to sow chaos on the roads she pulled her unmarked Ford Taurus into a parking lot that served a cluster of white shingled townhouses with green trim. The property was University-owned but about an eighth of a mile off the campus proper.

Two Fairfax County police cruisers waited for her in response to her call advising them of her intention to question Dawn Tandy. She didn't expect trouble, but given the nature of the crime, Fairfax thought the precaution was a good idea, and she hadn't objected.

A young woman who was definitely not Dawn Tandy sat on the rough wooden steps leading to the townhouse entrance. She was petite with skin the color mahogany.

Murphy identified herself and asked to speak with Dawn.

With obvious suspicion the girl eyed Murphy's gun and badge and the two police cruisers before answering. "She's not here."

Her name was Jasmine Robinson, and her accent was pure Jamaican. She had no idea where Tandy might have been the previous Friday night. "It was Friday night, you know. We were all out somewhere."

There was, of course, no question of looking inside the house without a warrant, least of all poking around Dawn's room.

Jasmine reluctantly told her that Dawn had received a phone call from her father in Florida and had piled her stuff into her old VW and taken off several hours ago, saying she was going home. The girl went inside and closed the door firmly behind her.

So her father had warned Dawn that the police were looking for her, and she'd done a runner out of town. Terrific.

She thanked the Fairfax cops for their help and called Sara Hampton on her cell.

The Commonwealth Attorney did not receive the news with grace. "Crap. We need to question that girl. How far do you think she's gotten?"

"Her roommate says she only left a couple of hours ago, so she's can't have gotten far. There are two possible routes: one down I-95, a straight shot to Florida, and I-81 through western Virginia."

"As yet there is not sufficient probable cause for me to present in an affidavit to a judge and get an arrest warrant. But we can have her detained temporarily for questioning. Can you put out an APB for the State Police to pick her up?"

"Yes. She's driving an old VW Beetle with Florida tags. Should be easy to spot. I'll get onto the State Police right away."

Two hours later Murphy was flying down I-81 with lights flashing on her way to the Virginia State Police post at Wytheville letting loose a string of epithets at the eighteen-wheelers that were slow to get out of her way. I-81 like I-95 is a major north-south transportation corridor that is eternally clogged with eighteen wheelers and frustrated "four-wheeler" drivers. The drivers' pain is amplified by the fact that the Virginia State Police enjoy unlimited hunting rights along both routes. It hadn't taken them long to locate Dawn Tandy.

Even at speed the 300 mile drive would take at least four hours. Murphy wouldn't get back home tonight.

She'd advised Ray Velazquez in Miami of developments, and that worthy had not been happy as he realized the Fernandez case was about to drop its messy baggage into the lap of the MDPD. He promised to set up a watch on the Tandy's and await developments.

Michael R. Davidson

The State Police had picked Dawn Tandy up on I-81 and deposited her in a holding room at their barracks in Wytheville, a clean red brick building with well-tended grounds in the far southwestern corner of Virginia. They'd provided her with a sandwich and coke from the canteen, neither of which improved her mood.

When Krystal entered the room it was already past seven in the evening, and Dawn had been waiting since early afternoon. She looked up as the door opened, a sullen expression marring her natural beauty. She was athletically trim and round where girls want to be round. She had movie star looks with high cheek bones and large, blue eyes in which waxed the same fire Krystal had seen in Frank Tandy's eyes on television.

"Hello, Dawn. I'm Detective Murphy from the Arlington County Police. I'd like to ask you a few questions."

Dawn continued to glare. "Why have I been arrested?"

After three years at university there was barely a trace of her father's Florida cracker accent.

"You weren't arrested. You were simply detained for questioning in connection with a crime."

"I don't see much difference. Either way, I'm being held against my will, and I've committed no crime."

In fact, Murphy could not "hold" her "against her will" nor compel her to return to Arlington in the absence of a formal charge of murder and subsequent arrest. Even if formal charges were brought at this point in the investigation Dawn's detention would last only until arraignment when any decent criminal defense lawyer would shred the charges. Of course, Dawn might just admit her guilt which would make Krystal's job a lot easier. But she had a feeling that was not going to happen.

"Like I said, I just want to ask you a few questions."

"I called my father, and he told me I don't have to say anything, and you can't make me."

"Look, Dawn, I know what your family went through and I don't want to make things any harder. Your father called to tell you the Miami police were asking about you, didn't he? You know I need to ask about the murder of Judge Fernandez."

Dawn stuck out her lower lip and remained silent as she eyed Krystal.

"You participated in a demonstration at the Washington Hilton Hotel where Judge Fernandez spoke."

"It's a free country."

"Did you see the judge at the hotel?"

Dawn bit her lip, the first lapse in her defiance. She was, after all, only twenty, and she had to be scared behind the tough façade. She finally nodded. "Yes, I saw him when he arrived."

"Did it make you angry to see him?"

The defiance returned. "What do you think? The sonuvabitch as much as murdered my sister."

"What did you do then?"

"What do you mean?"

"After you saw the judge – what did you do? Did you have any contact with him?"

Dawn's eyes grew wide with incomprehension. "Contact with him? Are you kidding? I wanted to get as far away from him as possible."

"Where were you Friday night?"

"You think I killed him?" The girl's voice was tinged with disbelief.

"Did you?"

"Fuck no!" She clapped a hand over her mouth, but the four-letter word had already escaped and a flush rose from her neck to her hairline. Murphy remembered her parents were staunch Baptists.

The girl was clearly frightened now, and Murphy pursued the advantage. "So where were you? Was anyone with you?"

Dawn said she had been upset by seeing Fernandez, that it brought back all the terrible memories. When the demonstration ended she had gotten in her car and driven out of Washington south on I-95 with no particular destination in mind. She'd pulled into a rest stop and just sat there until she calmed down then drove to the townhouse in Fairfax. She thought she had arrived around ten PM. She'd seen no one she knew.

And there it was: Dawn had no alibi for the time of the murder.

"Why did you leave today? Where were you going?"

"My father called and told me to come home. My mother is upset. The media's dredged up all the bad memories and it's just like Melissa's been killed again. My parents are having a hard time."

"And he also told you the police had asked about you."

Dawn sat up straight and one eye released a fat tear that rolled down her cheek. Murphy watched the girl closely. Tears are inspired by sorrow, joy, or guilt. Sometimes they precede a confession.

Dawn shook her head and opened her eyes. The girl was angry with herself, and the defiance was back. "I'm saying nothing more. Either arrest me or let me go."

Murphy put on her tough face. "You're not going anywhere until I say so. We've only just started."

"I'm a fourth year criminology major, Detective, and I know my rights." She stood. "I'm leaving – now."

The girl couldn't be held without a warrant and knew it. Krystal held out one of her cards, and Dawn reluctantly took it. "That gives you both my office and cell numbers. Please call if you change your mind about talking. If not, I may see you soon in Florida."

Dawn paused at the door and turned. "Come on down, Detective. The weather's nice."

And she was gone.

CHAPTER 11

The interview with Dawn Tandy provided nothing but confirmation of motive. Krystal spent the night in Wytheville and was back in Arlington by noon Wednesday. Velazquez in Miami would advise when Dawn arrived at her parents' home. If that was where she was really heading - if she was not making a bee-line for the Mexican border.

But that wasn't her primary concern at the moment. On the drive back from Wytheville she'd received calls from Sara Hampton, the Chief of Police, and Marty Jefferson all on the same subject. The proverbial excrement had hit the fan, and when she walked into her office she found a message to see Sara immediately. There also were numerous messages requesting her to call various news services to provide comments on the Fernie Fernandez case.

The news was all over radio and television, and the Post had printed a front page story by Tim Reiner, their star crime reporter. The gist of the story was that Dawn Tandy was a "person of interest" in the murder of Judge Fernie Fernandez. What was worse, Reiner somehow had learned that the police had a photo of the Judge's killer. The clear implication was that the photo was of Dawn Tandy.

Krystal called ahead to make sure Sara was in her office and then took the elevator up two floors. She found Sara wearing her snake face and drumming her fingernails on her desk. Dustin Smiley, the head of Media Relations, sat across from her with his leg swinging nervously over one knee.

"How could this have happened?" Sara demanded before Krystal could take a seat. "Who knew about the video besides us?"

Before Krystal could answer Smiley interjected, "I didn't even know about the hotel video! So the leak could not have come from Media Relations." His normally carefully modulated voice was an octave high and quivered slightly. Righteous indignation was not his forte judging from his plaintive denial.

Dustin Smiley was slightly chubby around the middle and had sandy hair that was beginning to thin noticeably in front, a problem he attempted to ameliorate by combing his hair forward. Krystal saw him as a definite future comb over. A sheen of sweat glistened on his forehead. He had his job thanks to the fact that he had a degree in media relations and could display a toothy smile to the cameras. He'd never been a cop, never walked a beat. But he knew all the local reporters and Sara's suspicious had fallen naturally on him.

Sara squinted at Krystal. "Is that right? Media Relations was not informed of the video?"

"Depends on which video you're talking about. Media knew nothing about the hotel security cams, but they were aware of the video and photos Metro gave us from the demonstration. The Metro material showed a clearly identifiable Dawn Tandy. Could that be what they're talking about? I sent a copy of that to the MDPD via EOS, too." She was answering Sara's question but fixed Smiley in her sights.

Sara turned her reptilian gaze back on him. Murphy could almost hear a warning rattle. "Well?"

Smiley seemed to grow smaller, like cornered prey.

"I didn't say anything to anybody about any videos or photos." And with somewhat less assurance added, "And neither did anyone else in Media Relations. I'd bet on the Metro police. You know what a sieve that outfit is."

He had a good point – if it was the Metro material the media was feeding from.

Sara reclined in her executive chair, the warning rattle subsiding, as she considered the situation. After several seconds she said, "Tim Reiner at the Post broke the story this morning. Krystal, I want you to talk to him, see what you can find out, and see if you can gain his confidence and cooperation. We need to seal this leak right away or at least control what Reiner reports going forward."

"Me!" Murphy was surprised. "I'm trying to conduct an investigation here, and I don't talk to the media. I never do. Let Dustin do it."

"I'll be glad to make a call." Smiley was eager to please now, and Tim Reiner was a big deal in Washington.

"No," said Sara. "I want Krystal to do it. I think Reiner would be more interested in talking to her. She's heading the investigation, and he won't be able to resist a meeting."

"C'mon, Sara. This isn't my thing. Let Dustin do it."

Smiley turned to Sara like a puppy hoping for a treat.

"The decision is made," said Sara, pointing a manicured finger at Krystal, "You're it."

The thick carpeting of Sara's office turned into an oozing morass of Everglades mud into which Krystal could feel herself sinking. Tim Reiner was a huge alligator sliding across the mud with every intention to devour her. She distrusted the media, distrusted its easy way with the truth. Anything you say to them can come back to bite you.

"He's going to distort whatever I say, and he's too cagey to reveal any sources to me."

There was a hint of condescension in the smile Sara sent her way. "You're a lieutenant now, Krystal. It's part of the job. Just be sure to get him to agree beforehand that everything you say is off the record.

Show him how it would be to his benefit to cooperate with us and not work against us as things go forward. Even those slobs have a few ethics left, isn't that so, Dustin?"

Smiley nodded glumly. "Yeah, make sure he agrees it's all off the record. He'll ask if he can use what you say as background from an anonymous source. Insist it's off the record."

Krystal was incredulous. Did Sara expect Tim Reiner just to roll over and reveal the source of his story? Why had she ordered Krystal to waste her time on this when there was so much more to do? They'd known one another for a few years now, and Krystal had been a guest at the big Hampton house just off of Military Road in North Arlington. Sara was a great mom to the two Hampton kids, Sally and little Freddy, named for Sara's husband. Sara liked to joke that they had named their children after government agencies. On such occasions Sara was always warm, vivacious, and charming.

But in the office the Commonwealth Attorney was all business and ambition. Krystal had heard about her rattlesnake act from others and laughed it off as an exaggeration. But now she'd witnessed it firsthand. It could definitely be a bad thing to get on the wrong side of Sara Hampton. She could appeal to the Chief of Police or Marty Jefferson, but neither would be willing to cross the Commonwealth Attorney.

Back in her third floor office the phone squatted on Murphy's desk, waiting for her like some repulsive black toad with poisonous skin.

First she called Velazquez in Miami who swore there had been no leaks there. The Fernandez case already was messy enough, and the judge had been important in Miami political circles, important enough that leaking information to the press would not be above some of his colleagues. For this reason, he said, he'd kept the material Murphy had sent to himself.

That put the Metro Police at the top of her suspect list, and she knew she would get nowhere calling them. That left Reiner. Maybe he would refuse to meet her when she told him what she wanted. He had no obligation to talk to the police, least of all about news sources. Nevertheless he would likely believe he had nothing to lose and a new source to gain if he agreed to meet. She sighed and placed the call.

The Post switchboard put her directly through to Reiner when she identified herself. His voice when he came on the line was younger than she expected. "Lieutenant Murphy? What can I do for you?"

Best get right to the point. With luck he would turn her down quickly. "I'd like to talk to you about the source of your story in today's paper."

Reiner didn't answer immediately. She could hear him breathing.

"Name the place and time," he said.

Murphy's heart sank.

"This has to be off the record," she said, still hoping against hope he could be discouraged from meeting her altogether.

Reiner chuckled. "Whatever you say, Lieutenant."

When she suggested he come to police headquarters in Arlington he demurred. "I really don't think that's such a good idea."

"Why not? Surely you've been in police stations before."

"Maybe, but don't you think it would be a bad idea in this case?" he insisted. "Pick another spot, someplace with a lower profile."

She unhappily proposed a small sports bar she knew on North Fairfax Street. There would not be many patrons in the middle of the afternoon.

She had no idea what Reiner looked like, but he said he would recognize her from photos that had appeared in the press last year when she had killed a serial murderer who had broken into the home of her friends, the Stracheys. The fact that she was wearing a badge and carrying a gun also would help him identify her.

The bar featured several flat screen TV's mounted high on the walls. Krystal was never certain whether the sporting events displayed were taped or broadcast. She chose a booth as far as she could find from the bar where a couple of afternoon drinkers were parked on high stools. Solitary drinkers, she guessed, three barstools apart, each staring blankly into half-finished beers. She ordered a coke and waited.

She'd visualized Reiner as a middle-aged with a paunch and a fringe of stringy, gray hair, wearing a shapeless suit like the archetypical movie reporter. So she was surprised when he appeared -- middle-aged, yes, but with a full head of longish silver hair, not very tall with a thin, lanky body. He wore designer jeans and a black T-shirt, topped by a blue blazer. He scanned the interior of the bar, zeroed in on her and came to the booth.

"Lieutenant Murphy?" He raised his eyebrows, also silver. His skin was ruddy, like that of someone who spent a lot of time out of doors, and his eyes were startlingly blue behind stylish tortoise shell glasses.

She nodded and he stuck out his hand. "Glad to meet you." The same voice as on the phone with the timbre of a much younger man that now carried a hint of enthusiasm.

His grip was dry and strong when she took his hand. "Please, sit down."

He brazenly scrutinized her for a few seconds before saying, "I was surprised to receive your call, but I'm sure glad to meet you."

Krystal was uncertain how to begin. Speaking unofficially to reporters was for her an obscure art, and not one she especially wanted to learn. She was the one who was supposed to be asking questions.

He smiled at her hesitation and seemed to read her thoughts. "This must be something new to you. I assure you there's nothing to worry about. What is it you wanted to tell me?"

"It's more like what I hope you'll tell me. Like I said on the phone, I want to talk about your source of your story."

He knit his snowy eyebrows. "I don't understand."

"I realize you aren't likely to reveal the source of the information, but ..."

He interrupted her with a flash of teeth so white they had to be caps. "Oh, you needn't worry about that. I completely understand your concern. It's not unusual. But I don't have to tell anyone, not even at the Post." He paused as a thought occurred to him and he frowned at her. "Has there been some problem on your end?"

There was real concern in his voice now, and his question made no sense. "Of course there's a problem. Your story naming Dawn Tandy as a person of interest jeopardizes our investigation. Your claim to have a photo suggests there is a serious leak in the Department."

"I promise you I don't reveal sources. There's nothing to worry about." He tilted his head, his concern of a moment ago was replaced by puzzlement.

"I think there's a lot to worry about if your reporting gets in the way of the investigation."

He sat back in the booth, cocked his head to the other side. "I'm afraid I don't understand."

Talking to the reporter was like chasing a hare down a hole. Try as she might to be specific, his obtuse responses just drew her in farther. "What is there not to understand? Can I get just a little cooperation here?"

"Cooperation? I really don't understand what you're trying to say. If you didn't want the story published, why did you send me the computer disks?"

Now it was her turn to be confused. "What did you say?"

"Oh, come on, Krystal – may I call you Krystal? – I appreciate the fact that you're concerned for your safety. Maybe you've had a change of heart. It happens all the time. But what's done is done. The story is out there now, and it's going to get even bigger."

"Jesus, try to be specific, will you? What did you mean when you asked why I sent the disks?" She emphasized the word "I." Krystal's heart had begun thumping. Something was definitely upside down in this conversation.

"I'm talking about the manila envelope delivered to my office yesterday, the envelope with two computer disks containing photos and video and a short note signed by you saying making the evidence public was the only way to move your case forward and maybe flush out the killer. You said you were sending the material without the knowledge of your superiors and wanted to remain anonymous. And as I said, you have nothing to worry about on that score."

Krystal could feel her jaw go slack as the energy momentarily drained from her body and a panicked bird fluttered inside her rib cage.

Her reaction did not escape Reiner's notice. "Krystal, you've gone all white. What's wrong?"

She gulped in some oxygen, and her transient discomfiture was pushed aside by what her mother had called her 'Irish.' "I didn't send anything to your office or to you. In fact, I was out of town until noon today."

"You're claiming you did NOT send that envelope?"

"Damn straight!"

Reiner put his elbows on the table and leaned toward her. His complacency vanished. "If you're telling the truth it's a problem for both of us. I don't publish allegations from anonymous sources, at least not from sources that are anonymous to me." His face had turned hard.

"If I'm telling the truth? Then, as you say, we both have a problem. That envelope sure as hell didn't come from me. No way."

"What about the pictures and video? Are they genuine? What about Dawn Tandy? Is the information accurate?"

Reiner was still leaning forward, elbows and forearms on the table, and now Murphy did the same, bringing her face to within inches of his. "Now you're asking me questions? Whatever it is you received, it didn't come from me. That compromises the integrity of the material you have, doesn't it?"

Reiner didn't back off. "It looks genuine to me."

"But now you have nothing to back it up."

He leaned back into the booth and folded his arms. "Not exactly 'nothing,'" he smirked. "The disk of the demonstration at the ACLU event has Metro Police time stamps all over it. I have some pretty good contacts at Metro, and I confirmed the authenticity with them. The other disk has a Crowne Plaza time stamp. That's where the Judge was murdered, and I can always get confirmation from the hotel that the disk is genuine. So no matter who sent the disks to me, I can confirm their authenticity. It's definitely Dawn Tandy at the demonstration, and the woman in the hotel video sure looks a lot like her."

He was right. If he really had the disks, he held the only two pieces of evidence aside from forensics in the case. Who the hell had sent them to him, and who had tried to pin the blame on her? It had to be someone in the Department, and she did have enemies there. But knowledge of the disks had been tightly held. The originals were in her desk drawer where she had left them when she drove to Wytheville to see Dawn Tandy. She'd checked as soon as she had returned, and they were exactly where she had placed them. She had made no copies. But someone else obviously had gone through her desk and done so.

"Mr. Reiner, I need to see the disks you have."

"Why, I assume you have the originals."

"I need to confirm that what you have is the same."

"I don't doubt that they are, but if I agree what do I get?"

The Commonwealth Attorney had told her to win the reporter's cooperation, hadn't she? "I'll provide you with non-attributable background as the case progresses, providing it does not jeopardize prosecution."

The bleached smile lit his face again. "That's more like it. I also need your promise of exclusivity."

"OK. And I have another condition, too."

The silver eyebrows rose.

"Anything you find out you share with me. It's got to be a two-way street."

"Done. Shake on it." He stretched a sinewy hand across the table, and she took it.

He reached into a pocket and withdrew a business card. "I'll have copies sent to your office," he said.

"Complete copies."

"Of course."

He laid the card on the table and wrote a number on its back before passing it to her. "This is my cell phone. Feel free to call any time."

CHAPTER 12

The early rush hour traffic was just beginning to spill into Arlington's major arteries, the drivers vying for position like salmon racing to headwaters to spawn. This gave Krystal more than sufficient time to reflect on the irony of the phrase "luck of the Irish." By the time she had parked and walked through the big glass doors into the lobby she was angry. By the time she pushed her way unannounced into Sara Hampton's office she was seething.

The Commonwealth Attorney looked up from her desk. "There are thunderclouds circling your head, and I get the feeling lightning is about to strike."

Krystal related her conversation with Tim Reiner. "Someone is not only trying to screw up the investigation, they're trying to screw me, too," she concluded.

"Looks like it." Sara's face was inscrutable. "I'm glad Reiner agreed to cooperate, but no matter what, public pressure for an indictment is going to grow now."

"We have very little for an indictment."

"We have Dawn Tandy, we have motive, we have her fleeing the area, and last but not least, we have the pictures."

"All of which taken together prove nothing."

"Good circumstantial evidence, though. Do you have any other leads, anyplace else to look?"

"You know we don't."

"Then get after this one, develop the evidence, and I'll make the charges stick."

"You make it sound so easy." Her words were steeped in sarcasm, the result of a day that had begun badly and steadily grown worse.

Murphy imagined she heard a warning rattle as Sara's head jerked up to reveal suddenly obsidian eyes. The Commonwealth Attorney's voice slashed at her with a sharp edge. "Krystal, if you don't think you can handle the pressure we can find someone else."

It was tempting to say yes, to walk away from the shit storm this case was turning into. Sara might be a friend, but her ambition would win in any contest between career and friendship. Krystal flashed on her own relationships, especially the one with Thomas Stewart and the reticence she felt about becoming emotionally entangled with him. Was she really so different from Sara?

She held Sara's gaze. "I didn't say I wanted out, did I?"

Chameleon-quick, the Commonwealth Attorney morphed back into friendly Sara Hampton. She smiled, "Good. That's the Krystal I want on this case."

Everyone was trying to manipulate her today.

As Krystal turned back to go out the door, Sara said softly, "Whether it was you or someone else who leaked the material to the Post, it forces the pace. It may turn out to be a good thing."

It was an ambiguous statement that might mean that Sara harbored a suspicion that Krystal might actually have been Reiner's original source. Words of denial rose to her lips, but she clamped her jaw to prevent them escaping and stalked her way to the elevator fists clenched at her sides. When the doors closed and the car began to slide downward, she howled in frustration.

CHAPTER 13

The first time Frank Tandy saw his future wife was in a small diner near Homestead, Florida, where he had stopped for breakfast on the way to work at a near-by construction site. She was slender and blond with a shy smile, and he knew as soon as he saw her that she was the one for him. He'd actually nudged the man sitting next to him and pointed her out.

"That's the girl I'm going to marry," he'd said.

He didn't know her name, hadn't even spoken to her. She hadn't waited on his table at all that morning, but his mind was made up, and he was persistent. He went to the restaurant every morning for days, always making sure he sat in the area where she was serving. The tag sewn onto her uniform told him her name was Charlotte. It was three weeks before he screwed up the courage to ask her out. It was another month before the shy, strictly religious girl agreed to marry him.

In the days before he met Charlotte, he'd thought he was living well. He had a good job in construction, a second-hand Mustang convertible, and good looks. Naturally thin, he was not a large man, but the kind of work he did gave him well-developed muscles and all the time outdoors in the Florida sun left him with a deep tan and sun-streaked hair. Work was plentiful and paid well, and in those days there was no end in sight to Florida's building boom. There was no thought of putting money into savings. Frank shared a furnished apartment with two other men, and they spent carefree week-ends drinking beer, chasing girls, and fishing off the coast.

Charlotte got him involved in the church, and they began their married life in a small, rented house in Coconut Grove. Dawn was born a few years later, and Melissa came along five years after that. Frank had been grateful that his daughters favored their mother's angelic looks. Both girls had shown remarkable athletic talent, especially in soccer. Frank was totally unfamiliar with the game but quickly came to appreciate it, and he and Charlotte attended the girls' matches and cheered them on. Life settled into a happy routine.

Melissa's death changed all that and augured the family's decline. When public interest in the case waned they'd tried to regain some semblance of family life, but the economy turned down, the housing boom crashed, and work for Frank became scarce. When they could no longer afford the house, they were forced to rent the trailer where they now resided.

Frank Tandy's skull had become a cauldron that seethed with unreleased anger, confusion, and resentment. There was, he concluded, no justice for the likes of him in America. He imagined he knew what people saw when they looked his way. There was a cruel name for it: trailer trash. He'd worked hard all his life, but with a limited education the best work he had been able to find these days earned him only fifteen dollars an hour for backbreaking labor at a tire recycling plant outside of town.

He worked alongside illegal immigrants from Central America whose language he did not understand and who earned the same as he. They lived in communal groups that pooled money for food and sent the rest to their families in Guatemala and El Salvador. After a few years' work they would return to their home countries where they could build a better life on the dollars they had earned illegally in the U.S.

But for Frank there was no longer any hope of building a nest egg or ever really retiring. He knew he would work until the day he died. He and his wife lived from meager paycheck to meager paycheck, and in the present economy they were lucky to have any work at all. Charlotte found a part-time job as a waitress in a local diner to help make ends meet, a fact that shamed him even more.

The only bright spot was Dawn whose athletic prowess had earned her a full boat university scholarship. The idea that she would be so far away in Virginia had terrified Frank, and he had at first resisted the idea, but Charlotte managed to calm his fears and keep him on an even keel. Dawn, she said, had the possibility of a better life. Still, he had stood at the entrance to the trailer park and watched Dawn's old VW Beetle dwindle into the distance until it disappeared.

And now the safety of his remaining daughter was threatened, not by some criminal predator, but by the very same kind of people who had set Melissa's killer loose on an unsuspecting community – the Establishment, the Authorities. The murder of Fernie Fernandez had set the media's pack of jackals on the family again, and this time it was Charlotte who was breaking under the strain. He needed Dawn to be with them to prevent his wife's complete break-down.

When she'd arrived she'd quietly told him of her temporary detention by the Virginia State Police and the interview with the detective from Arlington. And the very next day the media caught fire with the story that Dawn was a so-called "person of interest" in the Fernandez murder investigation. The jackals renewed their attack, circling ever more closely.

The fragile reed of Frank Tandy's self-control finally snapped.

CHAPTER 14

Jack Freidman worked for Channel Five in Miami as a cameraman. They'd set up the remote site just outside the entrance to the mobile home park on SW 70th Avenue, right in front of the Tandy trailer. They were playing the old media waiting game along with every other outlet in the greater Miami area. The person now considered the prime suspect in the cold-blooded murder of Judge Fernie Fernandez was in Miami. This had been confirmed when Dawn Tandy was spotted parking her old Volkswagen beside the trailer and carrying a small bag inside.

Frequent knocks on the door by eager reporters had been met with shouted obscenities, and the police had finally placed all media behind a barrier at the entrance to the mobile home park. Channel Five had been fortunate enough to secure a location for its van so near the Tandy trailer. Their coverage would be the best.

A few moments earlier Jack had climbed to the roof of the van to set up his camera, but now he lay dazed on the hard surface of the street. He didn't understand what had happened to him. He had been setting up the camera rig when something powerful had punched him in the chest and knocked him to the ground. It was strange that he could feel nothing. He sensed that people had gathered around him and were speaking to him, but he couldn't understand what they were saying. He made an effort to focus his eyes but failed as darkness closed in around him.

Murphy was at her desk reviewing duty rosters and crime reports from on-going cases. She'd decided to try to clear her mind by taking a break from the Fernandez murder, if only for the morning. It was nearing noon when her phone rang. It was Marty Jefferson.

"Krystal, do you have your TV on?"

"No. I needed some peace and quiet."

"Well, you'd better tune in to a news channel right now. You'll want to see this."

"What?"

"Just turn on your TV before the Commonwealth Attorney's office calls you."

She replaced the receiver in its cradle and picked up the TV remote. Whatever it was, she knew it was bad news. She clicked the set on and tuned to an all-news channel. The screen showed a chaotic scene on a street lined on both sides by mobile homes identified by the caption as SW 70th Avenue in Miami. In the background were several media vans and police vehicles with lights flashing. There was a lot of movement. An earnest young woman with carefully coiffed blond hair faced the camera.

"... at approximately 10:45 this morning a cameraman from a local television station was killed by a gunshot police believe was fired from the Tandy family trailer. Preliminary reports indicate the shot was fired from a high powered rifle. No shots have been fired since, but police have closed off the street and sealed the mobile home park. We are fairly certain that the entire Tandy family is in the trailer. The MDPD S.W.A.T. team arrived at the scene several minutes ago and is moving to take up positions surrounding the trailer. Police officers are evacuating other residents."

The reporter went on to identify the dead cameraman, and his picture flashed on the screen. This was followed by old photos of the Tandy family members and a clip from an earlier interview with Frank Tandy.

Murphy could only gape at the screen. She should call Velazquez back immediately, but before she could pick up the phone it rang again, and this time it was Sara Hampton.

"Have you seen this?" Murphy could hear Sara's television in the background.

"Yeah, I'm watching."

"I think you should fly down to Miami."

"They won't welcome any interference while this is going on."

"Like it or not, our only lead in the Fernandez murder is in the middle of whatever is going on in that trailer park. I'd like you to be there to protect our interests. I'll clear it with Jefferson and the Chief."

It was not an unreasonable position for the Commonwealth Attorney to take, and it would be interesting to view developments first hand. Before she could reply, Sara continued, "I want to see you before you leave. Book the earliest flight you can find. They used to fly out of National every hour or so. Pack a bag, and then come see me before you go to the airport."

"OK, but I'm going to call my contact in the MDPD first to smooth the way."

"Of course. See you later."

Velazquez answered his cell on the first ring.

"That you, Murphy?" Caller I.D. was alive and well in Miami.

"Yeah. Where are you?" She could hear sirens in the background.

"Guess you've seen the news. I'm here at the site. This is bad, Murphy, really bad, and it could get worse. Like I told you before, I think Frank is off his rocker."

"Are you certain the shot came from the Tandy trailer?"

"Yup." His voice was glum. "There's been no response to our calls or to the bullhorn. We know the entire family is inside, but nothing's stirring."

"I've been ordered to fly down there. That OK with you?'

She would be welcome, he told her. He thought that as she had met Dawn Tandy she might be of some help if they could establish contact with the family. The MDPD would have a car waiting for her at the airport.

There was an American Airlines flight to Miami at 3:15 that she could make. It wouldn't land until around six P.M., but that was the best she could do. She could have left an hour earlier if Sara Hampton had not demanded a meeting. Going home to pack was unnecessary. Murphy kept a go kit ready in her office: toiletries, toothbrush, blue jeans, polo shirts, a light Arlington County Police windbreaker, socks, underwear, plus gun, extra clip, and badge. The military had taught her to travel light. If she needed anything else she would pick it up in Miami.

Sara was in a much better mood when Murphy entered her office. "Hi, Krystal. Take a seat. I cleared your travel with everyone who counts."

"I spoke with Ray Velazquez, the detective in charge in Miami. He's really worried about the situation. He thinks Frank Tandy's gone around the bend. They haven't been able to establish contact with anyone inside the trailer. At least no more shots have been fired."

"Lord, can it get any worse? Our only suspect is holed up and shooting it out with the police." Sara's upbeat demeanor belied her words. The violent turn of events seemed to please her.

"There's no reason to believe Dawn fired the shot."

"I was speaking generically, dear. I suspect that entire cracker family is nuts, judging from Frank's statements and the way Dawn behaved when you questioned her."

Murphy hid her surprise at the slur Sara had tossed at the Tandy's. "Maybe. But we still don't have any hard evidence against Dawn."

Sara reclined behind her desk and steepled her fingers. "True, but the situation means someone has broken down, and that's an indicator of guilt. When it's all over I suspect you'll get a confession. Emotions will be running high, and that's when people say things they might otherwise keep to themselves. I've seen it happen."

"What are my marching orders?"

"Krystal, you have our full backing and confidence, whatever happens down there. Use your best judgment. Gain the trust of the locals."

"I don't think we'll have any problems with the locals. It's their show entirely until they get everybody out of that trailer."

"Good luck, Krystal. You'd better get out of here now and catch that plane." She stood and came around the desk to walk Murphy to the door. "You packed quickly."

"I always keep a go-kit ready in the office."

"Did you pack rain gear?"

"Just a light jacket."

"It rains almost every afternoon down there this time of year. Better pick up an umbrella at the airport. If you get a chance, try the Cuban food. You'll like it. Get one of your MDPD buddies to take you to Versailles. It's the best."

"You know Miami?"

"I went to school down there for a while – The University of Miami."

"I thought you went to Georgetown."

"Just the graduate work. Miami can be a lot of fun. Take some personal time, if you can."

"I doubt there'll be much time for fun."

Sara chuckled softly and came around her desk to give her a hug and light kiss on the cheek. "That's our super woman cop," she said. "You need to enjoy life a little more, I think, and Miami's the place to do it. Let's get together for dinner at our place when you get back. Fred and I will try to come up with a suitable dinner mate for you."

Murphy groaned. "I already have friends trying to set me up."

Sara looked at her with wide eyes. "And how's that going?"

"It's complicated."

Sara sighed. "Oh, Krystal, someday we're going to straighten you out."

The domed glass roof gave Reagan National Airport an air of lightness that contrasted sharply with the sullen lines of passengers going through the security checkpoints below. Murphy's status and her contacts in the airport security office got her past the lines with a minimum of fuss. It also got her upgraded to a First Class seat, for whatever that was worth in domestic air travel these days. She bought a small, folding umbrella at a kiosk and stuffed it into her bag and took a seat in the American departure lounge. She'd gotten to the airport with an hour to spare and now sat in an uncomfortable, hard plastic seat waiting for her flight to be called.

Flying was a lot like the Army, she decided. Hurry up and wait.

Her cell phone rang, and the caller i.d. showed a number with a 305 area code – Miami. She assumed it must be Ray Velazquez with an update, but when she answered, she heard only fast breathing at first, then a voice that it took her a second to recognize as Dawn Tandy's. "Detective Murphy," she whispered, "is that you?"

Her heart began to thud. "Dawn? Yes, this is Murphy. What's going on?"

"I still have the card you gave me. I didn't know who else to call."

"Dawn, where are you? Are you in the trailer?"

"Yes. I'm in the bathroom, but I don't have long. Daddy's gone crazy. He won't let us out. And I think he shot someone this morning. I don't know what to do."

"You need to get him to answer the phone, communicate with the authorities."

"He's torn out the phone line. He doesn't know I have a cell phone."

"Are you saying your father is holding you against your will?"

"Mama and I tried to talk sense into him, but he won't listen."

Murphy had to figure a way to get Dawn in touch with the Miami-Dade Police. She had to let Velazquez know the situation inside the trailer.

"Dawn, listen to me. Will you be able to use your phone again?"

"I don't know. Daddy doesn't like us to get out of his sight."

"In a few minutes I'm going to text to you the number of a friend in Miami. He's a policeman, too, and he's near-by and will help figure a way out for you. His name is Ray Velazquez. Make sure your phone is set to vibrate."

"I don't know ..."

Murphy heard a pounding sound and a man's voice, lifted an octave by hysteria: "Dawn, you come out of there right now. You been in there long enough, you hear me?"

Dawn said, "OK, Daddy, just a second." Her voice teetered on the edge of terror.

Murphy waited, her heart in her throat, then she heard Dawn's whisper. "I'm scared," she said, "and I want you to know something. I did not kill Judge Fernandez."

The pounding on the door resumed, and Dawn whispered, "I've got to go. Remember what I said." There was a click, and she was gone.

Murphy sat still for a moment absorbing what had just happened before dialing Ray Velazquez's cell number. He answered after three rings, and she filled him in on the call from Dawn Tandy. "Basically, you have a hostage situation in that trailer. You have to concentrate on finding a way to get the two women out of there."

"He's keeping the women close to him?"

"Yes, that's what it sounded like."

"Thanks, Murphy. We'll work on a strategy. Can you forward your cell phone to mine for the time you're in the air? Dawn might get another chance to call out. I don't want to risk trying a call to her just yet. Frank may have discovered her phone."

Boarding for her flight was announced and Murphy punched in the appropriate numbers to forward her calls to Velazquez as she walked through the jetway. She would have no way of knowing what was happening on the ground until she landed in Miami.

CHAPTER 15

Sara Hampton's knowledge of Miami meteorology was accurate. It was raining when the plane landed and cooler than expected. She had no checked luggage so she hurried through the terminal to the exit where she found an MDPD squad car waiting for her.

There was maybe an hour of daylight left, and she hoped she would reach the trailer park before dark. She disabled the call-forward on her phone and called Velazquez as soon as the cruiser pulled away from the terminal.

The situation remained unchanged. S.W.A.T. was making plans for the night when they could approach the trailer unseen. All attempts at communication had failed, and there had been no more contact with Dawn. Had it not been for her call to Murphy they would have known nothing about the situation inside the trailer.

Frank Tandy prowled the trailer from one end to the other, checking out every window, rifle in hand. Since shooting the man off the top of the van this morning, no other targets had presented themselves. Had they done so, he would have fired. He had only one box of the 30-07 ammunition his hunting rifle required, and he wanted to make it last.

Thank God he'd bought a carton of cigarettes the day before, but even so, he was down to his last pack. The peckerwoods outside had not cut electricity to the trailer, which meant he could make plenty of coffee, and between the nicotine and the caffeine he had quite a buzz on. That was good. It kept him alert.

He kept the television on, switching from channel to channel to follow what was going on outside.

The women did not understand, but that did not surprise him. Women could not know how a man felt when his world crumbled, when the high and mighty conspired to make his life a nightmare, when he was forced to sweat for subsistence wages alongside short, dark-skinned men who did not even speak his language, men who excluded him and made him feel like a foreigner in his own land. He had been reduced to the same level as illegal workers who had no right even to be in this country, who would work for peanuts and thus bring the wages of everyone else down to their level. What kind of world was it where the irresponsible, rich bankers got all the money while people like him sank deeper into poverty? He'd come to feel like less than a man.

And as if that weren't enough the only good news he'd had in years, the death of that evil sonuvabitch judge, had been turned against him and his innocent family, the family he could no longer adequately provide for. The same high and mighty authorities who welcomed illegal workers, foreclosed on the homes of working Americans, and abandoned any pretense of Christian principles now had declared war on his family, on his remaining daughter. They would use false allegations to drag her through the gutter and destroy her life as his had been destroyed. They would kill her just as they had killed his youngest daughter, Melissa.

No more. Frank Tandy would make his last stand, and the people would understand his rage.

They would come when night fell with all their armed might to silence his voice, end his rebellion. But they would not succeed. Frank knew what he had to do. He would make a statement the world would not soon forget, a statement the fat cats could not refute, a statement they could do nothing about. He would make certain the two women he loved would be safe from more persecution. The only way left for men like Frank Tandy to make their voices heard was through violence.

The drive from the airport to the crime scene was not long, in fact just a few blocks, but the sun was lowering toward the horizon by the time the squad car had worked its way through the crowds and deposited Krystal at the site. The rain had stopped leaving puddles in the roadway, and people were standing in groups outside police barriers that had been set up at each end of the block. The puddles captured reflections of the blue and red lights that flashed everywhere and no fewer than five helicopters jousted for position in the sky.

The mobile home park itself was bordered on the east by the weed-infested remains of long-abandoned railroad tracks and on the west by a set of tracks that from what she could see were still in use. She imagined trains rumbling past only a few feet away from the flimsy trailers, sending deep tremors through the inhabitants. SW 70th Avenue, a name that struck her as incongruous with the narrow, blacktopped street, bisected the trailer park north to south.

This clearly was not the most desirable address in Miami, and she flinched when she thought how such flimsy dwellings must fair in hurricanes. The few trees and scruffy palms that grew among the trailers, if anything, made the place more pitiable.

The Miami-Dade police had set up their command post at the north end of the park in a vacant lot that was strewn with large pieces of abandoned construction materials in various stages of decomposition. She showed her badge and asked for Ray Velazquez and was directed toward a white, 28-foot vehicle with the words Miami-Dade Police emblazoned on its side in large green letters. The behemoth looked brand new. Parked near-by was a military-style vehicle, around which a dozen men in olive drab uniforms and helmets were gathered for what looked like a briefing.

She banged on the door of the command center, and it was opened by a uniformed officer with sergeant's stripes. He looked her up and down, his eyes coming to rest on the gun and badge at her hip. "Who are you?" he asked.

"Detective Lieutenant Krystal Murphy from Arlington, Virginia. Is Ray Velazquez inside? He's expecting me."

The sergeant called over his shoulder, "Detective, you got a visitor."

She'd wondered what Velazquez looked like and was surprised when a well-built man with a mop of blond hair that hung in a loose tangle around his head appeared behind the sergeant. He was probably in his mid to late thirties and looked more like a surfer than a cop in his khaki cargo pants and loose, Hawaiian-style shirt. She wondered if he consciously dressed himself like a character from a TV show about Miami cops.

"You must be Murphy," he said with a welcoming smile. "Come in and join the party. You made it just in time."

She jerked her head in the direction of the men in olive drab. "Is that your S.W.A.T. unit?"

"We call them S.R.T., Special Response Team. They're good."

"I don't doubt it."

He beckoned her to step inside where he introduced her around. There were two other officers besides the sergeant, one manning a communications console. The other was dressed in S.R.T. military gear with a large pistol Krystal recognized as a .44 caliber Desert Eagle in a holster rig attached to the front of his Kevlar vest. Velazquez introduced him as Captain Jerry Smith, the leader of the S.R.T. contingent.

Smith was as tanned and trim as Velazquez and about the same age, but with close-cropped, dark hair and a thousand mile stare that Krystal recognized from her Army days. After shaking hands all around, Velazquez explained that Captain Smith was now in charge of the operation. There still had been no communication with Frank Tandy, and the information Krystal had been able to provide made it clear they were dealing with a volatile hostage situation.

There was general agreement that things could spiral out of control at any moment, and for that reason the S.R.T. would breach the trailer soon after dark. Power would first be cut both inside and out to give the S.R.T. the cover of darkness. As soon as they had taken up positions, the trailer's windows would be knocked out and flash-bang grenades tossed inside, followed immediately by a breach of the door. It was a simple plan, one that these men had carried out hundreds of times, and Smith had a high degree of confidence in success. His men were well-practiced in raiding drug gangs that possessed highly lethal weaponry and weren't afraid to use it.   In this instance, they would be up against only a single lightly armed and irrational man.

There had been a hysterical note in Frank Tandy's voice as he shouted at his daughter through the bathroom door, and Krystal shivered now as she recalled it. She agreed with the MDPD assessment. The situation in the trailer could become much, much worse very quickly. They had to get the women out of there, and there was a good chance that Frank Tandy would not survive the action.

Darkness was falling fast, and Captain Smith stepped out of the command post to join his men. They checked their weapons and started to deploy. In the gathering dusk, Murphy could still see three empty media vans about a hundred yards away marking where the Tandy trailer sat.

The sun set at precisely 6:58 PM, and a half-hour later, when dusk had turned to darkness, the commencement of the operation was signaled when the electrical power to the mobile home park was cut at Captain Smith's command. The S.R.T. moved up quickly to positions at each corner of the Tandy trailer, giving them complete control of the exterior, and the men designated for the flash-bang maneuver began to move in, crouching as they ran.

Murphy and Velazquez were in the command post observing the action on screens served by night-vision cameras set up to cover all four sides of the trailer, and one camera mounted on Captain Smith's helmet.

Several things happened in quick succession. Two shots sounded a few seconds apart from inside the trailer, causing the S.R.T. men approaching with the grenades to freeze momentarily, but the shots did not seem to have been directed at them. After a few beats a third shot sounded, and Smith shouted at his men to move. Within seconds windows were broken, grenades tossed inside, and the door breached by a large man wielding a sledgehammer.

Smith charged through the door, shotgun in hand, followed by three of his men, but there was no more shooting.

In the command center Krystal got a sick feeling in her stomach. The reports of Frank Tandy's rifle had been audible to everyone. Three shots. Two followed by one. Murphy hoped she was wrong about what that meant. She and Velazquez looked at one another in silence, neither wanting to say what they were thinking.

Without warning, lights flashed on outside as power was restored to the site, and the Tandy trailer, windows and door smashed, was washed in the white glare of police projectors. Murphy and Velazquez left the command center and ran the hundred yards down SW 70th Avenue to the trailer. They arrived in time to see Smith and his men emerge and remove their helmets, shaking their heads.

Smith saw them and waved them over. The look on his face told Krystal all she needed to know.

The S.R.T. leader's shoulders slumped in defeat, and the taut lines in his face were deepened by the glaring light from the projectors. "It's a sad sight in there," he said, jerking his thumb toward the trailer. "As sad a sight as I've seen. The women didn't have a chance. You'd better have a look for yourselves."

Sometimes imagined horror is worse than the experience itself, but not this time. Krystal let Velazquez precede her into the trailer. Both carried flashlights.

Dawn and Charlotte Tandy must have been sitting huddled together when Frank shot them both from behind, one at a time but mercifully quickly. The bodies of the two women, both blond, one young and lithe, one older and heavier, sprawled face down on the floor in front of a sofa. In the harsh glare of their flashlights the blood from their broken heads glistened wetly and bright red.

Frank was behind the sofa. He's placed the barrel of the high-powered rifle in his mouth and pulled the trigger. The combined shock of the bullet and pressure from the blast had torn his head to pieces and distorted what was left of his face into something unrecognizable as human.

Krystal wanted to retch but did not permit herself the weakness, forced herself to look at the bodies. She remembered Dawn as she had been when they met in Wytheville, scared but defiant, full of spirit, with an ethereal beauty. No longer. Her face had been destroyed by the bullet that had entered the back of her head. She'd said she was going home to Florida because her father had pleaded for her help claiming her mother was falling apart. Obviously it had been Frank Tandy who was falling apart. She wondered if Frank had planned this all along, if he had purposely lured his remaining daughter home to her death.

She flashed her light around the room, wanted to look anywhere but at the bodies, and it came to rest on a group of family photos in gilt frames. There were Dawn and her sister, Melissa, five years earlier in their soccer uniforms, carefree youngsters with their arms around one another's shoulders grinning into the lens. And there was a photo of the whole family in obviously more prosperous times dressed in their Sunday best standing in front of a small adobe house with palm trees and flowers in the yard. She picked up the photo and studied Frank's face. Whenever it had been taken he had not been the angry, taught man she had seen a few days ago on television. His hair was neatly parted and his face suffused with a look of pride and contentment. Violent, unreasonable death had stolen that contentment away from him. As angry as she was at Frank she could not help but think that he, too, was a victim.

The effluvia of death filled the small space inside the trailer with the strong, coppery scent of fresh blood mixed with the bowel release of one of the corpses finally drove her back outside soon to be joined by Ray Velazquez.

"Are you OK?" he asked.

"No, of course I'm not OK. Are you OK?" She realized that her anger was misdirected at Velazquez, and she struggled to moderate her tone. "It's just all so senseless and yet so horribly inevitable, as if Melissa's murder was the first domino to fall in a chain reaction that led to tonight."

"We'll never know what was in that man's mind, whether he planned this all along or whether it was a sudden impulse. He must have known we would have to try to get them out."

"I don't think it was the S.R.T. assault that set him off," said Krystal. "He shot them as soon as the lights went off, before they could even toss the flash-bangs. He knew it was coming, and he planned for it."

"You may be right, and I hope you are. Smith is probably blaming himself, and the media will sure as hell heap some shit on the S.R.T."

"The fucking media," she said. "We all dance to their tune, don't we, one way or another." She was thinking about Tim Reiner and the leak that had put Dawn Tandy in the media spotlight, something that might well have pushed her father all the way around the bend. She vowed to find out who had stolen the disks from her desk while she was away interviewing Dawn.

"I'm told it's a necessary evil," said Velazquez.

"They're free to toss information, sometimes not even factual information, to the public and then claim to have no responsibility for the consequences, like that Wikileaks jackass." Men and women like Thomas Stewart put their lives on the line for their country while sophomoric idiots revealed secrets that could kill them all in the name of "openness." She would never want to become a part of Thomas's secret world, but she understood why it had to be secret.

They had walked some distance away from the trailer back toward the mobile command center before Krystal's anger subsided sufficiently for her to remember she needed to inform Arlington of events before they saw it on television. She remained outside the command center and punched the speed dial for Sara Hampton's home phone. A glance at her watch showed it was not yet eight P.M., less than a half-hour since the atrocity in the Tandy trailer a hundred yards behind her.

Sara answered on the third ring. "Hi, Krystal. How's it going down there? We were just sitting down for dinner."

The Commonwealth Attorney's reaction to the news was a quick intake of breath, "My God, all of them."

"Yes. Those women never had a chance. I just hope they didn't see it coming."

"And so the Fernie Fernandez case ends there in Miami where it all started." Sara sounded more interested in the impact of events on her case than the three deaths that Murphy had just witnessed, and it did not improve Krystal's mood. Sara wanted to wrap up a difficult case; Murphy wanted to know the truth.

"You think this is the end of it?"

"It could well be. I told you the family's actions looked a lot like an admission of guilt."

"We don't have enough evidence to say that yet."

"And with all the principals dead, we're not likely to get any, don't you think?" Rattle, rattle. Krystal decided then and there that Sara was fast becoming less Commonwealth Attorney and more politician, the sort of politician that is uninterested in facts that conflict with their personal ambitions. This was not the Sara Hampton she had come to know over the years of their association. It was an unwelcome and sad change but perhaps inevitable. Politics these days is all about appearances.

Dawn Tandy's last, desperate words haunted Krystal's thoughts. The girl had denied any guilt in the Fernandez murder. Had she known she was going to die? The fear had certainly been in her voice.

"You could be right," she said into the phone, "we may never know. What do you plan to do now?"

"If no other leads are developed Fernandez will go into the cold case files."

"That would make it the 18th unsolved Arlington County murder since 1970. I don't think we should put it on the shelf just yet."

"We'll talk about it when you get back. Why don't you take a couple of days down there to clear your head? You can use the time to finalize everything with the Miami-Dade folks." The rattle subsided as Sara injected sympathy into her voice.

She could use some more time in Miami. She was unlikely to get another chance to look around in Fernie Fernandez's backyard.

CHAPTER 16

Ray Velazquez was holding a phone attached by a curly cord to one of the control panels of the command center van when she climbed back inside. When he was finished he turned and said, "That was our forensics unit. Uniforms will keep the area secure until they can go over the trailer and remove the bodies. Then we'll cordon off the trailer and let the residents back in."

"I'd like to see what your people come up with."

"Sure, no problem. As for me, I'm leaving the paperwork for tomorrow and going off in search of a stiff drink. Care to come along?"

It had been a long day that had begun in Arlington with her trying to clear her mind of the Fernandez case and ended here in Miami where the case flooded her thoughts to the exclusion of all else, and after the carnage in the trailer it was a battle to hold her emotions at bay. The chat with Sara Hampton had not helped.

She could most certainly do with a drink, maybe two.

She gave him a lop-sided smile. "That sounds like a good idea."

Krystal's luggage consisted of a single, small canvas carry-on bag, and now Velazquez bent to retrieve it from the floor of the command center. He held it up and raised an eyebrow in her direction. "This is all you brought?"

"I travel light."

"Amazing," he said, heading for the door, bag in hand. "Most of the women I know would need something this size just for their make-up."

Krystal wondered how many women he knew. He didn't wear a wedding band.

They stepped outside into a freshening breeze that brought with it the muted timpani of distant thunder. She felt a few drops of moisture that quickly multiplied into an evening shower. The rain felt good on Murphy's face as she dogtrotted after Velazquez to his car, which turned out to be a fire engine red Porsche 911. By the time they had settled into the buttery leather seats the rain had begun in earnest.

Velazquez laughed at her surprised reaction to the car. "It belonged to a drug dealer. We keep rounding them up and confiscating their property, so we have a pretty good selection of cars in the police motor pool. Porsche's are pretty common in Miami."

She replied, "I suddenly feel like I'm in an episode of 'Miami Vice.' I'll bet there aren't very many Porsches in this neighborhood."

She stared through the rain-streaked side window at the trailer park as they passed. It was one of the dreariest places she'd ever seen, a dead-end, and Dawn Tandy seemed so out of place there. She had been such a pretty girl, and she would have graduated from college next year. Yes, her parents, too, had died, but they at least had had more of life while Dawn's was cut tragically short.

When she commented on this Velazquez said, "To make it even sadder, did you know she was a hopeful for the U.S. Olympic women's soccer team? She was apparently very talented."

"Jesus! Doesn't sound like someone who would commit cold-blooded murder, does it?"

"What was she like when you met her?"

"Defiant, scared. She definitely had a temper, but she was surprised when she figured out she was a suspect."

"Do you have any other leads?"

"It's early days yet. Dawn was the only one to make the list so far. She was in town when Fernandez was murdered, and she has no alibi. The woman shown in the video entering the judge's hotel room resembled her."

"But ...?"

"But it's all circumstantial. The Tandy's certainly had motive to go after the judge, but maybe there's someone else with their own motive. I want to dig into Fernandez's background. The key to what happened is more likely to be found down here than in Virginia."

"Want some help?"

She turned to study Velazquez's profile as he concentrated on navigating the small, fast car through the pouring rain, shifting through the gears with practiced precision. He was a handsome man if you could look past the surfer image. The short-sleeved Hawaiian shirt displayed well-muscled arms. With his long, blond hair bleached almost white by the sun he wouldn't look out of place on an advertising poster for South Beach. He'd been very helpful from the beginning. She'd need an ally in Miami where the information on Fernandez resided.

"That would be great," she answered.

He steered a course east and south, and told her they were heading for Coconut Grove. They finally emerged onto South Biscayne Drive, a wide tree-lined boulevard with Biscayne Bay stretching into the night to the east, its surface now choppy with the rain, and a line of impressive high rise buildings on the other side. Within a few minutes he turned into a narrow drive leading toward a marina, then pulled to a stop at the entrance to a restaurant called Monty's where a valet parking attendant with a large umbrella opened their doors and escorted them through the abating rain to the canopy awning that protected the restaurant entrance.

The parking lot in front was filled with a shiny array of cars, none of which could possibly have cost less than $40,000. Large boats that Murphy thought might fairly be called yachts were moored at the marina next door. This was a different world entirely from the trailer park they had left fifteen minutes earlier. She'd thought they were going to a quiet little bar.

"Are you sure I'm dressed properly for this place," she asked, uncharacteristically concerned about her jeans and polo shirt.

He laughed, the first time she had seen him do so, displaying large, white teeth that contrasted sharply with his deep tan. "This is Miami, remember? Folks are pretty casual down here. You look fine. And," he continued sweeping an arm at the restaurant, "this place serves the best stone crab in town. I've not eaten since noon, and I'm starved. I assumed you were, too."

Aside from her usual coffee that morning the only meal she'd had all day was a tasteless cardboard sandwich and a coke on the flight down, for both of which the airline had the audacity to demand payment. Food was a compelling idea, and it made her feel guilty after what she had witnessed. Somehow it seemed only right that appetites should be demolished by such scenes, but if cops permitted such squeamishness, they might never eat.

Inside, they were shown to a table beside a window overlooking the yacht basin. Velazquez waved the menu away and ordered stone crab for two. Krystal was unfamiliar with the cold delicacy and admired the large pink claws with black tips when they were placed on the table along with a stainless steel bowl for discarded shell, dishes of melted butter, a sauce for dipping, and a sturdy metal implement to crack the thick, stone hard shells.

Velazquez grinned as he grabbed a claw and cracked it to extract the firm, white meat. "I ordered the 'all you can eat' platter. They'll keep bringing these babies until we either surrender or collapse." He waved the waitress to the table and ordered cold beers.

It didn't take long for her to get the knack of cracking the huge pincers to get at the flesh inside, and they ate in silence for several minutes.

Velazquez broke the silence. "What kind of help?"

Krystal had been lost in her thoughts as she concentrated on cracking the surprisingly hard crab shell. She couldn't get Dawn Tandy's final denial of guilt out of her mind. Had the young girl known she was about to die? Hopefully not. Hopefully death had come suddenly without warning. Krystal was not particularly religious, but she had been raised a Methodist, and she found herself hoping that Dawn Tandy had seen that fabled light, had been drawn into it and was now at peace.

"What did you say?"

"I asked what kind of help you would like."

She shot him a speculative look. "I want to dig into Fernandez's past for another suspect. There must be something there."

"You're convinced that Dawn didn't do it?"

"Like I said before, there was only circumstantial stuff, not enough to get an indictment in my opinion, despite the rush to judgment up north." She told him about the growing dissonance between herself and Sara Hampton, how she thought the Commonwealth Attorney's political ambitions were behind the desire to conclude the investigation. "She wants this all out of the way by the time elections come around, and she seems willing to indict Dawn Tandy in the public mind even if she can't bring her to trial."

"She could be right, you know."

"You didn't hear Dawn's denial to me. And I don't think what happened today was some kind of macabre Tandy family admission of collective guilt. I think the father just went nuts."

"You're the only one who heard what Dawn said on the phone. People will reach their own conclusions."

"You don't think I'm telling the truth about that call?" she bridled.

He raised his hands and pushed his palms toward her. "Of course, I believe you. I'm just drawing a distinction between what we know and what the public might think. The press will have a field day with this."

Mention of the press made her wonder if she somehow might turn Tim Reiner into an ally. According to the terms of their pact she should contact him soon. The veteran newspaperman would have his own sources.

She said, "The more I think about it the more questions I have. For example, how would Dawn Tandy have arranged to get into Fernandez's room? He surely would have recognized her, but he was certainly expecting the woman who killed him, and judging from the big grin on his face and what he was wearing when he opened the door he was looking forward to a night of nooky, not a confrontation."

"Do you think it was a hooker?"

"That's what it looked like, but nothing of value was taken from the room, and she wasn't inside longer than the few minutes it took to kill the judge. I think it was premeditated. The woman went into that room with the intent to kill. And she did a good job concealing her face from the cameras."

He nodded thoughtfully. "How long can you stay down here?"

"The Commonwealth Attorney seems to think I need a few days in the sun."

"That's enough time to look through the files. Have you found a place to stay yet?"

"There wasn't time to make a reservation. But there are plenty of hotels in Miami."

"How about bunking at my place?"

"'Bunking?'"

The big smile split his tanned face again. "Well, 'bunking' would contribute to a wonderful working relationship."

She didn't look forward to a night in an antiseptic hotel room alone with her thoughts, especially after the incident at the trailer park. She felt her defenses weakening but then thought of

Thomas and felt guilty. Wherever he was, she was certain it was nowhere near as pleasant as a hotel room.

She smiled back at Velazquez and shook her head. "Sorry, Ray, but there's someone else."

Velazquez shrugged his shoulders and gave a low, good-natured chuckle. "Too bad, but he's a lucky guy. As my mother always told me, 'It's a man's prerogative to ask and a woman's right to refuse.' At least I tried."

"Your mom would be proud," she said, "I hope this doesn't change your mind about helping me out."

"Of course not. What kind of guy would I be if I made conditions like that? But I do reserve the right to try again sometime."

She was relieved, and at the same time flattered by his attention. Maybe she'd stumbled upon a good man in Miami. *About time she had some luck.*

"Come on," he said, rising, "I know a spot near-by, and it has a great bar where we can have a nightcap. I'll introduce you to the mojito."

"Just one. And don't think you can break down my resistance with alcohol. I'm Irish."

"The thought never crossed my mind," he said with an evil smirk and waggled his eyebrows.

They recovered the Porsche and he drove a few blocks back along the shore before turning off and pulling under the portico of the Ritz-Carlton Hotel. Krystal looked at him in disbelief. "Are you nuts? I can't afford a place like this. You must know someplace cheaper."

He slid out from behind the wheel and came around to open her door as the inevitable valet parking attendant trotted up. "Policeman's discount guaranteed," he said with a flourish of his hand toward the entrance. "Not as nice as my place, of course." He waggled his eyebrows again.

"You're kidding."

Ten minutes later she was checked into a room at a steeply discounted rate, breakfast included.

The bar was every bit as glitzy as he had promised, and she felt out of place in her jeans despite Miami's contrived nonchalance about casual dress. She didn't have much else in her bag. She'd have to buy a more suitable outfit. Velazquez assured her she could find everything she needed at a shopping area a few blocks from the hotel and promised to take her there in the morning.

After drinks she walked out with him to the car and gave him a chaste peck on the cheek. "Thanks, Ray, for everything."

The room was luxurious and the bed like a cloud, but still she tossed through the night with the memory of Dawn Tandy's words of denial.

CHAPTER 17

The shopping center was called Coco Walk. It was a colorful multi-story arcade surrounding an attractive court in the center of Coconut Grove. Krystal selected a sleeveless blue cotton print dress and sandals that Velazquez assured her would be acceptable in any Miami establishment.

"I've picked a place for dinner tonight that I think you'll like," he said as they walked back to the car. He'd put the top down, and she was glad she'd pulled her hair back into a ponytail.

Michael R. Davidson

"Whoa, buster, that meal last night must have cost a fortune. I can't let you keep buying food for me."

"I insist. I'm going to introduce you to the food of my people, and it will be a pleasure."

"Your people?"

"*Si, señorita, mi pueblo – los Cubanos.*" His Spanish sounded authentic.

His ethnicity had not occurred to her. With his light hair and blue eyes he looked nothing like Ricky Ricardo. "You're Cuban?"

"Me and half of Miami. My folks escaped from the island before I was born."

Miami-Dade Police Headquarters was in what looked like an up-scale section of town called Doral. According to Velazquez a famous golf course was located just to the north. The building itself was a sprawling, modern structure with a flat roof and extensive grounds that made Arlington's multi-use building seem small. But once inside she recognized the familiar bustle of a working police department.

The Homicide Bureau wherein resided Velazquez's Specialized Investigations Squad occupied a warren of offices and cubicle space in the North West corner of the second floor. Velazquez guided her to his desk amid the curious stares of his fellow officers who took note of Murphy's badge and gun. There were, she saw, more than a few colorful Hawaiian-style shirts in the room. Not for the first time she envied men whose clothing choices offered so much more variety for weapon concealment. The loose shirts would be practical in Miami's sticky weather, too.

Velazquez brought her coffee in a cup emblazoned with the number twenty-six. "What's the number for?" she asked. The coffee was strong and good.

He sat back and put his feet up on his desk. "About thirty years ago things got so wild and wooly in Florida that the DEA funded a bunch of tactical units to fight all the drug-related violence. Here in South Florida the unit was called Centac 26, Centralized Tactical Unit 26. The unit eventually became the squad of super-duper elite crime fighters you see here today."

She couldn't suppress a laugh.

"How do you want to start?" he asked, still leaning back sipping black coffee.

"Something you said when I called you for the first time right after the murder seems pretty relevant. I believe your exact words were 'he had a reputation with the ladies.'"

"Yeah, old Fernie was a player, all right. He always was from what I hear."

"Did it ever cause him any problems?"

"Only when his wife wised up to his philandering several years ago and divorced him."

"That seems a long time for her to hold a grudge strong enough to kill her ex."

"I think she got even in the property settlement."

"Is she still in the area? If she is, it's as good a place as any to start."

A half-hour later the red Porsche carried them along Brickell Avenue through downtown Miami, an

Michael R. Davidson

area that reminded Krystal vaguely of Crystal City in Arlington except that here there were actually people strolling along the broad sidewalks, the blindingly white buildings seemed taller, there were palm trees everywhere, and the air smelt of the ocean. Definitely not Crystal City and its exhaust-infused atmosphere.

Velazquez turned right onto South East 8th Street and across a bridge that took them to a triangular-shaped island that seemed to sit barely above sea-level no higher than a sandbar, perhaps because it was weighed down with yet another phalanx of Florida high-rises. Velazquez said the area was comprised of two islands, one called Burlingame and the other Claughton. Eventually he pulled into the parking area of a tall condominium at the northern shoreline. Krystal guessed the condos must sell for around a half-million a pop, even in the present economy.

They'd telephoned before leaving police headquarters, so the former Mrs. Fernandez was expecting them. The concierge directed them to an elevator that swept them noiselessly to a floor mid-way up the building. Alerted by the concierge, Adele Fernandez stood at her open door waiting for them at the end of the hall. She was mid-60-ish, petite, with bottle-blond hair and skin the color of tanned leather. Murphy attributed the lineless face to plastic surgery or a surfeit of Botox. She was dressed in a sleeveless, pink blouse, white cotton slacks and sandals that showed toes with nails painted pink to match the fingernails.

The spacious apartment faced northward, toward Dodge Island and the Port of Miami and was filled with mid-morning light. Their hostess led them out onto a broad balcony where a pitcher of lemonade and tall, ice-filled glasses waited on a table where she invited them to sit.

"It's been a long time since I had police in my house," she said. Her voice was unexpectedly girlish. "In the old days when I was still with Fernie, we had police in quite often." As she spoke Adele poured the lemonade into the glasses causing the ice to crackle invitingly. She picked up a glass and raised it toward them. "Cheers."

They obligingly retrieved their own drinks from the table and sipped the lemonade that to their surprise tasted strongly of rum. Seeing their surprise, Adele said, "Oh, don't worry, officers. It's just a little Bacardi. It does wonders to liven up the mornings." It was ten A.M. Krystal estimated the ratio of lemonade to rum at 50/50 and surmised it was a good thing they had come while the day was still young. The old lady would be comatose by afternoon if she kept pounding these things down.

Velazquez smiled engagingly and took a healthy swallow. "Best lemonade I've had for a long time Mrs. Fernandez."

"Please, call me Adele. I kept Fernie's name just to spite him. I did enjoy how it discomfited Fernie, especially when he wrote out the maintenance checks." She showed the row of small, white teeth she had used to gnaw at her ex-husband. They looked sharp.

Krystal cast a glance at their surroundings. "The judge was well-off, then?"

Adele threw back her head and laughed. "Oh, not really, not at first. My family has money, and I really didn't need anything from him. I just felt he owed me, and the court agreed.

"Who might benefit from the judge's death, Adele?" Krystal risked a cautious sip of the "lemonade."

"Why, mankind, I suppose, and women, in particular. The man was an absolute goat. All he thought about was rutting."

"I mean, is there an estate?"

"Yes, he had some real-estate investments set up by his political cronies and made decent money as a judge. He drove one of those little sports cars, too. He liked to zoom through South Beach with the top down. He probably thought it made him look younger."

"Do you know who inherits his estate?"

"There are no children, at least as far as I know, and certainly not with me. As his ex-wife, I suppose I might have a claim. The man was a judge; he must have left a will."

Velazquez finished his drink and held out the glass. "May I have another, Adele? Rum is like mother's milk to me." He winked at Krystal.

Adele beamed at Velazquez. "You're one of those handsome Cuban boys, aren't you? Where were you twenty years ago?" She batted heavily mascaraed eyes at him, and Krystal thought that twenty years was cutting it pretty thin.

"We all have our regrets, Adele." Velazquez raised his refilled glass to salute her.

A delighted Adele topped off her own glass and leaned back with a sigh. "Fernie was such a handsome young man. He was Cuban, too, you know. He and his parents came over to Florida on a raft made of oil drums and scrap lumber. They didn't have a cent and Fernie went to work shining shoes on the street and worked his way up from there. In many ways he was a brilliant man, but his good looks did him in. They did me in, too, so far as it goes. Lord, but he was an Adonis when he was young. Girls couldn't keep their hands off him, and when he asked me to marry him I thought I was the luckiest girl in the world. I was quite a number in those days myself, but I think he must really have been attracted by the money and my family's political connections. He was ambitious, and he was smart. We were together ten years before the other women became just too much to bear. I'm not sure he was ever faithful to me. At first I was proud that all the women fawned on him believing he was mine. But finally, when his career really took off, I found out about the others. A dalliance or two I might have managed, but not that."

"There were a lot of women after his money?"

"Women? More like young girls looking for a good time. He was in his mid-forties. Those girls were still in their late teens or early twenties. A man like Fernie just couldn't resist."

Krystal wasn't sure this was leading anywhere. Adele was describing things that had taken place twenty years ago. She needed more recent information. But before she could speak Velazquez chimed in. "This rings a bell, Adele. When you refer to 'girls' do you mean an escort service?"

"Of course. I suppose the old satyr got tired of trolling the bars for girls to pick up and found out about Daddy's Girls."

Krystal looked inquiringly at Velazquez.

He explained, "Daddy's Girls is an escort service that specializes in placing girls with well-to-do gentlemen. The girls, many of them college students, aren't looking for marriage. They just want a sugar daddy to take care of them financially and provide expensive gifts and cars. It's all perfectly legal because it's set up as an 'introduction' service. Clients pay a one-time fee for an introduction, and what happens afterwards is entirely private between consenting adults."

Adele slitted her eyes. "That's the one."

"I think we may be straying off course," said Krystal. "What about more recently? Can you think of anything that could be related to the judge's death?"

"Well, my heavens. I thought it was that Tandy girl in the papers."

"We have to look at every possibility, ma'am."

"I'd like to help, but I've not been involved in Fernie's life for quite some time now. You might talk to Brian Cottrell. He was Fernie's law partner when they first started out, and they stayed close, especially when it came to politics. Fernie was planning to run for office, you know, and Brian was helping."

They thanked Adele for her time and asked if she could tell them where to find Cottrell. She walked them back into the apartment on surprisingly steady legs and dug in a drawer until she found a business card.

CHAPTER 18

Brian Cottrell's law offices were near-by in yet another of the ubiquitous high-rises that lined Brickell Avenue, and their badges got them inside. The rich décor was intended to project success and did, and the blonde behind the reception desk veritably glowed with tanned good health. The girl possessed all the attributes required for a *Playboy* centerfold, a fact that obviously was not lost on Velazquez, who displayed his broadest smile as he explained their business and requested to see Cotrell.

The receptionist reciprocated with her own dazzling display of perfect white teeth before reaching to punch a button on her phone to advise her boss of their presence. She listened a moment, then said, "Mr. Cottrell will see you right away."

She pointed at a door with a brass plaque bearing the attorney's name.

Velazquez introduced them, and the hefty lawyer leveraged himself to his feet and lumbered around his enormous desk extending his hand first to Murphy and then to Velazquez. His meaty hand was firm and dry, and his smile was as authentic as a $25 Rolex. If a visit from members of the Homicide Squad bothered him he certainly wasn't showing it.

Gesturing for them to sit down in the comfortable leather chairs in front of his desk, he returned to his throne-like position behind it. The late morning sunlight through the large window behind him masked his features in shadow.

"How can I help you, officers?" he asked. "I'm always happy to be of assistance to the police."

They had agreed that Velazquez would do the talking. "Thanks for receiving us on such short notice, Mr. Cottrell. We're investigating the murder of Judge Fernando Fernandez. We understand you were close friends with him and were hoping you might have some information that would help us out."

"Poor Fernie! What a tragedy." He shook his head slowly back and forth. "But I understood from the media reports that the case was resolved. That girl ..."

"We're not quite finished with the investigation despite what the press might say. There is a strong possibility that the Tandy girl was innocent."

"The circumstances of her and her parents' death would indicate otherwise. But it's not my place to second-guess your investigation."

Lawyers, thought Krystal. Their job was argumentation. Sides didn't matter. Velazquez had filled her in on Cottrell's less than savory clientele, and she had taken an instant dislike to the man.

Velazquez didn't bat an eye and continued smoothly. "Much appreciated, Mr. Cottrell. Can you think of any enemies the judge may have had, anyone with a motive strong enough to want to do him in?"

Cottrell pulled a long face. "Well, he was a judge, and as such developed the usual list of people with grudges. But strong enough to provoke murder? The only people who come readily to mind were the Tandys. Beyond that, I don't think I can help you."

Velazquez gave the lawyer a long, silent look before standing up. "Thanks, Mr. Cottrell. We appreciate your help."

"Any time, Detective, any time." Cottrell offered up a wan smile, but didn't bother to rise as they left.

Cottrell sat in silent thought for several minutes after door had closed behind the detectives. The fact that they were questioning him about Fernandez did not sit well with him. When news of the judge's murder appeared in the media and that girl was named as his killer, he'd almost laughed at the irony of having paid someone else to do the job.

But now, if the dead girl were innocent, he was frankly flabbergasted that the Puerto Rican beaner he had hired to do the job had pulled it off so smoothly. He had never expected that Gutierrez might sub-contract the job, but evidently he had, unless he had disguised himself as a girl. The guy was slender enough to have done so. A wig and a dress maybe? Ten thousand dollars were more than enough for a hired killing with a lot left over.

But now the cops had come to Cottrell's door, and that presented an urgent problem that had to be taken care of before Gutierrez found his way back to his office in search of the second half of his payment. The beaner might be smart enough to pull off a murder, but that didn't guarantee he wouldn't bring the cops to Cottrell's door again.

"I really don't like that guy."

They were back out on the street. Velazquez said, "Neither do I, but he's a big fish down here, and people tread lightly around him."

"Even cops?"

"Even cops. So, what now?"

"I'd like to know what Fernandez spent all his money on. It's all dead ends so far, but I still think we're more likely to find leads to the murder down here than in Arlington. He was only there for a day before he was killed. This is where he lived, and he was surely not without enemies. There seem to have been a lot of women. Jealousy can become lethal."

"I'm sure there were dozens of women over the years, both before and after the divorce. It'll take a bit of digging."

"Where will you start?"

"With his friends and acquaintances. I'll try to find out all I can about his latest squeeze, or squeezes, and then track them down."

"Will your management give you the time?"

"I think I can convince them, especially if you request it formally. I agree with your analysis. The Tandy girl doesn't look like a viable suspect anymore."

"She's more like a victim. Murder by media, I'd say."

Tim Reiner's story in the Post had been tragically premature. Whoever had leaked Dawn Tandy's name to him had precipitated three gruesome deaths in a squalid trailer on a wet Miami night. Reiner and his source might as well have pulled the trigger themselves.

"How about lunch?" Velazquez interrupted her morbid train of thought.

"It's a little early."

"OK, how about I introduce you to Little Havana and some Cuban coffee first?"

"Sure."

"You don't sound very enthusiastic."

"I can't stop thinking about this case."

"You need a distraction. Clear your mind. Something will turn up."

Velazquez let the top down on the Porsche and zoomed away from Brickell to SW 8th Street, known locally as *Calle Ocho*, and Little Havana. To Murphy it was like entering a foreign country. The street bustled with activity under a sun that cast dark shadows, giving the scene an almost cinematic quality. There were old men sitting at card tables in the open air playing dominoes, numerous small restaurants and shops with signs in Spanish. The place did not appear overly prosperous, but it had a comfortable, welcoming feel, like someplace you'd been before. Velazquez parked and led her to a small corner shop where in rapid Spanish he ordered small, sticky pastries and thick, sweet coffee that came in thimble-sized paper cups. It was perhaps the best coffee she had ever tasted.

They sat at a table set up on the sidewalk in front of the shop and she soaked up the atmosphere, the conversations in rapid Spanish from the people who flowed around them, the rich aroma of cigar smoke that wafted from a table near-by, accompanied by the slap and click of dominoes. In the Washington area the summer sun was punishing and the air heavy with humidity. People there scurried from one air-conditioned refuge to another, and everything was rushed. Here, life seemed more leisurely, people mingled and laughed, and the sun was friendly and embracing. She turned her face skyward and closed her eyes, letting the warmth seep into her body and relax her muscles.

"Welcome to Miami." She opened her eyes to see Velazquez looking at her with that gleaming smile of his that caused even Murphy's armored heart to beat a little faster.

She smiled back at him. "I see what you mean."

When they'd finished the pastries and coffee, he drove them to the other end of SW 8th Street and pulled into a parking lot next to a neatly maintained, rambling, white building. Green letters on the tall sign outside spelled out "Versailles." This was the restaurant Sara Hampton had recommended. It was still before noon, so finding a table was no problem. The place was standing room only by the time they left an hour and half later.

Velazquez introduced her to the delights of *mariquitas con mojo*, yucca, *moros y cristianos*, and *ropa vieja*, followed by custard and more Cuban coffee. It was more food than Krystal could handle, but Velazquez didn't seem to mind.

"Tonight we'll try out some real Spanish cuisine," he said.

"Jeez, we've just finished one meal and you're already talking about the next?"

"We think a lot about food. It's a common trait among Spanish speaking people. We like to gather and talk around tables groaning with wonderful food. And my ulterior motive is to make Miami so attractive that you'll return sometime soon."

She had to smile at his persistence.

He continued, "Another tradition is the *siesta*, and you look like you could use one."

She looked at him sharply with vexation-widened eyes. *Doesn't this guy ever give up? Now he suggests a nooner?*

He read her thoughts immediately and for the first time since they'd met looked discomfited as the words tumbled out of his mouth. "I didn't mean what you're thinking. I have to get back to HQS now and start sifting through what we have on Fernandez's acquaintances, see if anything was discovered at his residence, make a few phone calls. I'll drop you back at the hotel and maybe have some new info for you when I pick you up for dinner."

He was taking it for granted that she accepted the dinner invitation.

Actually, an afternoon break sounded like a good idea. She would only be in the way at MDPD HQS, and she should check in with her own people in Arlington, which she could do from the hotel. The dinner invitation was acceptable, too.

Back in her room, she took a quick shower and wrapped her head in a towel and her body in the in the luxury of the thick terrycloth robe the hotel provided. Velazquez's suggestion of a siesta was appealing, and she lay on the bed and stacked a couple of pillows behind her head. She grabbed the TV remote and tuned into a news channel just in time to catch the tail end of a report on another terrorist bombing in Afghanistan that had killed several people.

The flirtation with Ray Velazquez was immediately crowded out of her mind by concern for Thomas Stewart. She had no way of knowing if he was even in Afghanistan or if his work brought him into contact with terrorists, at all. His mysterious trips had annoyed but not frightened her because Thomas himself never betrayed concern. But macho

nonchalance was something she had noted in her
friend, former CIA officer Robert Strachey, as well. It
seemed to go with the job. Strachey had once
explained to her that espionage was an esoteric art
with an ethos and culture all its own that few could
master.

If she and Thomas carried their relationship to
the next level and perhaps beyond she would
undoubtedly be permitted a glimpse into that arcane
world. Police work provided a view of the human
character that was seldom pleasant, but cases had
beginnings and endings. For people like Thomas, the
battle was perpetual and fluid. Was anything ever
really resolved in his world?

Her thoughts were interrupted by the sound of
a familiar voice, and she jerked her head toward the
television. Sara Hampton's face filled the screen. She
was making an announcement to the media, and
Krystal recognized the façade of Arlington County
Police Headquarters in the background.

The camera zoomed out to show the
Commonwealth Attorney behind a bank of
microphones.

"As you know, the sole suspect in the murder of
Judge Fernando Fernandez, Dawn Tandy, was killed
along with her mother by her father, a man with a
fanatical hatred of Judge Fernandez. We can only
suppose that his daughter shared the hatred that
provided the motive for the judge's murder. We know
that the young lady was in Washington at the time of
the murder, that she was aware of the judge's
presence, and the Arlington Police have determined

that she had no alibi for the time the crime was committed. In the absence of other leads and given the facts just outlined, the tragic deaths last night in Miami must bring to a conclusion the Arlington County Police investigation into this case."

Krystal sat straight up on the bed, the reporters' questions drowned out by the blood drumming in her ears. How could Sara be doing this? She'd not even called to consult before going ahead. *Politics.* Sara wanted to tie a neat ribbon around the case and move on rather than be saddled with an ongoing, open-ended investigation of a notorious murder that might never be resolved.

She leapt from the bed and threw her belongings into her bag. She had to get back to Arlington pronto if she were to salvage the case. Surely Sara would listen to reason.

Dinner with Ray Velazquez was forgotten.

CHAPTER 19

It was after seven P.M. by the time Krystal walked out of the National Airport terminal and grabbed a taxi from the queue. It was still daylight and the smell of jet fuel infused the air around the terminal. Having made certain the Pakistani cabbie understood where she wanted to go she punched the speed dial on her cell phone for Sara Hampton. She had tried numerous times without success to contact Sara before leaving Miami. The Commonwealth Attorney was away from her desk at a meeting, she had been told. *Which meant she didn't want to talk to Krystal.*

Sara's office number this time responded with voice-mail, and a call to her home was answered by Fred Hampton, Sara's husband. Fred was a former Democratic Congressman from Maryland who had lost his seat in the Reagan landslide of 1980 and moved seamlessly to a prestigious K Street lobbying firm. He and Sara had met at a party rally in the 90's, and it had been kismet according to what Sara had told Krystal. Fred was rolling in money, had no further political ambitions for himself, and was more than happy to bankroll his wife's climb up the party ranks.

"Fred, I've been trying to call Sara all afternoon. Is she there?"

There was an awkward pause that quivered Krystal's detective antennae. He was conjuring up an answer. The politician's talent for quick and natural dissimulation seemed temporarily to have abandoned Fred.

"She's not here, Krystal. I don't know when she'll be home," he said at last. Krystal had a sudden vision of Sara standing beside Fred waving her hands and shaking her head.

Her response was thick with sarcasm. "Whatever you say, Fred." She was angry and not about to let him get away with thinking he was deceiving her. "When you do see her, please let her know that we need to talk as soon as possible."

She stewed in the back of the cab the rest of the way home. Sara had good cause to avoid a conversation. The Commonwealth Attorney, no matter how grand her title, had had no right to declare the Fernandez case closed when in actuality it was just

Michael R. Davidson

getting underway in Miami, a much more likely place to discover leads. What was worse, Sara had thrown Dawn Tandy's still bleeding corpse under the bus for more abuse, all but declaring her to have murdered the judge in collusion with her crazy father.

Tossing the matter into the cold case files might be convenient for Sara Hampton's political ambitions, but Krystal resolved to plead her case with Deputy Chief Jefferson and even the Chief of Police.

The light on her answering machine was blinking like a bloodshot eye in a cave when she entered her darkened apartment. Maybe Sara had left a message. She dropped her traveling bag to the floor, switched on the light and headed for the kitchen where she pulled the nearly depleted Laphroaig from under the counter, plopped a couple of ice cubes in a glass, and poured a healthy measure of the peaty whisky, reflecting a she did so that Bob Strachey would frown on the ice. After the experiences of the past few days she felt she owed herself the indulgence. She felt a generalized sense of foreboding that she couldn't shake. She pulled a frozen meal from the fridge and popped it into the microwave without even checking to see what it was, which brought to mind the wonderful meals she'd enjoyed in Miami with Ray Velazquez and how much she had enjoyed the handsome Cuban's attentions, droll and forward though they had been. Her mouth curled upward at the corners at the thought.

Glass in hand, ice cubes clinking in time with her footsteps, she returned to the living room to check her messages, and was surprised at how pleased she was to find one was from Velazquez. The time stamp told her he'd called about the same time her plane was landing at Reagan National.

"Tried to call your cell, but you must still have been aboard the plane," he said, "I saw the news from Arlington. What the hell is going on up there with your prosecutor? It's not sitting well with our guys, and my boss gave me the green light to keep digging, so you don't have to worry if you can't send an official request." He paused then continued, his voice dropping to a throatier pitch. "Krystal, I really enjoyed meeting you and getting to spend some down time with you. I hope that somehow you can find a way to come back to Miami so we can take up where we left off. Take care."

He might have been referring to the investigation, but Krystal was certain his interest was not confined to professional activities. He was a bloody Latin lothario! She raised her glass to the answering machine. "Salud, amigo." He'd taught her that much Spanish, and she couldn't repress a smile.

There was an earlier call from the Strachey's that was probably a dinner invitation. Amy was a fantastic cook, and Murphy was a frequent guest at their table. But the voice on the message was Robert Strachey's, and he sounded somber.

"Krystal, give me a call as soon as you can. It's important," was all he said.

The tone of his voice chilled her mood, and she took another sip of her drink before setting the glass on the coffee table and punching the speed dial for the

Strachey home in McLean. A glance at her watch told her it was nearly 8:00 PM.

Robert answered. "Krystal, thank Heaven you got my message. I'm afraid I have some bad news. Thomas Stewart has been seriously injured and is *en route* to Walter Reed from overseas. I thought you would want to know."

The air rushed out of her lungs as though she'd been punched in the stomach. The flirtation with Ray Velazquez that only seconds ago had brought a smile to her face was transformed into a guilty memory. She recalled the news broadcast she'd heard in Miami about the deaths in Afghanistan. She caught her breath and asked Strachey, "Was he in Afghanistan? I heard about a bombing. How bad is it?"

"I'm afraid I can't say a lot right now. But the medevac plane is due at Andrews sometime tomorrow. He was initially treated at a field facility and then airlifted to Germany. I really don't know the nature or extent of his injuries, I'm afraid. Amy's still at the office trying to find out. We should know soon."

Amy Strachey was in charge of a top secret computer program at CIA Headquarters.

"Please call as soon as you find out anything. I'll want to see him at Walter Reed. And, thank you, Bob, for letting me know."

It had to have been the bombing in Afghanistan.

CHAPTER 20

Ramon Gutierrez was frightened. His arm where the knife had sliced it left a trail of crimson splotches behind as he raced down the sidewalk. Behind him, his attacker lay doubled into a fetal position with several knife wounds that were likely to prove fatal.

Sudden wealth had become a curse. Friends had warned him that word on the street was that there was a contract out on him. At first he'd laughed it off. Who would have reason to kill him? And then it hit him – that lawyer, Cottrell. Cottrell had the means and capability to order him killed, and the reason was apparent now that he took the time to think about it.

Cottrell had hired him to kill Judge Fernie Fernandez and handed him a ten thousand dollar down payment, but before he could even make plans, that crazy girl they talked about on television had bumped the old guy off up in Washington, and that made Ramon a loose end. The consequences had now been made painfully clear.

He'd been standing with his girlfriend, Marisol, on the sidewalk in front of their favorite bodega in South Miami when some guy he'd never laid eyes on before appeared out of nowhere wielding a knife. Ramon instinctively raised his arm in defense and received a deep gash. Had his girlfriend not grabbed the assailant's arm as he drew it back for a second blow Ramon would never have had the time to pull his own blade and jam it between the guy's ribs and again into his stomach. He could not remember how many times.

Marisol's scream had brought him out of his stupor as he stared down at the body leaking blood all over the sidewalk. He told Marisol to get away as fast as she could, and he ran in the opposite direction. But he knew there was no place he could hide, not in Miami. If Cottrell had gone to his boss instead of hiring a freelancer, no place in Miami would be safe for Ramon.

He'd blown the down payment from the lawyer on the biggest diamond ring he could find for Marisol. He didn't dare go back to his apartment, and he didn't have enough money to get out of town. There was only one thing he could do.

CHAPTER 21

Thomas had been transported in an Army MI-17 helicopter to a battlefield hospital, a facility that had saved the lives of countless American wounded. A trauma team worked late into the night, and before dawn the next morning Thomas was placed on a plane to Landstuhl Regional Medical Center in Germany for further evaluation and preparation for transport to the States.

The U.S. Air Force Aeromedical Evacuation System is highly efficient. CCATT patients are initially stabilized in the field and then evacuated from the combat zone and through a series of increasingly sophisticated medical facilities. The shrapnel wound to his chest had been diagnosed as life-threatening before evacuation to Landstuhl.

By evening his condition had stabilized, and he was placed aboard an Air Force C9 Nightingale for transport to Walter Reed National Military Medical Center in Bethesda, Maryland.

Krystal and the Stracheys drove in a car filled with apprehensive silence to Bethesda as soon as Amy confirmed that the plane had landed at Andrews Air Force Base and he had been transferred. This was a big deal for the CIA, and according to Amy Agency brass had been at the base to meet the plane.

Ominously, Thomas had been sent immediately to surgery.

His parents and his sister joined them, and now the group waited in aching silence for more information. It was nearly six P.M. before a doctor in scrubs found them in the waiting area. He introduced himself as Colonel Mills, Chief Neurological Surgeon, and the news was not encouraging.

"Thomas is resting comfortably, but he is unconscious, and we plan to keep him that way for some time. He suffered three shrapnel wounds, one to his shoulder which has been treated and should present no serious problem. The second wound is much more serious: a piece of shrapnel penetrated his chest. But it's the third wound that has us worried: shrapnel also penetrated his skull, and the surgery to remove it will be very delicate. We won't attempt it until he's a little stronger. You should be prepared for a long and unpredictable recovery."

Thomas's mother and sister were hugging one another and softly sobbing, somewhere between relief that Thomas would live and dread of what a traumatic brain injury might imply for his future.

The surgeon was not being unkind by his straightforward presentation of the facts. Krystal suspected he had had many such conversations with grieving relatives discovered that forthrightness was the best method of preparing loved ones for the rigors that lay ahead.

In a softer voice he continued, "There was a deep penetration to the left side of his brain, the part that controls language and cognition. We won't know the full extent of the damage until he regains consciousness. We'll keep him in an induced coma for a few days to allow as much healing as possible and reduce stress and swelling. But it's important that you realize that once brain cells are damaged or destroyed, they will never return. You should be prepared for some possible paralysis of his right side, as well, but it's too early to tell."

After another hour they were permitted into Thomas's room. Family went first, two at a time, ushered by a nurse in military fatigues. When she entered the room with Amy, Krystal girded her emotions. She'd seen trauma before, but her feelings on this occasion were confused. Was she here at Walter Reed because she had developed an emotional attachment to the dashing CIA officer beyond mere physical attraction? Or was she here because these people, Robert and Amy, expected her to be involved, assumed that she and Thomas were closer than they really were? It felt like stepping into a dark pool without knowing its depth. A few more steps and she would be over her head.

Thomas lay still as death in the hospital bed. He head was swathed in bandages, and his breathing was regulated by a respirator, the tube of which was taped to the side of his face. Sophisticated monitoring equipment recorded his life signs, transmitted by wires that snaked out from under the crisp, white sheet. The tube from a saline drip was taped to the back of his hand. The click and wheeze of the respirator were the only sounds in the room as she approached his bedside. The handsome face was sallow beneath the tan. Krystal swallowed a sob that involuntarily jerked at her chest. She noticed that the nurse discreetly held a box of Kleenex in one hand and resolved that she would not need one. She waved the nurse away.

This was not the case with Amy Strachey, a gentle soul who had known Thomas much longer. Tears coursed freely down her cheeks, and she gratefully accepted the offer of a tissue.

"How long will it be before he wakes up?" croaked Krystal.

"The Doctor will probably will not bring him out of the induced coma until after the surgery." The nurse glanced at the monitoring read-outs. "His vital signs are not where we would like to see them."

"But how about mentally? This was a brain injury." Krystal was a detective. She had to ask questions.

The nurse frowned slightly. "That's something to discuss with the doctor. We see lots of TBI's, traumatic brain injuries, here, and results vary considerably. He's strong and he's young, so there's every reason to hope for the best."

How many times had the nurse said the same thing to distressed relatives of the severely wounded?

CHAPTER 22

Krystal flung herself onto the sofa in a depressed and vaguely confused state that was unusual for her. She cast her eyes around the apartment, alighting on old family photographs, her miniature cow collection, and finally coming to rest on a photo of herself as a pigtailed Hoosier teenager with her arms around the family German shepherd, Ozzie. She'd loved that dog, now long gone, and the unbidden thought that now she did not even have a pet to comfort her provoked a gush of tears that surprised and embarrassed her.

The tall, easy-going CIA man had burrowed more deeply under her skin than she had been willing to admit even to herself, and the realization left her distrustful of her own feelings. She felt smothered under the oppressive weight of Thomas's condition and uncertain prognosis, a prognosis that could well color her own future. She had to sort this out, sort herself out.

She didn't know how long she sat there in the semi-darkness when the trill of the phone brought her back into focus. She rubbed her eyes with both hands and gulped a couple of deep breaths before lifting the receiver.

"Krystal?" It was Ray Velazquez's voice.

She cleared her throat before daring to speak. "Yeah. What's up, Ray?"

"Are you okay? Your voice is different."

"I'm okay. I just got back from visiting a friend in the hospital. It was kind of a downer."

"Sorry to hear that." She detected authentic concern in his voice, some natural Latino talent for empathy. "I have some news about the Fernandez case and thought you'd want to hear it."

She sat up, eager to divert her thoughts away from Thomas Stewart. "I'm all ears, Ray."

"You remember that lawyer, Brian Cottrell?"

"Of course."

"Well, one of his former clients, a small-time lowlife named Ramon Gutierrez, walked into the station late today to volunteer that Cottrell paid him to kill Fernie Fernandez."

The news cleared the fog from her mind like a stiff breeze. This could be the break they were looking for, the game changer that would clear Dawn Tandy. She sat straight up pressing the receiver more tightly against her ear. "No shit? What are you going to do?"

"You already know that Cottrell is a big wheel in South Florida politics, so we have to tread carefully. We're going to polygraph Gutierrez tomorrow. If it looks like he's telling the truth, I'm going to interview Cottrell. Wanna come down for the fun?"

There was barely disguised eagerness in his question, like a kid asking a girl to the prom.

"I'd love to, Ray, but I don't think I can do right now." It was hard to turn down the invitation. She almost had said yes. She wanted to say yes. Until today the Fernandez murder had been foremost in her thoughts. But right now, she'd give anything to jump on a plane for almost any destination to get as far away from Washington and its complications as possible.

Velazquez was disappointed. "But ...? Is it your friend in the hospital?" He emphasized the word friend.

"Yes. I just can't leave right now."

"I understand." There was a moment's silence. "This friend is the man you told me about?" She could hear his breathing at the other end of the line.

She'd told Velazquez that she was involved with someone else and almost had regretted it at the time.

"Yes, it is."

"Is it serious?"

She paused before answering, irrationally wondering for a wild second whether Velazquez was asking about Tom's condition or the way she felt about him. *Idiot, of course he was asking about Tom's condition!* "I'm afraid it is."

"I'm really sorry, Krystal. I hope things work out." He sounded like he meant it.

"I do too. Will you keep me in the loop anyhow?"

"Of course."

She felt ridiculously grateful for the positive response.

She replaced the phone in its cradle, her mind a battleground of opposing priorities. Finally, a new thought forced its way to the surface like a bubble rising through thick oil. She grabbed the phone again and punched in the number for Ray Velazquez's cell phone.

"Ray, Fernandez was murdered by a woman, and she didn't look like a guy in drag. Has this guy you have in custody said anything about a woman?"

The connection was good, and Krystal heard Velazquez chuckle softly. "I was going to discuss it with you, but you have bigger things to worry about right now."

She needed, really needed to focus her attention on the case, to force her thoughts back into the proper groove.

"That doesn't mean I'm not still interested. So, what's the skinny on this guy?"

"Atta girl." He sounded encouraged. "Like I said, Gutierrez is a lowlife with a minor record. He's an enforcer for a South Miami drug family, but he's never done time. He might now, though. It looks like he killed a man before coming to us."

"So this criminal killed someone and ran straight to the cops? We need more criminals like him. It'd save a lot of street work."

Velazquez chuckled again. "He came to us for safety. He thinks Cottrell put a contract on him to keep him quiet."

"This case just gets weirder by the moment."
And deadlier, too. Counting the person Gutierrez allegedly had killed, the toll was now at five bodies. "We know for a fact that your guy didn't kill the judge. What about a girlfriend?"

"He has one, and we're looking for her now. Gutierrez claims she can testify that he killed the man in self-defense."

"Good. We can compare her to the woman in the video."

"Her name is Marisol Alonso, and I doubt she's a blonde. And Gutierrez is not exactly a matinee idol, so Marisol is unlikely to be a looker like your killer."

"You'll let me know when you find her?"

"Wouldn't think of doing otherwise, Krystal. Look after yourself and do what you have to do."

"Thanks, Ray."

She ended the call and wished she were in Miami instead of Arlington and that Thomas Stewart were not in a hospital bed fighting for his life.

CHAPTER 23

The rain fell steadily all morning, beating a martial tattoo onto the unfurled black umbrellas. Scudding clouds blocked the sun, draining color and leaving only shades of gray and pools of darker shadow that covered like mourning veils the faces of those beneath the umbrellas. The small, marble markers stretched into the distance in straight lines of crosses and stars of David until they disappeared into the mist that clung still low to the earth reminding Krystal of the lines of an old song her dad had liked: "Old soldiers never die; they just fade away." Even the reports from the rifles of the honor guard sounded muted by the oppressive mist.

Death had overwhelmed hope and prayer to claim Thomas Stewart. Now, three days later, lingering disbelief laden with grief etched the faces of his friends and family as they gathered around the grave at Arlington National Cemetery. The CIA, of course, had sent a representative of appropriate rank, and many of Thomas's Agency colleagues were present, as well.

Krystal had chosen to wear her Army Reserves dress blues. Thomas's mother had hugged her tightly and whispered that her son had written so much about her to the family.

The Strachey's drove her home afterwards, the atmosphere in the car filled with an opaque silence that isolated each of them with their own thoughts. The Stracheys and Thomas's family had expressed condolences to her as though the loss should be affecting her more than them.

Alone in her apartment she sorted through her feelings. There was sorrow, there was regret, but also there was that most painful companion of death -- guilt.

She had cared for Thomas Stewart, and something deeper had been stirring, but whatever it had been it had blossomed for Thomas before fully developing for Murphy. She had made no promises, and he, perhaps sensing her hesitation, had made no demands. The fact that his family and the Strachey's *assumed* there had been something more only added to the burden and left her adrift in unfamiliar waters.

A tiny spark of anger finally was kindled and waxed bright. Were things that had never happened, an incomplete relationship, fair cause for guilt? Thomas had been a fine and admirable man. Might they have developed a deep and lasting bond? Perhaps, and she could rightfully mourn losing the possibility.

She recognized that the guilt did not arise from her relationship with Thomas, but rather from what others assumed that relationship to have been. They had placed her in a position where it was impossible to tell the truth, where she had to pretend, if only through lack of denial, that she had been in love with Thomas. To give voice to denial would be hurtful to all those grieving people. She would have to live with this for a long time.

Jefferson called her to his office the day after funeral and invited her to take a seat. He had lined the wall behind his desk with plaques, diplomas, awards, and nicely framed photos of himself with various prominent people, including several with Sara Hampton. This was a bureaucratic twitch common in Washington among those who saw themselves on the ladder to success and eager to demonstrate that they enjoyed influential contacts. People in government sought trinkets like presidential cuff links that the Secret Service handed out like candy. Such trinkets and photos became totems of magically transferred power to be displayed. The displays were known derisively as "vanity walls."

Jefferson composed his face into somber lines and his voice when he spoke was solicitous and an octave below his usual tone, the remnants of his southern drawl becoming more pronounced.

"Krystal, I received a call from Sara Hampton last night informing me of your loss. I'm very sorry. I didn't even know you were engaged. Please accept my and the Department's condolences."

"I wasn't ..." She had not been engaged to Thomas, not even close.

Before she could finish, Jefferson shushed her and plowed ahead. "I can't imagine what you're feeling right now, but after a tragedy like this you have no business being on the job. I admire your famous grit, but you need to take some time off."

She choked back the denial that had risen in her throat like bitter bile. "I'd rather stay on the job, Marty. There's this new lead in Miami."

Jefferson leaned back in his chair and contemplated her for a few beats before shaking his head. "That's an admirable attitude, Krystal, and very brave, but I've discussed this with the Commonwealth Attorney and the Chief of Police, and we've decided to grant you two weeks administrative leave. You've been working at a tremendous pace and under great strain, and we think this would be the best thing for you and for the Department."

"But ..." She wanted to fill him in on developments in Miami.

Jefferson rose to his feet and came around the desk. "No arguments, Krystal. It's been decided." He placed his hand lightly on her shoulder, something the diplomatic and politically correct Marty Jefferson had never done before. "Come on. I'll walk you to your car."

Half an hour later, Murphy pulled into her usual space in the parking lot of her apartment building and braked the car to a jolting halt. As her mother would have described it, she "had her Irish up," but in this instance had no convenient target against which to vent it. She felt victimized by assumptions she dare not refute. But why not? Thomas Stewart's parents and family had left Washington the same day as the funeral. There was no logical reason she couldn't tell the Stracheys or anybody else that they were mistaken about her and Thomas. This thought was refuted immediately when the realization hit her with the force of a speeding locomotive that she was protecting Thomas. To contradict the fantasy his family had concocted that he had known happiness and love before his untimely death would somehow diminish his memory. It would be a selfish act.

Her empty apartment offered no solace. She was most fearful that people would start calling to offer condolences and baked goods. There was no way she could remain here. She made flight reservations, packed her bags, and drove to Reagan National Airport where she caught a flight to Miami.

CHAPTER 24

Ray Velazquez was surprised and his voice colored with pleasure when she called him from Miami International Airport. He agreed instantly to pick her up. "I'll be there in fifteen minutes," he said and added, "and I'll get your room back in Coconut Grove, too. How long will you be staying?"

"I don't know. Maybe a week."

"I'm on the way."

MDPD headquarters was only a short distance from the airport on NW 25th St., and she soon saw his car weaving through the airport traffic. Velazquez was still driving the Porsche and had the top down. She could see that he was wearing a short-sleeved, white *guayabera* that contrasted sharply with his sun-darkened skin, and his thick, blond hair was tousled by the wind. He sprang out almost before the wheels had stopped spinning to grab Murphy's bag and open the passenger side door for her. "Seeing you back down here is an unexpected pleasure," he grinned. "Is this another official visit?"

"Not exactly." She settled into the seat and fiddled with the seat-belt more than necessary in order not to meet his eyes. She knew the question was coming but could think of no way to avoid it. She closed her eyes and rested her head back against the sun-warmed, creamy leather of the headrest.

His brow creased behind his sunglasses but he said nothing as he slid behind the wheel and engaged the gears. They slipped away from the curb out into the slowly moving line of cars circling to pick up arriving passengers. Once they were away from the terminal he shot her a sidewise glance and asked, "What about your friend in the hospital?"

There it was – her permanent baggage. Without turning her head, she said, "He died."

"Oh." He was silent, processing her words, then, "I'm very sorry, Krystal. When did this happen?"

"The day after we last spoke on the phone. The funeral was yesterday."

Velazquez, for once, was at a loss for words. He drove silently out of the airport and pulled onto the Dolphin Expressway heading east. As he accelerated the exhaust of the Porsche left a high-pitched, guttering Doppler trail in their wake. He retreated to safer ground. "I'm taking you straight to the hotel, OK?"

"Yep." She wasn't going to talk about it if she didn't have to.

Velazquez negotiated the cloverleaf off the highway onto SW 27th St. and headed south toward Coconut Grove. Murphy lifted her face to the clear, blue sky and enjoyed the wind and the sun in her face. Miami really did have its own feel, like a tropical island. Neither said a word until he pulled to a stop under the portico at the Ritz Carleton.

He switched off the engine and slid his frame out from under the wheel with a lithe, practiced movement, then circled around to open her door, ever the Latin gentleman. Krystal's mother would have commented that he had been "raised proper."

He waited until she had twisted her way out of the low, bucket seat onto the pavement before retrieving her single bag from the boot. "Still travelling light, I see. Let's get you checked in, and it's still at the policeman's discount rate." A crooked, uncertain smile carefully arranged itself on his face.

"Thanks, Ray. I really appreciate it."

And she did.

The registration formalities complete, Velazquez escorted her to the elevator and reached out to touch her shoulder. "Just give me a call if you need anything, Krystal."

She looked up at him, shaking off the thick patina of gloom with which she had armored herself against any discussion of Thomas. "Don't go anywhere until I can dump my bag in the room. I want to go back to police headquarters with you. I want to see where you are on the Fernandez case."

It was the third time that day she had surprised him, and she was glad to banish if only temporarily the shade of Thomas Stewart.

"You're here officially, after all?" he asked.

"Not exactly. But the case is on the far back burner in Arlington and all the action is down here."

He cocked his head and repeated. "'Not exactly?' That's the second time you've said that."

She nodded. "No one in Arlington even knows I'm here."

He frowned for a second before his face was cleared by a characteristic flash of white teeth. "Well, we don't have to tell that to anyone down here, do we?"

In the room she didn't have to change clothes as she had flown in her standard jeans and polo shirt combo. She pulled her service pistol from her bag (cops are allowed to bring their weapons onto planes) and clipped the holster to her belt along with her badge. An Arlington Police baseball cap completed her wardrobe. Before leaving the room she unfolded the blue print dress she'd bought on her last trip to Miami and put it on a hanger it in the closet. She'd folded it carefully and placed it in her bag at the last moment.

Velazquez eyed her weapon when she stepped out of the elevator. "Now you really look official."

Back in the Porsche, she removed her baseball cap and leaned back to catch the sun on her face, welcoming the Miami warmth that penetrated her clothing and skin and sank down to her bones. She wondered why the heat in Miami should seem so different from the heat in Washington. There it was oppressive; here it felt welcoming. Maybe it was the palm trees.

Velazquez said, "I thought redheads tried to avoid the sun."

She opened one eye in his direction. "You mean like vampires and albinos? I grew up in farm country, and I'm used to the sun. And I guess I'm lucky that my skin doesn't freckle."

"There must be some Latino blood in you, then."

"Not unless they somehow found their way to Ireland before the 19th century."

"Oh, we Latinos get around. Some survivors of the Spanish Armada landed in Ireland, you know."

"You have enough blarney to be Irish," she said, beginning to feel more like a normal person. She closed her eyes again, and more of the tension drained away. The Cuban cop's company was a good antidote to gloom.

"You said you were going to polygraph Gutierrez. How did that turn out?"

Velazquez kept his eyes on the road as he maneuvered the sports car in and out of traffic. "He passed with flying colors. That did not please the MDPD brass."

"Why not?"

"I told you Cottrell is a mover and shaker in Miami politics. I'm still waiting for permission to interview him."

Politics and police work are uneasy bedfellows, and the Fernie Fernandez murder was a case in point. "The brass isn't going to hold you up too much longer, are they?"

"I'm pushing them as much as I can. I don't see how they can stop it, but they'll lay down some ground rules for sure."

"I'd like to tag along on that interview."

Velazquez took his eyes off the road long enough for a quick squint at her from behind his Ray Bans. "Are you sure? I get the impression it could get you in trouble at home."

"Maybe," she shrugged, "but I still want in if you can do it. It ain't over 'til it's over, and it's still a long way from over." *Sara Hampton's political ambitions be damned.*

"Shouldn't be a problem."

Velazquez slipped the Porsche into a space in the headquarters parking lot and raised the top before they went inside.

"Last thing we want is to sit on boiling hot leather when we come out," he said.

Krystal accompanied him to the Specialized Investigations Squad premises on the second floor. They navigated their way past Velazquez's guayabera and Hawaiian shirt clad fellow officers to his desk where he found a memo providing clearance to interview Brian Cottrell. A handwritten note was scrawled across the top instructing him to check in with the head of the Homicide Bureau before taking action.

It was another twenty minutes before Velazquez returned. He jerked his head toward the exit, and Krystal snatched her baseball cap from his desk and followed. Catching up to him she sensed he was not an entirely happy camper.

"What's up?"

He waved a hand in the air, fingers splayed. "Do you see it?"

"See what?"

"The kid glove. I can interview Cottrell again, but I have to do it *politely*."

"Let's look on the bright side. At least it's a start."

"Apparently the results of Gutierrez' polygraph are worth next to nothing as evidence. Without corroboration it's still just his word against Cottrell's, and Cottrell carries a lot more weight."

"So all Cottrell has to do is deny knowledge."

"*Si, señorita. ¡Me cago en la leche!*"

"What does that mean?"

"You don't want to know."

The lawyer was clearly not happy to see them again.

"To what do I owe the honor of a second visit? Has there been progress in your investigation?" The expression on his face belied the tone of polite interest.

Michael R. Davidson

Velazquez said, "We've come across an individual with whom you might be familiar. His name is Ramon Gutierrez. Does the name mean anything to you?"

Krystal watched the lawyer for any signs that may betray guilt or concern but detected nothing as his demeanor remained unruffled.

After a moment's theatrical thought, Cottrell replied, "Yes. He is a former client. I defended him in court some time ago."

Velazquez continued, "Have you had any recent contact with him?"

Cottrell smiled. "That's why I remember him so well. He came here to see me a couple of weeks ago."

"For what reason?"

"I'm afraid that falls under attorney-client privilege, detective. May I ask the reason for your interest?"

Velazquez ignored the question. "So he came to you regarding a legal matter?"

"Yes, he did." Cottrell shifted slightly in his chair, impatience registering in his body language. "Can we please get to the point of your visit, detective? I have other obligations this afternoon."

Velazquez offered up a friendly smile. "Of course, sir, no problem. Gutierrez was recently the target of a murder attempt that he feels was somehow connected to his relationship with you. But more to the point, he alleges that you contracted him to kill Fernie Fernandez. Would you care to comment on the allegation?"

Cottrell sucked in his breath and leaned back to survey them from beneath shaded lids. When at last he spoke his voice had acquired an edge. "That's the most preposterous thing I've ever heard, detective. I'm surprised you're wasting your time and mine with such an absurd story. What proof does Gutierrez offer to back up his claim?"

Krystal wondered if this was an attorney's question or the question of a man who wanted to confirm he had not made a mistake.

"He passed a polygraph examination."

Cottrell shook his head in disgust. "A polygraph examination! And you come to my office with only that? You know as well as I that the polygraph is a fickle and legally useless instrument." He rose ponderously behind the desk. "I unequivocally deny the allegation, and I will be making some phone calls to register my displeasure that you should even come to my office on such a flimsy pretext. Fernie was a good friend of mine of long standing. This interview is over." He gestured dismissively toward the door behind them.

Velazquez and Krystal stood.

"Thanks for your time, Mr. Cottrell," said Velazquez.

Half-way to the door Krystal grabbed Velazquez's elbow and turned back to Cottrell.

"Mr. Cottrell," she said, "just one more question, please. Did you attend the ACLU meeting in Washington with Judge Fernandez?"

The lawyer pursed his lips and stared at her with eyes as cold as a cobra's, but a cobra confronted by a mongoose. She thought he actually swayed a bit, as though the question put him slightly off balance. He'd paid little attention to her other than a quick leer when they'd entered his office, but now she commanded his full attention. He answered through clenched teeth. "Yes, as a matter of fact I was at the conference."

She persisted. "So you were in Washington when he was killed, perhaps in the same hotel?"

Cottrell snarled, "I left Washington immediately after the conference ended and did not spend the night. Now, please leave."

When the door closed behind the two detectives Cottrell sat heavily behind his desk where he remained unmoving and deep in thought for a long while. Something had occurred to him, something Fernie Fernandez had mentioned at the ACLU conference that he had nearly forgotten until now. He barked a laugh out loud as the way out of his dilemma fell into place.

Cottrell pressed a button on his intercom and instructing his receptionist to bring him a Washington, D.C. area phone book. After finding the number he sought, he opened a desk drawer that contained a dozen pre-paid "burner" cell phones. Such untraceable phones were useful for communications with certain of his less savory clients. He selected one and dialed the number he had found.

When the call was answered he identified himself and asked to speak with someone he knew would be particularly interested in the Fernie Fernandez case.

Chapter 25

"Well, that was fun," said Velazquez.

They contorted themselves back into the Porsche's low-slung seats. He started the engine and lowered the top again. Krystal found it curious but logical that while the lowered top exposed them to the tropical sun Velazquez simultaneously ran the air conditioner, creating their own micro climate. She decided that if there was ever a city made for convertibles it had to be Miami.

"I hope I didn't get you into any trouble with those questions." She had had no business questioning a suspect on Velazquez's turf, especially a suspect who was to be handled "delicately." But the question had clicked in her mind like a piece snapping into a jigsaw puzzle.

"I don't think so," he replied as he pulled out into the stream of traffic on Brickell. "It was a logical question, one I should have thought of myself, and it puts him physically close to the murder." Velazquez smiled grimly as he turned over the possibilities. "I'll have to check the manifests for flights from Washington to Miami the day of the murder to confirm his story."

Her question opened a whole new line of inquiry. She said, "If he hired Gutierrez here in Miami, he could have hired someone in Washington, as well."

"Maybe. But if that's what happened, Cottrell is not going to tell us, and we have no other leads. Let's sit down somewhere and talk this over."

He drove the short distance to Calle Ocho and the coffee shop where he had taken her on her previous visit. The same old men sat at the same tables under large umbrellas playing dominoes and sipping *mojitos*, beer, or sweet Cuban coffee from tiny, thimble sized paper cups.

Velazquez brought pastries and coffee to their table and sat opposite her. She couldn't get a read on his eyes because of the glare reflected from his sunglasses. She squinted in the bright sun picturing her own RayBans on the dresser in her bedroom in Arlington where she had forgotten them. She'd have to buy another pair down here soon or go blind from the reflection of sunlight from every surface.

She took a small sip of the thick and sweet black Cuban coffee, holding it on her tongue before swallowing slowly so the rich flavor would linger. "Well," she ventured, "it's beginning to quack."

He tipped his sunglasses down over his nose and crinkled his eyes before replying. "It quacks, yes, but I don't see anyone walking like a duck just yet."

"Maybe not. But there is a trail leading away from the Dawn Tandy theory. I just can't accept the idea that that girl was a killer and that the case ended with her death."

She shuddered involuntarily, recalling the bloody scene they had found inside the Tandy trailer. It clawed at her like a feral animal determined to subjugate its prey. The image of that destroyed young life, a life she believed was innocent, was why she clung so determinedly to this case.

Should she let go, release herself from yet another self-imposed obligation? The Arlington Police had all but relinquished control to the MDPD. She was expected to go with the flow because her friend did not want an unsolved murder to mar her record and spoil her chances to enter big-time politics. Where her loyalties, both professional and personal lay was the question she had to answer now. She hoped they would not be put to a more rigorous test.

"What do we know about Cottrell?" she asked. "Why would he want to have his old friend Fernie murdered?"

Velazquez raised his sunglasses back to bridge of his nose. "That's a good question."

"Gutierrez doesn't know?"

Velazquez popped a pastry into his mouth and chewed contemplatively for a moment. "I asked him about that, but he claimed to have no idea."

"There must be a motive."

"Duh! And that's where we're falling flat. The only strong motive related to the case belonged to the Tandy family, at least the only one we know about."

"Are you confident Gutierrez is telling the truth?"

"He passed the poly."

"Cottrell was right. It's not really a reliable measure of the truth," she said. "There are all sorts of ways to beat the machine. But why would he lie about such a thing?"

"Maybe to bargain his way out of a manslaughter charge."

Murphy didn't like the implications. The circumstances made it way too easy for Cottrell to squirm out of trouble, and he had the wherewithal to create trouble for Velazquez and her. "If Cottrell really did have a grudge against Fernandez, there is one person who might be able to shed some light on it," she said.

He grinned at her. "Adele."

Murphy was pleased that their thoughts coincided. The dead judge's ex-wife could well have more information than they had gleaned from their first, brief encounter with her. "Let's go over there right now."

He shook his head. "No, not now. Let's make it tomorrow morning."

"Why not now?"

Velazquez held out his arm to display his watch. "See what time it is? The sun is well past the yard-arm. She was already half tipsy when we saw her the last time. Let's try to catch her in the morning before she's had too much lemonade."

Chapter 26

Her cell phone warbled out a tinny version of the "Mission Impossible" theme just as she and Velazquez were finishing lunch. He had taken her to a small restaurant on Calle Ocho where he introduced her to the Cuban sandwich and *yucca frita*, which she discovered to her surprise that she preferred to French fries.

Thanks to the ring tone she didn't have to check caller i.d. to know it was Captain Marty Jefferson calling. Vclazquez shot a quizzical look as she brought the phone to her ear. Her face must have betrayed her surprise.

Jefferson got to the point without his usual "let's relax and reason together" preamble. "Murphy, what the hell are you doing conducting a murder investigation in Miami?"

And how the hell had Jefferson discovered where she was, let alone what she was doing? "Erm ..."

The Deputy Chief continued before she could think of an appropriate response. "You're supposed to be on leave taking it easy. I thought we were doing you a favor, but instead you went to Miami and stirred up trouble?" The tenor of his voice rose at the end, made it sound like a question.

She couldn't think of an answer or an evasion that would satisfy him, so she opted for frankness. "You gave me two weeks off, Marty. There weren't any conditions on where I could go or how I would spend the time."

"Goddamnit, Murphy, don't give me that bullshit! You know you're not supposed to spend any more time on the Fernandez case. I thought I made that clear."

The profanities were very unlike the normally urbane, politically correct Marty Jefferson. Someone had put a burr under his saddle. "That's not the way I remember our conversation, Marty. I don't remember your saying anything at all about the Fernandez case. And besides, I'm only tagging along with a buddy down here."

Velazquez cocked his head at the term "buddy."

"You're doing more than that from what I hear," he said. Was that anger or frustration in his voice?

Now they were getting to the nub of it. "What did you hear, Marty?"

"That you've been asking inappropriate questions of powerful people."

"And where did you hear this?"

"You don't deny it?"

"I might have asked one question."

"Yes, one inappropriate question."

"You mean Brian Cottrell. He may be a powerhouse down here, Marty, but he doesn't pull any weight in Arlington. And the question I asked was certainly not inappropriate. The guy admitted he was in Washington on the day Fernandez was murdered. And the MDPD have a guy who says Cottrell hired him to kill Fernandez."

"Really?" *That set him a tad back on his heels.*

"Really."

Jefferson was silent for a beat, maybe two, as he absorbed this news. Then, "Well, that may be fine and good, but it's not any business of ours. It's the MDPD's job to follow that up. You stay out of it."

"I don't understand, Marty," she said. But she thought she did. "Who told you about this?"

"That's not your concern. You've already disobeyed orders, and you know what could mean."

Had Cottrell somehow engineered this? Krystal wondered whether he also had contacted Velazquez's superiors. Given the circumstances, a bleat to the Miami authorities should have been his first move.

"No, Marty, I don't know. What exactly does that mean?" She'd make him say it out loud.

"It means Detective Lieutenant Murphy," he emphasized her title, "that as far as Arlington is concerned the Fernandez murder is a case that is now entirely in the hands of the MDPD, which will inform us when it is resolved. It means that you specifically are to butt out or there will be consequences."

"Me, specifically?"

"Emphatically."

"I don't see how what I'm doing could cause her a problem, politically or otherwise. And from the Commonwealth Attorney's point of view, solving a crime that happened on our turf should be a good thing." Maybe mentioning Sara would soften his position.

"Don't argue, Krystal. This case is no longer any of your concern. If the MDPD turns anything up that we can help with, they'll let us know. This is something to work through official channels. Since you're in Miami, why don't you just go to the beach and relax. You need to take it easy." He had reverted to a first name basis with her, and a pleading note that must have cost him a lot had appeared in his voice.

"And if I don't agree?" This was a dangerous question, but she couldn't help herself. She could feel her "Irish" rising.

"Then your administrative leave is cancelled, and you come home."

"Marty, four people have died so far, the judge and the three Tandy's – five if you count the guy Gutierrez knifed. We can't just drop the whole thing.

Dawn Tandy was not a murderer, no matter how inconvenient that might be for Sara Hampton."

Jefferson sighed heavily. "Krystal, Hampton has the ear of the Chief of Police. If they say it's over, that's it. We're out of it. If I hear one more report that you're still meddling in this case, you're coming back here. And if one word leaks to the 'Washington Post,' we'll know where to look."

This reference to Tim Reiner shocked her. "And that's it?"

"That's it."

She wasn't ready to surrender. Jefferson started to say something more, but she ended the call and sat stewing in her own thoughts. She had been hammered, and it did not feel good. She was being fed a strong dose of reality, the reality that she belonged to an organization and was subject to its hierarchy, even when she disagreed. So much for individual initiative. But the question that nagged at her was whether her perseverance was really so counterproductive as to justify such a reaction.

Velazquez was saying something.

"Earth to Krystal." His voice jolted her out of her reverie. "What was that all about? From the thunderclouds now circling your head it wasn't good news."

"That sonuvabitch Cottrell somehow pulled some strings in Arlington to get me off the case."

Velazquez sat back in surprise, both of his hands flat on the tabletop. "I gathered from your side of the conversation that it concerned the Fernandez case. But why did this load come down on you before it hit me? I expect to have an unpleasant conversation when I get back to headquarters this afternoon. Cottrell pulls a lot of weight in Dade County, but Arlington?"

"Your guess is as good as mine."

"What are you going to do?"

"I don't know yet. Can you drop me at my hotel now? I need to think about this."

"Do you still want to visit Adele Fernandez with me tomorrow morning?"

It didn't take a second for her to decide. "Damn straight!"

Chapter 27

The call from Brian Cottrell had been a surprise, a very unpleasant surprise. The Miami attorney had voiced more than a mere complaint about an inconvenient police investigation; the man had somehow guessed the truth about why Fernie Fernandez had been killed. The implied threat could not have been clearer. Things were spinning out of control.

Dawn Tandy's participation in the demonstration outside the ACLU meeting had been so fortuitous. She would appear on the Metropolitan Police videos, and Murphy would be on her scent like the faithful hound she was. The girl's death had been an unexpected gift. But the detective apparently had developed a deep sense of guilt about the Tandy affair and had become convinced that the girl was not responsible for the judge's death. And now she was back in Miami.

Brian Cottrell was another matter entirely. The man had no conscience at all and was more than willing to use blackmail to protect himself.

There was no way to impede the Miami-Dade Police Department investigation, an investigation that could conceivably lead to Cottrell's arrest. If that happened he would be beyond reach, and the man might say anything!

Everything teetered on a precipice high above a boiling cauldron of certain destruction. The forces of self-preservation were like the external stimuli that drove lab rats to unnatural acts.

There was really no other choice.

Chapter 28

Velazquez didn't ask her to dinner, either out of consideration for her recent "loss" or because he anticipated trouble when he returned to his office. And in truth that was a relief. She needed time alone to think. The hotel room boasted a large terrace with comfortable furniture, and she took advantage of it late in the day to watch the sun go down over Miami. A pair of parrots somersaulted in the air against the purpling sky, chattering at one another as she stretched out on a chaise lounge and sipped her drink.

She had grabbed a light meal in the hotel restaurant only to be shocked by the charges – no cop discount there. The bar where Velazquez had treated her to her first *mojito* was only a few steps away. She'd ordered scotch but hadn't finished before a male hotel guest had tried to make conversation, and she'd beat a retreat to the room.

Ignoring the prohibitive cost she'd poured two small bottles of scotch from the minibar over ice and now sipped it as she mentally dealt with the implications of Jefferson's call, adding it to the string of calamities beginning with the Fernandez murder. It was unpleasant to be torn between personal conviction and professional duty, two things that until now had been synonymous. She'd agreed without hesitation to accompany Velazquez the next morning to re-interview Adele Fernandez. She could do that with little fear that word would leak back to Arlington.

But the coquettish dipsomaniac might provide a clue leading elsewhere and draw her into further involvement with the investigation. This would be a personal choice. She should be able to walk away with a clear conscience, bowing to the decisions of her superiors, but this case was different. She'd broken a cardinal rule for crime investigators: don't become personally involved. She had linked Dawn to the case in the first place, she who had sparked the intrusion on the family in Miami, and who in the end had heard the desperation and fear in the girl's voice in that last phone call. The case had become very personal very quickly. Dawn had directed her final plea of innocence at Krystal, and somehow she was still watching, demanding vindication. The only way to exorcise the ghost was to solve the case.

Damn Sara Hampton's political ambition! What did political ambition have to do with the guilt or innocence of a suspect? Why were politics intruding so cripplingly on her investigation? She had played an underhanded game, not consulting with her as the investigating officer before declaring publicly that the only lead to the judge's killer ended with Dawn Tandy's death.

Krystal had long viewed the Commonwealth Attorney as a kindred spirit, another female with exceptional abilities who had won admiration and respect through her work. She had looked up to the older woman, had accepted her hospitality, knew her husband and children. They had exchanged small gifts at the Holidays. No matter their past relationship, she had to consider Sara an enemy in this matter.

Late in the evening as an inane late night show flickered on the television she lay in bed unable to sleep. One misstep and her career in the Arlington Police Department could be over. She was walking on a very high wire with no safety net to catch her if she slipped.

CHAPTER 29

At nine-thirty in the morning, she had been waiting fifteen minutes under the hotel's *porte cochère* when Velazquez appeared in the red Porsche. He had called an hour before to inform her that the meeting with Adele Fernandez was set for ten A.M. She had turned down his invitation to breakfast.

"All ready?" he asked.

"I hope Adele hasn't made her 'lemonade' yet."

Miami's morning traffic already was thinning, and it was only twenty minutes before they were crossing the curving causeway that connected Burlingame Island to the mainland. Several boats already were passing underneath, heading out to sea in search of fish or a rendezvous with narcotics traffickers. A few moments later Velazquez pulled to a stop at the entrance of Adele Fernandez's building on the north end of Burlingame Island.

The concierge again had been alerted to their arrival, and the elevator swept them noiselessly upward. As before, Adele waited for them in her open doorway. Today she wore yellow yoga pants and a lime green top that bared a narrow strip of 60-something belly, flip-flops revealing perfectly pedicured toes, and a bright yellow bandana in her hair. If the term "dressing your age" meant anything, Adele thought she was 22. Porcelain-capped teeth sparkled when she caught sight of Velazquez, and as soon as they reached her door, she grabbed his elbow like a bass striking a lure and pulled him inside, leaving Krystal standing in the doorway. Suppressing a snicker, she followed Adele and her captive across the expanse of the living room and through the double sliding glass doors onto the sun-drenched balcony where a large, sweating pitcher of "lemonade" waited on a table. Velazquez looked back over his shoulder and winked.

Adele struck a pose on a loveseat and pulled Velazquez down beside her. She belatedly acknowledged Krystal and waved a tanned and surprisingly well-toned arm at a chair on the opposite side of the table.

"Let's have some lemonade," she said. Krystal belatedly noticed that there were three tall ice filled glasses on the table confirming that Adele had known that Velazquez would not be alone. Adele poured the lemonade over the ice and sat each crackling glass carefully back on ceramic coasters decorated with a circle of small alligators each with the tail of another in its jaws. Adele looked up brightly from her task and raised her glass. "Welcome back," she said, "I do enjoy company."

Krystal took a cautious sip, having already caught the sweet scent of rum hovering over the lemonade. She thought seriously about purchasing some shares in Bacardi.

"How can I help you?" Adele cast an adoring glance at Velazquez and batted her eyes.

"We'd like just a little more information about your former husband, if that's all right," he replied.

"If it's necessary. I'll help any way I can." Not a twinge of regret that her former husband was dead. Just how much Adele had hated Fernie Fernandez?

"What can you tell us about the Judge's relationship with Brian Cottrell?"

"Oh, they've known one another for years. I think they went to college together or were in the same fraternity or something."

"That's a long time."

"They did practically everything together." She knit her brows. "To tell you the truth, I never liked Brian Cottrell. He had a tendency to get Fernie into trouble, and then there was the womanizing."

"Can you think of anything that might have soured the relationship, anything relatively recent?"

"Well, until recently Brian had been supporting Fernie's political ambitions ..."

Velazquez was instantly alert. "Until recently? You mean they had a falling out?"

"I don't know the details, but yes." Adele paused, and for just a moment her face was shaded by a calculating mien. "It could have been about a woman."

The way she said this made it obvious there was more.

Krystal's parents were the same age as Adele, but she could not imagine them harboring any remaining interest in sex. Adele, Cottrell, Fernandez ... these people were in a different category. Maybe it had something to do with the tropical climate. Miami oozed sex.

Velazquez caught the hint that Adele knew more. He leant forward and asked, "What woman would that be?"

Adele took a dainty sip of her lemonade and batted her eyes at the blond Cuban before replying. "Of course, it's just gossip, but knowing Fernie, I suspect it's true. They say he and Brian's wife were messing around."

"That does not sound like a very smart thing to do," said Velazquez.

Adele took another sip. "Fernie did not always think with his head," she said, a bitter undertone creeping into her voice. "He did a lot of his thinking below the belt." *Another sip.* "And he and Brian's wife had known one another before."

"How's that?" asked Velazquez.

"Didn't you know? Cynthia Cottrell was a Daddy's Girl. I think Fernie actually introduced her to Brian."

The Daddy's Girls escort service had come up during their previous meeting with Adele. "You mean," Krystal asked, "that Brian Cottrell married a call girl?"

"Oh," she giggled like a mischievous schoolgirl, "they weren't exactly call girls. For the most part they were young college girls who offered their, erm, 'companionship' to older, always wealthy men, who agreed to indulge their desire for fine clothes, cars, and apartments in exchange for favors."

"And by 'favors,' you mean sex?"

"Isn't that obvious, my dear?"

"And so you're saying that Judge Fernandez 'knew,' Cottrell's wife," Krystal emphasized the word 'knew,' "before he introduced her to Brian Cottrell?"

"That's the way I understand the story. I eventually found out that the two of them exchanged girls all the time. Only Brian seemed to settle down after his marriage. Apparently, neither Fernie nor Cynthia could adapt to the idea of fidelity. She's quite a bit younger than Brian."

Velazquez rose to his feet. "Thank you, Adele. You've been of considerable help to our investigation."

Adele's hand shot out to grab Velazquez's arm. "You're not leaving already!"

As Krystal stood, Velazquez patted the older woman's hand and said, "I'm afraid we must, but it's been a great pleasure seeing you again. If anything else occurs to you, please don't hesitate to give me a call."

As they rode the elevator back down, Krystal said, "There's no doubt she'll be calling, you know."

Velazquez waggled his eyebrows. "I hope you're right. She's loaded, and not only with rum."

Krystal snorted. "She'd like the Porsche."

The interview with Adele had lasted only about thirty minutes, so Velazquez swung north on the mainland and then headed west on 395 in the direction of the airport and MDPD HQS. With the Cuban behind the wheel, the ride consumed only 15 minutes. On the way, neither spoke as they considered the implications of what Adele had told them.

Back at the office, Velazquez fetched two cups of strong, black coffee to his battered metal desk and handed one to Krystal. "Wherever we look in this case there's a girl involved," she said. "The murderer, Dawn Tandy, and now Brian Cottrell's wife. There has to be a connection somewhere."

Velazquez squinted. "You think jealousy is the motive?"

"It sure as hell looks that way as far as Cottrell is concerned. Gutierrez claims he contracted a murder. Put that together with what Adele told us and you have a motive. We should talk to his wife."

"That would really put Cottrell on the warpath."

"What do you suggest?"

"Maybe we should dig a little deeper first and talk to someone who knows everyone involved."

Krystal raised an eyebrow in query.

Velazquez said, "Let's take a drive up to Palm Beach and have a chat with whoever's in charge of Daddy's Girls."

As they were rising to go, a white haired cop with a deep tan wearing a spotless *guayabera* intercepted them. "You're working on the Gutierrez case, right? The one involving Brian Cottrell?"

Velazquez cocked an eyebrow and nodded.

The cop continued. "You're gonna love this. Cottrell was found shot to death in the parking garage of his office building a couple of hours ago."

Chapter 30

The forensics team, a gaggle of uniformed officers, and two plain clothes detectives were swarming the crime scene when they arrived. Police cars with flashing blue lights and the coroner's wagon blocked all the entrances and exits to the parking garage of the building on Brickell Avenue they had visited just the day before.

They flashed their badges and pushed their way through the phalanx of uniforms. Brian Cottrell lay face down on the concrete floor beside the open passenger side door of a silver Mercedes sedan. The car keys were clutched in his right hand. He had been shot through the back of the head with a small caliber bullet. There was not much blood.

Velazquez introduced Krystal to the two detectives and asked, "What do you think happened?"

"What you see is what you get. Looks like an armed robbery gone bad," replied a white-haired, mustachioed detective with mischievous eyes who had been introduced to Murphy as Bob Hammond. He wore a bright green and white Hawaiian-style shirt with a palm tree motif. "Someone sneaked up behind him and pumped a bullet into his brain. The doc says he died instantly. Must have happened when he arrived for work this morning. There's stippling around the wound so the shot was fired from just a few inches away."

His partner, an olive-skinned man with carefully groomed hair whose name was Enrique Perez, said, "This guy had a lot of criminal connections. Could be he crossed one of his clients."

Krystal knelt to get a closer look at the corpse. "It looks like the shot was fired from a low angle. Whoever did it was considerably shorter than Cottrell."

"He was a big man," said Hammond, "a lot taller than most people."

"Yes, but this has a familiar look about it." She was reminded of the scene of the Fernandez murder. Cottrell's skull displayed the same kind of small caliber wound, and as was the case with Fernie Fernandez, the shot had been fired from a low angle. She didn't believe in coincidence.

"When forensics has the bullet," she continued, "it'll surely be a twenty-two, and they should contact the Arlington Police to compare it with the round recovered from the body of Judge Fernandez. I'll bet it's a match."

Another element of the crime scene caught her attention. "I wonder why the passenger side door is open rather than the driver's side."

Hammond glanced at the open door. "Maybe he was after something on the passenger seat and the killer sneaked up from behind. There's nothing there now. And his wallet and watch are missing."

"He was shot in the back of the head execution style," observed Velazquez.

"Yeah," replied Hammond laconically. He bent over the body and lifted the right side of Cottrell's suit jacket. "And take a look at this."

There was an empty holster on Cottrell's belt. "From the size of the holster," offered Perez, "he was carrying an automatic, maybe a nine millimeter or forty-five. He might have gone for the gun when he turned his back and the assailant saw it. Regardless, whoever it was has upped his payload from a twenty-two. A street punk would do something like that."

The detective was defending the armed robbery gone bad theory.

If Gutierrez were to be believed, the attorney had contracted the murder of his erstwhile friend, Fernie Fernandez, who had subsequently been killed in Arlington. Now Cottrell was dead, too, and likely by the same female hand. Whatever the motive, it had nothing to do with the Melissa Tandy case or Cottrell's wife or a robbery. There was something else, something that connected the two victims. If Adele

Fernandez's gossip were true, Cottrell's wife became suddenly important.

Cottrell's home was a large, white stuccoed, Spanish style house in a well-established, upscale neighborhood on Leonardo Street in Coral Gables. The property encompassed a walled half-acre, every square foot of which was meticulously landscaped and groomed. An MDPD black and white patrol car was parked at the gated driveway entrance when Krystal and Velazquez arrived. The uniforms would already have notified Mrs. Cottrell of her husband's death.

Adele Fernandez had intimated just a few hours earlier that Cottrell's current wife was involved in an affair with Fernie Fernandez. Now both Fernie and Cottrell were dead, possibly murdered by the same person. Was this the connection they sought, the final link in the chain? Cottrell's alleged motive for having Fernandez killed was jealousy, or perhaps simply pique. It was even conceivable that Cynthia Cottrell had killed her husband to avenge her lover, Fernandez. Maybe she had killed both.

They found Cynthia waiting for them in the living room. The place was enormous and decorated in what Krystal assumed was typical Floridian *nouveau riche* ostentation with marble floors and lots of gilded mirrors and fat furniture. A vast mahogany entertainment center with what must have been a 70-inch flat screen loomed against one wall. The woman's blond hair excited a brief *frisson* up Murphy's spine, but a second later she abandoned any thought that Cynthia could have been the woman in the Washington hotel video. She was taller and much more generously proportioned than the willowy figure who had visited death on Fernie Fernandez. Cynthia's was probably in her early to mid-forties. Her bosomy good looks would have been suitable eye candy on the arm of Brian Cottrell who was twenty years her senior. There was more than enough woman here to satisfy any man's ego ... and to bruise that same ego if she were stepping out on him.

Cynthia was seated when they entered, staring blankly out sliding glass doors that gave onto a stone patio with a pool beyond, but she rose to greet them. She wore low-cut Capri pants and a silk top short enough to reveal a lot of tanned, flat midriff, and Krystal couldn't help but be reminded of Adele's similar taste in clothes, which was apparently a common Miami affliction. Tears had smeared Cynthia's mascara and left dark tracks down her cheeks. A short, crystal glass dangled from thumb and forefinger of her left hand. It contained a clear liquid that might have been water or vodka. Krystal's money was on vodka.

Velazquez performed the introductions and invited Cynthia to resume her seat. They sat opposite across a large, glass-topped coffee table that squatted on fat, gilded Queen Anne legs.

"We're very sorry for your loss, Mrs. Cottrell," he began. "Can you think of anyone who might have wished your husband ill?"

Cynthia jerked out a short, bitter laugh before saying, "Take your pick. Brian was a powerful and well-known man, but I wouldn't say he was exactly loved. He was an attorney who took on unpopular cases."

"Did anything seem unusual this morning before he left for the office?"

"No. He swam laps in the pool, had breakfast, and drove away. He didn't say anything."

"He didn't say anything over breakfast?"

Cynthia lowered her eyes. "We didn't have breakfast together."

Velazquez shot a loaded, sidewise glance at Krystal. He leaned forward, elbows on knees, and asked softly, "Mrs. Cottrell, did you know Judge Fernando Fernandez?"

She raised her eyes to them again. "Yes." Her voice was flat.

"The judge was a good friend of your husband, wasn't he?" Velazquez persevered, keeping his tone mild, non-accusatory.

"They had known one another for a very long time."

"Had anything come between them recently?"

Several emotions flickered across Cynthia's face like the jerky frames of an old-time movie: fear, resentment, and finally shame.

"What do you mean?" asked the widow. She averted her eyes to stare through the glass doors toward the pool.

"We heard there was a falling out."

"They ... I don't know."

"Mrs. Cottrell, both men have been murdered, possibly by the same person. We have a man in custody who claims your husband hired him to kill Judge Fernandez."

Cynthia jerked her face back toward Velazquez, her eyes widened in shock and surprise and her hand flew to her mouth.

Velazquez bored through her resistance. "We're just trying to understand what might have happened. If there is something here, some commonality we don't know about, it could be important. Your own safety might be affected."

Cynthia's body remained rigid for a second before she asked, eyes still wide in a mascara-smeared field, a raccoon caught in a flashlight's beam, "What do you mean? You think I'm in some sort of danger?"

"Mrs. Cottrell, we simply can't be certain right now, but we think there is a connection between the two murders. The man we have in custody was not the person who committed the crimes. The judge, as you probably already know from the media, was murdered in Washington by a woman."

Cynthia looked from one to the other of them. "You surely don't think that I ... The woman who killed Fernie is dead, isn't she?"

Velazquez shook his head. "We don't think so. As I said, we have reason to believe your husband was shot by the same person who killed the judge."

Krystal was gratified by the question. If only the Arlington Police were similarly inclined to listen to her. Her esteem for Velazquez ratcheted up several notches.

Cynthia's lips twisted into a facsimile of a smile. "I wasn't surprised that it was a woman who killed Fernie. There were a lot of them."

Velazquez circled his objective in tightening rings. "Mrs. Cottrell, it's awkward to ask this, but how well did you know Judge Fernandez?"

Cynthia flushed deeply at the naked implication and bowed her head. She said nothing for several beats, and defiance had replaced shock when she looked up at them again.

"I've known both Brian and Fernie for years. I met them while I was still in college."

Murphy remembered what Adele had told them about Cynthia Cottrell's past.

"Daddy's Girls." Velazquez's words formed a statement rather than a question.

"It was a long time ago," said Cynthia, "and it paid my way through college. Better a few years on my back, a nice car to drive, and expensive gifts than ending up with a crushing student loan that I could never pay off. And I wasn't the only girl who made that decision and landed on her feet. At least I ended up marrying Brian."

Now they were getting somewhere. Krystal followed her intuition. "What about Fernandez?"

Cynthia gave them a lopsided smile. "Fernie introduced me to Brian. Fernie wasn't really a good fit with the agency. He never stayed long with anyone. Both he and Brian were in their late 30's, both up and coming Miami attorneys with money to burn. But Brian wasn't the womanizer Fernie was. He was a long-term kind of person. We continued our relationship after I had finished college and married. Brian was actually a very faithful husband."

"Mrs. Cottrell," Velazquez said, "I'm sorry to be so blunt, but were you having an affair with Judge Fernandez?"

She flushed again as her mouth turned down at the corners. "It was only a short fling, a mistake. Brian had become so distant and spent all of his time at the office. When it was over, I told him about it. He felt so betrayed, by both Fernie and me. I was ashamed."

"Were you at home all morning, Mrs. Cottrell?" Velazquez posed the inevitable question.

Cynthia sighed, "God, it's just like a cop show on TV. Yes, I spent a lot of time sunning at the pool. José, our yard man, can vouch for that."

Velazquez stood up. "Thank you, Mrs. Cottrell. We'll call if there are more questions."

Outside the mid-day sun hung over them, an intense ball of fire that pounded down rendering the landscape into sharp contrasts between dazzling light and impenetrable shadow.

"I think I see the link," she said.

"What do you see?"

"The thing the two victims had in common, besides Cynthia – Daddy's Girls. We were going to look into it earlier."

They reached the Porsche, and Velazquez was silent as he started the engine and switched the air conditioning to full blast. He put the car in gear and pulled away from the curb. "They were both in the legal profession, they were long-time friends, and they were involved in politics together. The Daddy's Girls connection is a couple of decades old. Don't you think we should be looking for something more recent?"

Her intuition running at full tilt, she was certain a woman was at the bottom of this, a woman who now had acquired a taste for murder. Whoever it was, the motivation had to be strong. "Currents run deep in this one, Ray. There's something else or someone else we haven't identified yet."

"You mean the shooter."

"Of course. And I think it has something to do with that so-called 'introduction service.'"

"It's worth a try. We don't have much else. I'll make a few calls this afternoon, and we can drive up to Palm Beach tomorrow. We'll make a day of it."

Krystal liked the sound of that. It would keep her below the Arlington radar.

CHAPTER 31

The drive required fourteen hours of high-speed combat with the brutal traffic on I-95, and she had done it overnight with no sleep. She arrived in Miami before even the first pink strip of dawn had cracked the sky over the Atlantic horizon. This made finding parking on all but deserted streets easy. A surge of adrenalin energized her metabolism and banished thought of rest. What seemed like an eternity ago she had meticulously planned how she would take care of Fernie Fernandez. It was her home turf. There had been nothing to connect her to the crime, and had there been a problem she was in a position to divert the investigation. The situation in Miami offered no such advantages.

She used the pedestrian street entrance to the parking garage to avoid the closed circuit TV camera at the vehicular entrance and waited with her hand on the grip of the old pistol inside her purse. Her memory of Cottrell's early-to-work habit did not betray her. She spotted him behind the wheel of a big Mercedes as it rolled down the ramp and into its assigned space with a squeal of rubber slipping against the smooth concrete floor.

When he emerged from the car she saw that he retained the broad shoulders and imposing height that had made him so attractive as a younger man. But he had put on pounds around the middle and the mane of long, dark hair had been replaced by a completely bald pate surrounded by a thin line of clipped gray.

She came out from behind a pillar and walked directly toward him. Brian Cottrell was surprised to see her, but he had no trouble recognizing her. At least, she had not changed so much.

"Brian, we have to talk."

He scrutinized her for a second over the roof of the car, his eyes narrow, deepening the lines on his face. Then a shark's grin replaced the scowl and he stepped around the car to stand in front of her. "What are you doing here?"

"Like I said, we need to talk."

"Did you pull that bitch cop off my ass?"

Cottrell had lost none of the directness of his youth, but it had acquired a rough, brutal edge.

"That's what we need to talk about, and I don't think we should do it here."

Her hastily devised plan was to get him to drive her to some remote location where she would kill him.

"Why not," he asked. "My office is just upstairs."

"I don't think it would be a good idea for us to be seen together, especially when the police are interested in you. It wouldn't be good for either one of us."

"You didn't answer my question. What about that female cop?"

Why, she wondered, did men find it necessary to define the gender of "female" cops? They would never have specified "male" cop.

"I'm working on it," she replied, "but I'll need your help. We need to coordinate a couple of things."

"Like?"

The parking garage was still deserted at this early hour. *Maybe she didn't have to get him anywhere else.*

"Come on," she urged, "let's just take a drive so we can talk undisturbed." She reached into her purse and wrapped her fingers around the butt of her grandfather's gun. The feel of the worn, wooden grip gave her confidence.

She could see that he was annoyed at the interruption to his daily routine, but he shrugged and turned to open the door for her, always the 'gentleman.' *And always one to underestimate a woman.*

As he turned away she stepped closer, raised the old revolver from her purse until it was only a few inches from the back of Cottrell's head and pulled the trigger. The pop of the .22's discharge echoed weakly from the enclosed walls of the parking garage, and Brian Cottrell dropped to the hard floor beside the car. His legs twitched for a few seconds before he lay still. She wondered if his face held a surprised expression.

It was like magic. One moment the man was there, and after she pulled the trigger only a vacated husk remained devoid of the threat that once had resided there. The threat vaporized into the air together with the life. Suddenly she could feel empathy for all those men who killed their nagging wives and those women who killed their unfaithful husbands.

She bent down quickly to feel for a pulse and found none. Thinking quickly she decided to make it look like a mugging. She removed the expensive, gold Rolex from his wrist and pulled his suit coat aside to get to his wallet. In doing so she discovered the large caliber pistol holstered on his belt and with some difficulty unsnapped the thumb safety strap and removed it, placing it in her purse along with the revolver.

It was time to leave. She'd already changed her plan and spent more time in the garage than was wise. Such luck could not hold. She walked quickly to the pedestrian exit to the street.

Chapter 32

It would have been wisest to clear the area and get out of Miami as quickly as possible to minimize the possibility that someone might remark on her car's Virginia license plates. The energy generated by her pent-up state should have dissipated by now, the tension of the endless overnight drive south and the adrenalin built up in anticipation of killing Cottrell should have receded and left her exhausted on a tide-drained shore, but the erasure of yet another threat had left her strangely invigorated.

She was on a roll. Something had changed within her, darkened her thoughts like a cloud of black ink dropped into clear water. She had turned back the threatening tide and no suspicion could fall on her. Unless ...

She had eliminated the immediate threats, but others remained. Lesser threats, indirect threats to be sure, but sufficiently potent to give her pause as she sat in her Prius a block from Cottrell's parking garage. That word, "threat," amplified by the echo chamber of her mind drowned all other thought. She retrieved the wallet she had taken from Cottrell's body and examined its contents. The information she wanted was easy to find.

She knew Miami well and headed south toward Coconut Grove. A short time later, she turned off of South Miami Avenue into the entrance of the Vizcaya Museum with its extensive grounds and isolated parking areas for tourists, surely empty at this early hour. An out of town car would attract little attention here, and she could get some sleep while she waited. Cottrell's body would be discovered soon. The cops would arrive. His wife would be notified. It would be several hours before an opportunity would present itself. It was a gamble, but there was no other way.

The museum grounds would not open to the public until 9:30 AM, over two hours later. She found a quiet side street and settled down to wait, reclining the driver's seat so her head was below the window line. When Vizcaya opened, she paid the $18 entrance fee and found an empty parking lot where she forced her charged body to rest.

It had been perfect until Krystal Murphy's nose had begun twitching. It had been a mistake to send her to Miami in the first place. But there had been no way to predict that the detective would somehow lurch into Brian Cottrell and discover a trail that could, after all that had happened, still possibly lead to the ruin of Sara Hampton. The Commonwealth Attorney was accustomed to being in control of events, of manipulating them to her advantage, both as a prosecutor and a politician. But now control was sliding down a slippery slope at the bottom of which certain destruction awaited unless she could halt the descent.

Cottrell had threatened her. Either he had guessed that Fernandez had attempted to blackmail her into renewing their sexual relationship or Fernie had told him about it during the Washington conference. Either way, Cottrell had to die. He was a man with many enemies and connections to the underworld, and she calculated that there would be no particular reason to connect her with his death.

Shortly after noon, Sara watched from her parked car a half block away as Krystal Murphy and a tall, blond man she assumed was a cop emerged from the entrance to the Cottrell house and got into a red Porsche. And that sealed the Arlington cop's fate.

She knew Krystal's bulldog character well, had seen her aggressive investigative style. Krystal would not let go until she had solved the crime. The gruesome deaths of the Tandy family had for some reason ignited a flame in her that had to be quenched.

But first things first. More waiting.

The MDPD black and white drove away in a few minutes. Sara left her Prius and walked the half-block to the Cottrell house. The streets were deserted in the heat of mid-day. The temperature had risen with the sun, now at its zenith in a clear blue Florida sky.

She rang the bell at the gate and stared into the CCTV camera mounted above it. She was worried that a housekeeper or another person might respond to the ring. She was acting recklessly again. She had not even considered whether Cynthia might have someone in the house with her. But within a few seconds Cynthia Cottrell's voice sounded from the speaker. "Yes?" She would find out soon enough.

"Cynthia, it's Sara, Sara Villeneuve." She used her maiden name, the name by which Cynthia had known her.

The surprise was evident in Cynthia's voice. "Sara? I can't believe it! What are you doing here?"

Sara could feel the other woman's eyes examining her. She smiled at the camera. "I was in Jacksonville visiting my parents when I heard about Brian. I drove straight down. I thought you could use some support."

"Please come in, Sara. It's really good to see you. The police just left." There was a tinge of uncertainty in Cynthia's voice. It had been so many years since the two had seen one another or even spoken. Hopefully, the shock of her husband's death would have dulled her thought processes somewhat.

The gate lock buzzed open, and Sara followed the walk to the front door where Cynthia waited. "I know I must look a mess," said Sara. Indeed, following the overnight drive from Washington she knew she must present a less than well-coiffed sight. "I just threw on some clothes and drove down here as fast as I could."

Cynthia, she noted, retained the spectacular good looks that had always been a magnet for men. The two embraced, and a tear escaped down Cynthia's cheek smearing her newly applied mascara.

She took Sara by the elbow to guide her into the living room. "However did you get here so quickly, Sara? The police informed me only an hour or so ago. You drove down from Jacksonville?"

"I'm a Virginia Commonwealth's Attorney now. I have my connections."

Indicating that Sara should take a seat, Cynthia said, "One of the police was from Virginia, a woman."

"Bingo. That was Krystal Murphy, one of mine. I hope she asked good questions."

"She didn't say much. The good-looking blond detective did most of the talking."

"What did they want to know?"

"They think the same person who killed Fernie Fernandez may have killed Brian."

"But we already knew who killed Fernie – that Tandy girl." Sara watched the other woman closely for a reaction to this statement.

"That's not the impression they gave," said Cynthia, screwing up her face. "They seemed quite interested in a Daddy's Girls connection."

Sara reached into her handbag and wrapped her hand around the butt of Brian Cottrell's pistol. It felt solid and reassuring. "What about Daddy's Girls?" she asked.

"They were looking for some way to connect Brian and Fernie's deaths." Cynthia got one of those looks that people get in their eyes when a new realization occurs suddenly to them.

Sara pressed ahead. "And what did you tell them about Daddy's Girls, Cynthia?"

Cynthia was evidently chasing some thought that still eluded her, like someone who sees a face in the crowd they think they recognize. When she answered her voice was distant. "Only that Fernie had introduced me to Brian. That was so long ago. We were only girls. You and I ..." She stopped in mid-sentence as the thought she had been pursuing finally coalesced. When she focused again on Sara, a large pistol had appeared in the Commonwealth's Attorney's hand and was pointed directly at her.

"Yes, Cynthia," said Sara, "I knew them both, too."

Cottrell's .45 auto was huge compared to the old .22 revolver, and much heavier, and Sara had to hold it with both hands. Even so, it wobbled, but she was only feet away from Cynthia Cottrell, frozen to immobility, over the top of a coffee table, and she couldn't possibly miss.

When she pulled the trigger she didn't expect the huge report of the big gun or the recoil that almost jerked the weapon from her grip. Her ears rang with the reverberations that bounced off the walls of the room. She shook her head and focused to see that she had hit Cynthia in the left shoulder where the hollow point slug had ripped flesh and broken bone. Bright crimson blood spilled over the white brocade of the loveseat, and a part of her brain thought it a shame to ruin such fine furniture.

Seated as she had been, the force of the bullet had not knocked Cynthia to the floor. The pain receptors in her brain were still blocked by the shock of the blow, and she now stared down uncomprehendingly at the ruin of her shoulder and then back at Sara. "It was you ..."

Her sentence remained unfinished as Sara's second shot silenced her forever, striking her squarely in the middle of the chest, and bloody froth replaced the words issuing from her mouth until there was no more air in her lungs and none would ever return.

Her ears still throbbing from the roar of the shots, Sara watched in fascination as Cynthia slumped first to the side and then slid slowly off the gory loveseat to the floor under the edge of the coffee table. Visible through the glass top of the table, the still body could have been part of a tableau in a museum display case had it not been for the spreading crimson stain. Oh, well, she thought. It's a tile floor. The blood will clean up nicely.

It was time to go. She had been careful to touch nothing inside the house. The gunshots had seemed preternaturally loud inside the room, bouncing from the tiled floor and solid walls. She would not have been surprised had the noise shattered the glass doors leading to the pool area. But it had not. Still, she could not be certain that the shots had not been audible outside. Fortunately, the grounds of the Cottrell home were spacious and surrounded by a high wall.

One more look at the corpse under the table assured her that Cynthia Cottrell, another threat, was indeed dead. The feeling was again liberating, even exhilarating. The trick now would be to escape unseen. She had been inside the house for less than ten minutes. With luck, the streets still would be deserted.

She closed the front door behind her as she left, hearing the click of the automatic lock, and used a handkerchief to wipe the knob. A peek through the bars of the gate confirmed that no one was in sight on the street. As she closed the gate, she remembered to wipe the bell button under the CCTV lens, and then crossed the street. She saw that the house opposite also had high walls, and she should not be visible from there.

Strangely, it felt to Sara more like she had been a spectator at Cynthia's death than the perpetrator, as though it were not Sara Hampton, Virginia Commonwealth's Attorney, who had committed murder, but rather someone else, some guardian angel of death sent to shield Sara Hampton from harm. The real Sara Hampton, she realized, was now only an observer safely ensconced in a far corner of her mind.

She had sensed this strange being inside her becoming stronger during the long drive from Washington as the endless lights of other vehicles and the long, straight highway had mesmerized her. The single-mindedness of her actions had blocked out the fact that Sara Hampton was no longer in control. Locked into the tiny refuge, Sara became frightened.

The murders of Fernandez and Cottrell could be rationalized by the former Sara Hampton as self-defense. Both had threatened her well-being and her future. But now she had killed Cynthia Cottrell, who had displayed no intent to do her harm, in cold blood. Sara Hampton nee Villeneuve, Virginia Commonwealth Attorney, wife, mother of two, would not have done such a thing – could not have done such a thing. But she, or the new being that had overwhelmed her and possessed her like some malign spirit, had done it.

The idea to kill Fernandez had been born of fright. He threatened to destroy her career and possibly her family with the knowledge he held. Those far away college days when becoming a Daddy's Girl had seemed both a lark and a way to off-set the costs of her education. She enjoyed sex, so why shouldn't she profit from it. It wasn't like being a prostitute, not really. There had only been Fernie, who was quite different in those days. There were definite benefits in the form of a car, jewelry, money. College boys could not offer the same benefits.

Fernie truly had liked her in those days and been generous. The "affair" had ended amicably. He eventually married some society woman, and that was that. Until that fateful day at the ACLU conference.

That was when the darkness had entered and grown like a malignancy until all thoughts other than self-preservation had been obscured. There was no right, no wrong, only threats to be eliminated – self-preservation. Somewhere in the deep recesses of her mind hope flickered that once she was safe, the black-winged angel would leave her.

Chapter 33

At nine A.M. the following morning, Krystal and Ray Velazquez were just leaving MDPD Headquarters with the intention of driving north to Palm Beach when his mobile phone rang. Still in the parking lot, he pulled the Porsche to a stop and took the call. When he had finished, he gripped the wheel tightly with both hands. "Cynthia Cottrell was found dead in her house this morning. She'd been shot."

Both sat in stunned silence for a moment as the news sank in. Then he asked, "What the hell's going on, Krystal? Two murders could be a coincidence; three makes it a serial killer."

Krystal thought of the Tandy family. The toll of the dead in this case was now six. "Who found the body?" she asked.

"The yard man. Today was his regular day at the Cottrell house. When he couldn't raise anyone at the door this morning he went around the house and spotted the body through the glass doors."

"We'd better get over there."

He shifted violently through the gears as they screeched out of the parking lot and headed for Coral Gables.

Three black and whites and a sheriff's car were clustered in front of the house when they arrived at Leonardo Street. Velazquez approached one of the uniformed officers standing near the driveway entrance. A battered pick-up truck with the word's 'José's Yard Service' stenciled on the doors stood in the drive. Krystal noted the sergeant's stripes on the cop's shoulder. Velazquez flashed his badge and asked, "What have we got?"

"We've secured the house and called the CSU. They should be here any minute. The front door was locked, but sliding doors in back to the pool area were unlocked. Nothing was taken that I could see. The TV's still there. Lots of valuable stuff. Nothing out of place other than the body on the floor. The guy who found her is with some of the guys around back."

"OK," said Velazquez. "Send a couple of uniforms around to canvass the neighbors. See if they saw or heard anything."

"Yes, sir."

"Come on, Krystal. Let's talk to the yard man."

His name was José Ferrer, and they found him sitting in a lawn chair beside the pool. One policeman stood alongside. There was dried blood on the yard man's hands and the front of his shirt.

Velazquez introduced himself.

José said, "*No hablo inglés, señor.*"

The fact that the witness did not speak English presented no problem in Miami where Spanish was a second, and as often as not a first language. Velazquez launched into a rapid torrent of Spanish that left Krystal in the dark, but José visibly brightened and rattled off his story. The man was clearly scared. Maybe he was illegal, but he had had the decency to notify the authorities. She waited. She wanted to get into the house, check out the scene, but she couldn't do that without Velazquez.

After fifteen minutes Velazquez was winding up his questions. "*Quedate aquí un rato más, Señor Ferrer,*" he said, "*Después tendrás que acompañar a los oficiales a la sede para darles una declaración escrita.*"

José didn't look happy, but he nodded a resigned assent.

Velazquez turned to Krystal and said, "To make a long story short, he's been working for the Cottrells for several years. When he arrived this morning and couldn't raise anybody, he came around back and knocked at the glass doors then peeked inside. He saw Mrs. Cottrell on the floor. The doors were unlocked so he went in to see what was wrong. That's when he discovered she was dead."

"Ergo the blood all over him."

"Yeah. Couldn't be helped. She might still have been alive."

The cop had been listening. He said, "Not this morning, she wasn't. The woman's been dead since sometime yesterday, if I don't miss my guess. I've seen enough stiffs to know."

"OK," said Velazquez. "Let's take a look, Krystal."

They pulled nitrile gloves and sterile booties from boxes that the police had placed on one of the patio tables.

The glass doors had been kept closed to preserve ambient temperature, which could affect the onset of *rigor mortis*. The glass-topped coffee table where they had sat with Cynthia only the day before had been shoved aside, apparently by José, so he could reach the body, but the scene left little doubt as to what had happened. The white brocade of the loveseat was red with blood, and there was a large hole in one of the cushions. A quick look at the body told them Cynthia had been shot twice, once in the shoulder and again center mass. The .45 caliber slugs had done extensive damage. The center mass shot had passed completely through the body and punched a ragged hole in the back of the loveseat.

"She was sitting when she was shot," said Krystal, "facing her killer. Those shots were point blank. The killer might have been sitting where we sat yesterday. I wonder if she knew the person who shot her."

Velazquez was taking in the rest of the room. "Nothing's out of place," he said. "The front door was locked. My guess is that Cynthia let the killer into house. Either the confrontation began at the door, and she was surprised, marched in here and shot, or she knew the killer and invited them in for a chat."

Krystal was still examining the body. "These wounds weren't made by a .22. The wound to the shoulder is strange. How could anyone miss at such close range?"

"You're right about the caliber." Velazquez bent to a shell casing lying on the tiled floor. "Looks like a forty-five," he said, "There should be another one around somewhere. They would have skittered across the tile when they were ejected. A pro would have retrieved his brass."

Krystal stepped to his side. It was clearly a .45 caliber shell casing.

Velazquez asked, "Do you think we could be dealing with a second murderer here?"

Krystal knit her brows. "You mean because a different weapon was used? It wouldn't make sense. Fernandez, Cottrell, and Cynthia were a love triangle. They were all closely connected. And remember that empty holster on Cottrell's body. I'm betting it was his gun, and if I'm right we're looking at the same person who killed both Fernandez and Cottrell. I wouldn't be surprised if Cottrell's own fingerprints are found on the brass."

This was the only explanation, the only way she could derive any sense from the events. Everyone involved in this case was connected by a common thread, a thread that did not include the Tandy family, but did include the killer. The task they faced was to identify the thread and follow where it led.

Chapter 34

Plans to drive up to Palm Beach were scrubbed, and they dashed back to MDPD headquarters to await results from the CSU examination of Cynthia Cottrell's residence. Someone had brought pizza to the office, and a couple of already cold slices served as lunch.

It was nearly 4:00 PM and many cups of coffee before the phone rang on Velazquez's desk. The conversation was short. When he finished and turned back to Krystal she could read triumph in his face.

"They found something," he said, "something important."

"What?"

"Let's go back over there," he replied, grinning, "You'll see when we get there."

Krystal was not a fan of teasing, especially when it involved withholding information from her, information she was desperate to have. Despite one polite request followed immediately by some choice Irish imprecations, Velazquez still refused to tell her more on the drive back to Coconut Grove. She wondered if it was a Latino thing. Whatever, his attitude did not win him any points.

By the time they arrived an afternoon thunderstorm had swept in from the bay, and Krystal's mood matched the cloud darkened sky.

The CSU van was parked in front, and one of the team met them at the door. "We've finished dusting and taking samples," he said, "so no more need for gloves or booties. Brenneman is waiting for you in the living room." Rain had begun to pelt them, and the tech ducked into the house, waving them after him.

"Where is it?" asked Velazquez.

"Over there in the entertainment center." The tech waved at the mahogany monstrosity that nearly covered one wall surrounding a 70-inch flat screen TV. Another CSU tech knelt before an open door at the bottom fiddling with some piece of electronic gear inside. He looked over his shoulder when they entered.

Velazquez jerked his head toward Krystal. "Tell her what you found."

The tech rose and extended his hand, pulling off his glove as he did so. He was African-American, probably in his mid-thirties, slender and about Krystal's height. He wore glasses with black plastic rims that only emphasized his resemblance to Urkel.

"I'm Doug Brenneman," he said, then added unnecessarily, "MDPD Forensics."

"Glad to meet you, Doug. What's that?" She was looking past him at the electronic equipment with which he had been fiddling when they entered.

"Brian Cottrell was a well-known attorney with a lot of heavy-duty criminal connections, as well as enemies." began Brenneman. "So it's only natural his house would be alarmed. As a matter of fact, the house was completely wired, including with video ..."

Krystal was suddenly excited. "You mean there's video of the murder?"

Brenneman shook his head. "No. Unfortunately, Mrs. Cottrell had not activated the system at the time of the murder. It's really a shame. There's video coverage of every room, as well as the perimeter of the house, all motion activated – if the system is switched on."

"So what's all the excitement? Why are we here?" She shot a venomous glance at Velazquez, who held up his hands in mock defense.

Oblivious to this exchange, Brenneman continued, "But one part of the system is permanently hard-wired on. You probably noticed the buzzer at the gate and the CCTV camera and microphone. They transmit to a small screen and speaker console beside the front door. Whenever the bell is pressed, the system is activated, and a recording is made of the person at the gate."

Krystal forgot her anger. "So there's a picture of someone at the gate?"

"Yep." Brenneman smiled widely, a happy geek.

"Can we see it?"

"No problem."

Brenneman turned and knelt again and pushed some buttons on the face of a large console. The TV flickered to life and coalesced to a black and white still image of a person staring into the lens at the gate.

Krystal gasped and turned, slack-jawed, to Velazquez, who was still studying the image on the screen. "I don't believe it!" she blurted.

There was a flash of light through the window followed by a loud clap of thunder as though God himself had chosen to dramatize the moment.

She became the center of attention.

"You know that person?" asked Velazquez.

She looked back at the screen, still unable to believe what she was seeing. "Yes," she said, "I do. That's Sara Hampton, a Virginia Commonwealth Attorney from Arlington that I work with sometimes. She's the same as a prosecuting attorney."

The dissonance of Sara's image associated with a murder was jarring. What was Sara doing here in Miami and what had she been doing at Cynthia Cottrell's house? Had Sara been so upset that Krystal had returned to Miami that she'd come herself to check up on her? How had she found her way to Cynthia's door so quickly?

There was a time stamp in the lower right hand corner of the image. It showed that Sara had arrived at the house at 12:15 PM the day before, only a few minutes after Krystal and Velazquez finished their interview with Cynthia Cottrell.

She realized that Velazquez was speaking to her. "Say that again? Our new prime suspect is a prosecuting attorney?"

The very idea was foreign. That such a question should be asked about Sara Hampton was akin to believing the moon was made of green cheese. It might look that way, but the facts were contrary.

Ignoring Velazquez, she directed a question at Brenneman, who was still kneeling at the console. "Are there any other images from the front gate?" Hope against hope.

"Yesterday morning, the uniforms who notified her of her husband's death, and this morning, only the yard man who discovered the body. He rang the bell, but when there was no response he used his own key."

"So it's possible that the killer found another way in?" *Grasping at straws.*

Brenneman rubbed his chin. "Well, the main system was switched off. Mrs. Cottrell probably didn't feel she needed it during the day. We found no evidence of anyone entering other than by the main entrance. It's not impossible that someone scaled the fence, but we found no footprints, and now ...." A hard rain now pelted the pool area and the yard beyond. If there had been traces of an entry, they would be obliterated in the soft soil by the time the rain stopped.

"From the beginning we've been pretty sure that the killer entered via the front door," said Velazquez, "that Cynthia let them in, and that it's possible she knew her killer. Is there any connection that you know of, Krystal, any chance that your prosecutor and Cynthia were acquainted?"

She shook her head. "None that I know of."

"Well, she's sure as hell a person of interest now. We need to find her pronto." Lacking any personal connection to Hampton, Velazquez had no trouble seeing her as a suspect or at the very least someone who might shed light on the crime. He wanted to know the reason for the Virginia Commonwealth Attorney's visit to Cynthia Cottrell on the day of her murder.

He's thinking like a good cop. But there has to be a logical explanation. "I can call her office," she said, reaching to the holster on her belt for her cell phone.

The call completed, she frowned at Velazquez. "They say she's been on leave for the past three days. I'm going to call her husband."

But Fred Hampton was not at home.

"He'll be at work, and I don't have that number," she informed Velazquez. The thought struck her that she should call Deputy Chief Jefferson, her immediate superior. After their last conversation, Jefferson surely would be unhappy to learn she was still on the case in Miami. She had disobeyed a direct order. There might be consequences. Or she could make another call to Sara's office and ask for Fred's number, which they might well refuse to provide. She was a squirrel that had run into the path of an oncoming car and couldn't make up its mind which way to jump.

She decided to wait until Fred would likely be home from work. At most it would mean only a couple of hours' delay.

Chapter 35

Krystal cut the connection on her cell phone, conscious of Velazquez's impatience rolling over her with a frenetic Cuban beat from the other side of the table. It was after six P.M. and the two were in a booth at a small bar in Coconut Grove, just a few blocks from her hotel, half-finished glasses of beer on the table between them. The storm had passed, leaving a hint of ozone in the air and puddles that shimmered in the fading, rose-hued light as they evaporated in the after-storm heat. Showers in Florida apparently did not necessarily cool the air.

Her words stumbled out like nervous actors reluctant to step onto the stage. "He said she drove down to Jacksonville yesterday. Something about an illness in the family. Her folks live there."

She mentally re-played the conversation with Sara just before her first trip to Miami, before the Tandy tragedy. Sara had recommended the restaurant, Versailles, where Ray Velazquez had introduced her to Cuban cuisine. Sara knew Miami well. Sara had done her undergrad college work in Florida before moving to Georgetown for the law degree. But had she studied in Jacksonville or Miami?

"Did he give you their number?"

"Whose?" She was too preoccupied to understand the question, unfocused on what Velazquez was saying.

"The number of her parents in Jacksonville."

Embarrassed and angry at both herself and Velazquez, she said, "Shit!" and punched the re-dial on her phone. A moment later she scribbled a Jacksonville phone number on a paper napkin.

Velazquez reached for the napkin. "Do you want me to call them?" The fact that he understood her inner conflict was implicit in his softer, no longer insistent, tone.

She placed a hand over his, preventing him from taking the napkin. "No, I'll do it. I know Sara, and a call from a Miami cop would probably spook her folks."

He turned his hand over so they were palm to palm and gave her a squeeze. "OK. But it's got to be now." The squeeze felt good.

"Yeah, I know." The cell phone, so quotidian, now became something fearful and alien, an instrument capable of sorting out pain from relief in the form of truth. She picked it up and punched in the numbers she'd written on the napkin, hitting each key with her index finger with more force than necessary. She raised it to her ear, listening to each ring, almost wishing no one would answer. But they did.

"Hello?" A female voice.

"Mrs. Villeneuve?"

"Yes, who is this, please?"

"My name is Krystal Murphy. I work with your daughter, Sara, in Arlington, and I'm trying to get in touch with her. Is she there with you?"

"Sara? Why no. Is something wrong?"

"Ma'am, her husband, Fred, said something about her coming down to visit you in Jacksonville, that someone was ill."

Krystal listened for a moment, said, "Thank you, Mrs. Villeneuve, there must have been some sort of mistake," and ended the call. Her expression told Velazquez all he needed to know.

"They've not seen her, have they?"

"No. She's not been there." Krystal shivered involuntarily.

"But we know she was in Miami yesterday, where two murders were committed within the space of a few hours."

"Damn it! I know that. I just don't see how the pieces fit together."

"Sherlock Holmes said, 'when you have eliminated the impossible, whatever remains, however improbable, must be the truth.' And what remains is that your friend is a murder suspect."

"But we haven't eliminated every other possibility. All we have is the circumstantial fact that Sara was at Cynthia Cottrell's gate sometime before Cynthia was murdered. We don't even know if Cynthia let her inside, and there is no hard evidence that she did."

"But she was there," he said, "and we need to find out why. And there is the fact that the same person, a woman, is likely to have killed both Fernandez and Brian Cottrell. You yourself insisted on that point. For the time being, Sara Hampton, a woman, is our best lead."

He was right. She knew he was right. And there was more: Sara's unseemly haste to put the Fernandez case to rest and blame the Tandy girl, the Commonwealth Attorney's dogged insistence that Krystal retire from the case and say away from Miami. In fact, it had been Sara who had suggested Dawn Tandy as a suspect in the first place. With Sara as a person of interest, those actions became suspect. There was also the fact that Sara had attended the ACLU conference where Fernandez had been a featured speaker, had told her about the judge's behavior there. Had there been some contact between her and the judge, as well? Suspicion had been thrown on Dawn Tandy for the very same reason. All of this was undeniable. But Dawn Tandy had had a motive. What motive could have driven Sara Hampton to murder? What was the connection between them all? Find a motive, find a murderer.

"A penny for your thoughts." Velazquez intruded on her confusion.

She sighed, expelling the indecision with the exhalation. She was a cop, a good cop, and sentiment only interfered in the kind of work cops had to do. Time to shake it off. So she told him about Sara's unorthodox behavior in connection with the Fernandez case, of how she had tried to wall Krystal off from the events in Miami following the Tandy family deaths.

The blond Miami detective listened intently, taking in the facts and sorting them. He chewed on his lower lip and took a draught of his now warm beer. At last, he said, "We're dealing with a serial killer."

Krystal had dealt with a serial killer only the year before, one who had taken pleasure in the slow torture and murder of innocent women.[2] She had worked on that case with the FBI's behavioral sciences unit and knew their theories.

"Listen, Ray," she replied, "I know Sara, have known her for a number of years. There is nothing about her that even hints at the type of sociopathic behavior associated with serial killers. Quite the opposite, as a matter of fact, so I don't think she fits into that category, at all. There's a difference between being driven by a psychosis and having a rational motivation for killing. In this case, IF Sara Hampton is the killer, you can bet she has a reason."

---

[2] "THE INCUBUS VENDETTA," Michael R. Davidson, 2014

"So we would not be dealing here with a crazy person, but with a smart lawyer who thinks rationally, a prosecutor who knows how to avoid leaving clues. What could drive someone like that to murder?"

"That's the problem we have, isn't it – motivation. Why would Sara have wanted these three people in particular out of the way? How could they have threatened her? The psychological cost to her would be extremely high."

"They could have had something on her, some information she would not want revealed. Blackmail?"

"By all three of the victims? Doesn't seem logical. If we can identify a motive, it's usually much easier to find a murderer. In this case, we have a possible murderer, but no known motive. And Cottrell had a lot of enemies down here. His and Cynthia's killer could have been local." Now she was arguing against her own theory.

He nodded. "And, as you so pointedly noted, there is only circumstantial evidence. But, as you also pointed out, Cottrell was killed by the same kind of small caliber weapon used on Fernandez."

Krystal remembered the times Sara had lectured her on the marginal value of circumstantial evidence in a courtroom. Who could be better versed in the law than a prosecuting attorney? Who would be better equipped to avoid leaving a trail of solid clues?

"You know what we have to do now, don't you, Krystal?" The bantering, Latino, tone to which she had become accustomed was gone. He was a cop on the scent, and he would not permit himself to be distracted by doubt or the fact that the "person of interest" was Krystal's friend.

"Yes. We have to find Sara and question her."

"I'm going to have a bolo put out on her, and the next step is to go public, plaster her picture all over the media and say she is wanted for questioning in connection with the murders."

"That will alert her. If she's guilty, she could run. She does have money." She realized she could no longer waver about calling Marty Jefferson in Arlington. Things had gone too far, too fast. "Let me make another call. There might be an easier way."

She punched the familiar numbers into her phone and waited for the answer. She'd dialed Jefferson's cell phone. He answered after only two rings. "Krystal?" The magic of caller i.d.

"Yeah, Marty, it's me."

"Are you still in Florida?"

"Yes, I am, and things are happening down here that you're not going to like very much."

"Damn it, Murphy, are you still messing around in that case? I warned you ..."

She didn't let him finish the sentence. "Marty, just listen to me. One, yes, I'm still involved. Two, there've been two more murders down here that may be related to the first one. Three, the only person of interest who has been identified is Sara Hampton."

Dead silence. Then, "You'd better explain that."

She told him about the two murders and the discovery that Sara had visited Cynthia Cottrell.

"That doesn't make her the killer." Jefferson was having the same trouble as Krystal. The words "murderer" and "Sara Hampton" were incompatible.

"I know what you're thinking, Marty. It struck me the same way. But surely you realize that we have to find Sara and question her as soon as possible."

"So, what's the problem?"

"We don't know where she is. She told her husband she was driving down to Jacksonville to her parents' because one of them was ill. I called her parents, and they've not seen nor heard from her. The only solid trace we have is her visit to the Cottrell house. Maybe she can explain it, maybe she can't, but we have to find her. The MDPD is about to put out a bolo on her, and they'll go public tomorrow if she doesn't turn up."

"Shit! There's a lot at stake here, Krystal. How do you know the murders down there are related to the Fernandez case? As far as we're concerned, that case is closed."

She knew exactly the "stakes" he meant – Sara Hampton's political ambitions. If he was anything, Marty Jefferson was a climber, a nice, polite climber, but nevertheless a moth unable to resist the temptation of the flame.

And that "case closed" comment ignited a flame so bright it temporarily blinded her, made her reckless. She couldn't get the grisly scene in the Tandy mobile home out of her mind. "Goddammit, Marty, that case is NOT closed, and you would damn well know it if you didn't have your nose so far up Sara Hampton's ass! I'm not going to give up until we catch the fucker who did this, even if it is our precious Commonwealth's Attorney."

Velazquez pressed his body against the back of the booth as though propelled there by a strong wind.

There was a stunned silence from Jefferson that lasted so long Krystal wondered if he had broken the connection. But then she caught the sound of heavy breathing. She instantly regretted her outburst, setting her "Irish" loose on an unsuspecting world. It was true that Marty Jefferson was a political animal, but he also had backed her strongly for her promotion to head the Homicide/Robbery Unit. She should not have thought so ill of him.

"Marty," she said, "I'm sorry. This thing has really gotten under my skin, and now there's this totally unexpected connection with Sara. We need to clear it up as soon as possible for all our sakes. If Sara has done nothing wrong, if she can satisfactorily explain her presence at the Cottrell house this morning, we can prevent the embarrassment a PSA[3] would bring, both to her and the Arlington government."

"I'm listening." Jefferson's voice was tight and had lost the hint of an amiable southern drawl that normally softened the edges when he spoke.

"We need to find her ourselves first. I don't think the MDPD will give us more than a few hours to do it." She shot an interrogatory look at Velazquez, who grimaced, nodded his assent, and mouthed the words, *until six o'clock tomorrow morning.*

---

[3] Public Service Announcement

"They'll give us twelve hours before all bets are off. And it's going to be all up to you, Marty. You'll need to find out her cell number, press Fred Hampton to do what he can, and ..."

"I know what I have to do, Murphy." He used her last name again, a sure sign of vexation. "I'll call you when I've found something out."

"Just one thing, Marty. The MDPD need the make, model and plate number of her car right away. That bolo is going out one way or the other."

"I'll see what I can do. And we're going to have a talk when you get back here, which had better be damned soon." Jefferson broke the connection before she could reply.

"I can't delay putting out a bolo, Krystal," said Velazquez. "The PSA, yes, but if she's guilty and still in Florida, we need cops on the look-out for her."

He was right, and she had no leverage that could stop him. Maybe she didn't want to. Time was already working against them.

Chapter 36

By nine o'clock the following morning nothing further had been heard from Marty Jefferson. Velazquez had given her an extra three hours past the deadline he had set the night before, but was now going through the motions necessary to alert the media that Sara Hampton was wanted for questioning in connection with an ongoing murder investigation. Another call to Jefferson had resulted in nothing but an order to wait. She tapped her foot impatiently on the floor of MDPD Headquarters as she watched Velazquez. The "Miami Vice" cop was transformed. He had abandoned his usual slacks and short sleeved shirt for a dark suit, starched white shirt, and tie. This was in deference to his planned appearance before the television cameras at a press conference that had been called for ten A.M. He'd caught her looking at him more than once, and she was embarrassed. But with that tan he looked like he'd just stepped off a Hollywood movie set!

Krystal's cell phone vibrated. She'd placed it on Velazquez's desk, having resisted the temptation to smash it against the wall after her last failure to contact Jefferson. The caller i.d. showed the Deputy Chief's number at Arlington Police HQS. She grabbed the phone while signaling frantically to Velazquez.

"Marty?"

Jefferson's voice, if anything, was colder than the night before. "Murphy, I have someone here who wants to speak with you. Are you with the Miami police now?"

"Yes, I'm here at Headquarters with Ray Velazquez."

"Can you put this on speaker, please?"

"Sure." She pushed the little button with the picture of a speaker and laid the phone back on the desk. Velazquez raised his eyebrows, but all she could do was shrug.

The next voice they heard was a surprise.

"Krystal, this is Sara Hampton."

There was no mistaking the Commonwealth Attorney's voice, and Krystal mouthed the words, *it's her,* to Velazquez.

Hampton's disembodied voice drifted out of the speaker again to infuse the air with her calm, firm, reassuring lawyer's voice. "What's going on down there, Krystal? What in the world is this crazy talk I hear from Deputy Chief Jefferson?"

Krystal, at a loss for words, was grateful when Velazquez spoke up. "Ms. Hampton, this is MDPD detective Ray Velazquez. I'm investigating the murders of Brian and Cynthia Cottrell. Can you tell me what you were doing at the Cottrell house the day before yesterday?"

Sara responded evenly, "Jefferson here informed me of Cynthia's death this morning as soon as I came into the office. I was, to put it mildly, shocked to the core. Cynthia is an old college friend of mine, and I went to pay her a visit but only talked to her at the door without going inside. She told me about her husband's unfortunate death and said she just wasn't up to visitors. So I gave her my condolences and left. I drove back up here yesterday. There's really nothing more I can tell you, detective."

"What were you doing in Miami, Ms. Hampton?" Velazquez persisted.

"Nothing in particular. Just visiting old haunts. Paying a visit to Cynthia was a spur of the moment idea."

"You were just driving around Miami aimlessly?"

"No, detective. As I just said, I was visiting old haunts, just relaxing. I'd planned to visit my parents in Jacksonville, but decided to go on down to Miami. I had no particular plans other than to get away from the office for a while and clear my head. I needed time to think about my upcoming campaign for the State

Senate. I do some of my best thinking when I'm driving."

"Do you own a firearm, Ms. Hampton? Is there a weapon registered in your name?"

"No, I do not. I abhor guns of all types."

"Did you know Brian Cottrell?"

"Slightly. I knew he had married Cynthia, of course, and we were both in the ACLU. I did know him by reputation."

"Where did you stay in Miami?"

"I think I'm done answering questions, detective. I've explained the reason I was at Cynthia's house, and that should be more than sufficient for your inquiry. Now I have something to ask you. I understand that a bolo was issued concerning me last night. I want that rescinded immediately with a clear explanation that I am no longer needed in connection with your investigation. And if any word of this is leaked to the press, I will take immediate legal action against your department and you personally. In fact, it's an insult to me and my position as a prosecuting attorney that you should harbor any suspicions whatsoever about me. I appreciate that you had to clarify the reason for my visit to Cynthia, but to go so far as to issue a bolo and insinuate that I could be a person of interest in a murder case is really beyond the pale. I would gladly have answered your questions without all this angst. Now let me speak with Detective Murphy, privately."

Krystal detected the rattlesnake timbre in Sara's voice and she hesitated before picking up the cell phone as though it might bite her. She switched off the speaker before raising it to her ear.

"I'm here, Sara," she said.

"Don't 'Sara' me, detective," the rattle definitely increased in intensity. "The Deputy Chief tells me that you seem almost convinced that I had a hand in these murders. I can't tell you how that makes me feel, but I'll tell you one thing: you get your ass on the next plane out of Miami and get back to your job here, a job, I might add, that you are lucky to still have. You have ignored the well-meaning advice of your superiors and, even worse, disobeyed their orders. The Fernandez case is closed as far as Arlington County is concerned, and you have no business interfering in an unrelated Miami police investigation. You've made a terrible mess of things. Do you understand?"

"Sara, we tried to contact you ..."

Sara cut her off. "I know. Fred called, and then my parents. They were frantic. You have no sensitivity, detective, you never did. And you lack discipline. It's your weakest point. That's all I have to say to you for the moment. Now get on that plane."

The connection was broken, and Krystal stared at the phone in her hand, half expecting it to burst into flames.

"From the look on your face," said Velazquez, "your conversation didn't go much better than mine."

"They've ordered me back to Arlington. They want me to leave today."

"I guess you'd better do it."

"What do you think about what she said?"

"It's pretty thin, and I don't like that vague 'driving around thinking' bit. And what about her husband thinking one of her parents was ill and that was the reason she came to Florida. Also, why would she drive all this way when she could have flown? I still have unanswered questions, Krystal, but unless we can come up with something more, we're left with only that video of her at Cottrell's gate. No one is going to press charges on the basis of that alone."

Krystal rubbed her temples. "I have a really bad feeling about this, Ray, really bad."

"Arrests and prosecutions can't be based on feelings."

"I know it, damn it!" Her gorge was rising. "Sara has tried to cut me off at the pass, prevent me from digging into the Fernandez case. You wait. Forensics will confirm that the gun that killed Fernandez was the same one used to kill Brian Cottrell. I'm sure it will. All of this is connected somehow. You know there has to be a thread."

"It's not a bad theory," said Velazquez. "But it's only a theory. It's possible something will come up concerning one of Cottrell's criminal clients, some sort of vendetta. He hired Gutierrez to kill Fernandez. Maybe Fernandez was one step ahead of him."

She shot him an exasperated look. "No, no, no. You forget the two of them were killed with the same gun."

"Maybe. If the forensics match. I'm ready to grasp at straws."

"Crap." And that was exactly how she felt.

Chapter 37

The flight was normal: whoosh up, something they called a sandwich that tasted like cardboard, whoosh down, screech as wheels hit tarmac, shuffle up the jetway into the airy space of Reagan National Airport. She retrieved her car from long term parking and opted for Route 1 rather than the GW Parkway to get back to Arlington. On the way through Crystal City she passed the Crowne Plaza Hotel where it had all begun, and this jogged her memory of its soulless, pastel interior and the half-naked body of Fernie Fernandez on the floor of his suite with a neat, round hole in the middle of his forehead.

Her thoughts were churning, had been since that conversation with Sara Hampton. If only she could start all over again from the moment she had entered the room. If only she had not been stampeded into hunting down Dawn Tandy, or, she chided herself, had she not so single-mindedly chased down the lead to Dawn. She couldn't avoid the fact that she'd been eager to follow that trail. She'd seen the charnel house that the Tandy mobile home in Miami had become, as well, heard the desperation in the girl's voice during that last, fateful phone call. Her young life had been ended by a 30-06 bullet through the back of her head that obliterated her brain and left her once fresh, beautiful face unrecognizable. If her feelings of guilt following the death of Thomas Stewart had been irrational, the burden she felt over Dawn Tandy was depressingly tangible. It weighed down upon her, a constant presence that suggested ghosts could be real.

It had been almost physically difficult for Krystal to board the plane in Miami. Something grasped at her, trying to hold her there. It was Dawn Tandy who had pulled her back to Miami. It was Dawn Tandy's insistent voice which seemed to say nothing but echoed in her thoughts like some howling animal dying in the forest, leaving her desperate to put an end to its misery. And the farther she got away from Miami, the more insistent it became, calling her back with its song of rage and frustration.

She concentrated on her driving, finally swinging onto Washington Boulevard toward Arlington. She wouldn't go to the office now. She would wait until morning, and she would not call Marty Jefferson to reassure him that she had obeyed the order to return. Let the bastard sweat. Let Sara Hampton sweat. Fuck them both!

Her phone vibrated, and she cursed aloud believing it must be Jefferson checking on her. Her mood changed when Ray Velazquez's name appeared on the caller-id.

"Hi, Ray," she said, "you probably saved me from ramming some civilian, I'm so pissed off."

Her greeting was met with silence for a few beats. "Well," said Velazquez at last, "maybe we'd better wait until you've stopped somewhere before talking."

Shit! What now? The good-natured bantering tone was absent from his voice.

"No, it's all right, I promise," she said. "What is it? You don't sound happy."

"I'm not. The good news is we got the ballistics report on the bullet that killed Cottrell -- .22 long rifle. The bad news is Arlington never sent the ballistics report on the bullet that killed Fernandez, so we have nothing to compare the Cottrell slug with."

"That's just not right," she said. "Arlington wouldn't refuse a request like that from the MDPD. What did the response say?"

"That's just it. We've still not received a response from Arlington. I didn't want to call anyone else up there until I'd spoken with you. This case seems to be especially sensitive for your folks. What do you think?"

"I don't know what to think. Let me check it out, and then I'll get back to you."

"Time flies when you don't have a clue," he said. "We're chasing our tails."

"I'll sort it out, Ray."

"I hope so. I'll wait for your call."

It would not be a simple matter of inquiring about the status of the MDPD request. *Hey, Marty, I know everyone is really pissed off that I went back to Miami, and I've been told to cease and desist, but first thing I'd like to talk about with you now that I'm back is that ballistics report that Miami is waiting for."*

Oh, yeah, that would go over really well. She'd be lucky to walk out of Jefferson's office with her head. She'd have to find another way to sort out the delay and make sure the report was sent to Ray. Funny, the Miami detective had now become "Ray" in her thoughts rather than just "Velazquez." Something had shifted there.

Maybe the report was just stuck somewhere in the system and eventually would turn up in Miami. If it didn't, there was no way she could appeal to Jefferson on the matter. One promising alternative was to appeal directly to Jeff Headley in the forensics unit. He would have direct access to the records and at the very least be able to provide some insight into how the MDPD request had been handled.

Her empty apartment provided an anticlimactic ending to her journey. It didn't really feel like "coming home," and never had. It was just a space she occupied on a more or less regular basis. A wave of nostalgia for the colors of Miami, the smell of strong,

Michael R. Davidson

Cuban coffee and cigars, and the exotic atmosphere of the town washed over her. At least in Miami she had had someone to talk over the case with who did not dismiss her views, someone who had no pre-conceptions about her, someone whose company she actually enjoyed. It had been like getting a fresh start after the trauma of Thomas Stewart's death and playing the unwonted role of grieving girlfriend.

She had turned off the answering machine before leaving because she didn't want to come home to a lot of messages she would feel obligated to answer. There was no one she wanted to see, certainly no one who would want to talk about Thomas. Even more, she dreaded going into the office tomorrow.

There was nothing edible in the refrigerator, so she ordered pizza and poured herself a scotch before sitting down to wait. Casting another glance around the apartment she suddenly found so unwelcoming, equally unwelcome tears started from her eyes. This was odd because she was not sobbing, her chest was not heaving, she was not, would not cry. There were just the tears, and she didn't know what to make of them. It was a symptom, she decided, but she was unsure of what. Sadness, frustration, jet-lag?

The apartment was just a place to crash after a long day's work, a space reserved for privacy. Did she have a home any longer? Her family was still in Indiana, and her brother and his wife were popping out children seemingly according to some sort of regular timetable. But that had not been for her. There were adventures to be had in a world much wider than the somnambulant Mid-west.

There had always been a dog when she was growing up. Her father was a firm believer that a man was not whole without a dog at his side and equally adamant that most dogs were better and more loyal than most people. Krystal never thought she would miss anything about Indiana, and she had escaped the flat fields as soon as the opportunity presented itself. No regrets. But she did miss dogs – Ozzie, the family German shepherd most of all. In all the years since leaving home, first the Army, then college, then the police, she had never been in a position to keep even a goldfish, let alone a dog that demanded a lot of personal time.

God, how she hated introspection, and involuntary introspection was worst of all. This was too much like self-pity, something Krystal Murphy simply never indulged. Then what the hell were these tears about?

Her mind conjured up an image of Thomas Stewart, and a sob finally escaped.

Chapter 38

The next day, the third of June, the Metropolitan Area awoke to a cloudless sky that promised the first real heat leading into summer. It had been a restless night. The pizza had not agreed with her, and she'd overdone it just enough with the scotch to bequeath her a morning headache to complement the stomach upset. The sunlight in her eyes as she drove east toward police headquarters did not improve her mood nor attenuate what remained of the headache.

She stopped at her favorite Starbucks, but found that the overpriced brew she had formerly enjoyed every morning now paled in comparison to the sweet strength of Cuban coffee served in tiny cups on Miami's Calle Ocho. In fact, nothing she saw in Arlington compared favorably with Miami's frenetic, Mambo environment. Arlington with its neat, clean streets and red brick faux colonial architecture seemed driven by the desire to avoid excitement while Miami sought to provoke it. This did not improve her mood as she mounted the steps to the glassed entrance to headquarters. Nothing good awaited her inside the building on this day. She had vowed to keep her "Irish" under control and take her lumps in silence.

She'd switched her cell phone off the night before, and when she'd turned it on this morning there had been several voicemails from Marty Jefferson wondering where she was. The man certainly had a burr under his saddle. Sara must really have come down on him, perhaps even complaining to the Chief of Police. She shook it off. The more she thought about it, the worse it became, and that was a no-win course of action. Best to face the music, get the facts, see where she stood ... see if she still had a future with the Arlington County Police.

She dropped the three-quarters full cup of Starbucks schlock into a trash receptacle in the foyer and rode the elevator to Jefferson's floor. When she knocked on the frame of his open door, Jefferson looked up with a flash of irritation. "There you are! Where have you been? I've been trying to get in touch with you since yesterday afternoon."

She did not drop into a chair as she normally would have done with Jefferson, but remained standing in front of his desk. "I got in late yesterday afternoon and went straight home. I was tired and switched my phone off. I just wanted to rest."

"Yes, you've apparently been quite busy, involving yourself in matters that do not concern you or the Arlington police."

He stared expectantly for a couple of beats, but if he was waiting for an apology, he would be disappointed.

Jefferson knit his brows and lowered his gaze to the papers on his desk and waved her out of the office. "Get back to work. You might receive a call to see the Commonwealth Attorney, but not for a while. She's pissed off at you, and for good reason."

Without a word, she turned on her heel and headed back for the elevator. She still had a job, apparently.

The half-hidden smirks she received when she entered her own office confirmed that news of her predicament were widespread. She said nothing and closed the door to the glass-walled office, and slumped behind her desk. Someone had opened her normally closed blinds, probably just to bug her more. She saw one of the guys in the common office area say something she couldn't hear, which apparently amused the rest, and she visualized them as hyenas circling a carcass preparing to dash in and rip off a hunk of dead meat.

She switched on her computer, wishing she had another cup of coffee, no matter how bad, but she didn't want to walk out through the bullpen again to fetch it from the coffee pot that was always kept full.

Her e-mail did not have much of a backlog, so she switched to open cases. The Arlington "most wanted" list remained about the same, mostly men wanted for rape, malicious wounding, or robbery. Six of the seven men on the list were Hispanic. Again, she was reminded of Miami where the MDPD's homicide unit was a relative cauldron of activity. Arlington County averaged was 5.6 murders per year, and thus far this year the Fernandez killing was the only one.

There was nothing to do except shuffle through the crime reports, paper correspondence and personnel matters that came with the job. She was surprised that so little had happened during her absence, but then realized that she had been away only a short time. Everything in Miami had transpired over the course of just a few days.

By noon the ghost of Dawn Tandy was tapping impatiently on her shoulder, whispering into her ear for justice, would not cease pestering, until she had been exonerated. Only then would she lift the pall of guilt she had draped over the detective who had suspected her of murder. Krystal decided to break the vow of the previous evening and pulled up the department's Law Enforcement on Line account to see if the forensics report on the bullet that had killed Judge Fernandez had been transmitted to Miami. It had not.

Now she would have to pay a visit to Jeff Headley, the head of the Forensics Unit. The question was could she do so without it coming to Jefferson's attention. She decided to take the chance.

Michael R. Davidson

It was strange to be ducking around corners, acting furtively as though she were behind enemy lines. This was her headquarters, her building, but today it had an unfamiliar feel, as though she were no longer welcome here.

Headley was at his desk in the Forensics Unit, strands of his thinning, too long red hair hanging over his forehead. The man came from Massachusetts and spoke with a Boston accent that broadened his vowels and omitted r's from the endings of words. Krystal had worked hard over the years to lose her midwestern twang that recognized no phonetic difference between the words "pin" and "pen." She privately berated herself for the attempt to conceal her roots; something she noticed was not a concern for people from the Deep South, New York, or New England. It was personal, a reflection of a deep-seated feeling of inferiority that resulted in colorless, character-free diction.

Headley's attention was focused on the computer screen in front of him, and he did not notice Krystal's quiet entrance. He started when she spoke.

"Hi, Jeff."

He swiveled his chair to face her. "Jeez, Krystal, you scared the shit out of me. When did you get back?"

"Sorry." So everyone knew about her sojourn in Miami. "Last night."

"I heard there are a lot of people pissed off at you."

Yep, everyone knows. "I suppose so. That's their problem more than mine."

"Not what I heard. They're REALLY pissed off."

"I can't understand why, Jeff. I really can't."

He scratched his head and flicked the hair out of his eyes. At least Headley was being up front about it, unlike the gloating monkeys in her own shop.

"The word is you disobeyed a direct order from the Deputy Chief and tried to mess up the Commonwealth Attorney's case, and I wouldn't wish it on my worst enemy to be on the wrong side of her." Maybe he wasn't exactly gloating, but he was enjoying prodding her a little too much.

"It wasn't exactly like that, Jeff. I didn't disobey any orders. As a matter of fact, Jefferson ordered me to take some time off." Why was she telling him this? She wasn't here looking for sympathy or to provide another faggot for her *auto da fe*. "Anyway, I have a question for you."

He eyed her as someone might regard a plague victim who had just entered his room and wanted to touch him. "Humph. What's the question?"

"No big deal. I was just wondering why the forensics report on the bullet from the Fernandez case has not been sent to Miami."

She got the impression that Headley would have made the sign of the cross had they lived in another age.

"Don't try to drag me into your Miami swamp, Murphy. I don't need any of your mud on my boots."

She hadn't realized that Headley was familiar with metaphors, and the use of her last name was a danger signal. "I don't know what you mean ...

HEADLEY. I know that the MDPD formally requested a copy of the report. So why haven't you sent it?"

He did not respond immediately, and she restrained herself from grabbing him by the shoulders and shaking an answer out, settling for crossing her arms and tapping her toe.

"Come on, Headley. It's a simple enough question, and I goddamn outrank you. So give me an answer." She put a hand on his desk and leaned over, her face inches from his.

His normally pale face developed bright red splotches, and sweat broke out on his forehead that might have been signs of fear or signals of an impending explosion of anger. But he finally capitulated.

"There is no forensics report on that bullet."

She was nonplussed. "How could that be? It's a murder case."

His mouth twitched up at one corner, evidently pleased at her confusion. "It's a closed case," he said. "No autopsy was performed, so there's no forensics report."

"But the body was sent to Manassas." Manassas was the location of the Northern Virginia office of the Virginia medical examiner system, charged with investigating all violent deaths in the Commonwealth.

"Yes," Headley conceded. "It was sent out there. Might still be there. But as far as we're concerned, the case was closed when the killer was identified and then died."

"It wasn't closed. It's an unsolved case."

"Not what I heard."

Then she remembered looking through the unsolved case files earlier. Fernie Fernandez's murder was not on the list.

After Krystal Murphy left his office, Headley picked up the phone and dialed Marty Jefferson's extension, just as the Deputy Chief had instructed him to do should the nosy female detective come snooping.

Chapter 39

She didn't hesitate. Stepping into her office only to switch off the computer, she retrieved her car from the parking lot and headed directly to Manassas. As usual, there was construction west bound on Interstate 66, but 45 minutes later she pulled into the visitors parking area in front of the ultramodern building at Pyramid Place that housed the Northern District offices of Virginia's Office of the Medical Examiner.

The office entrance was just off the main lobby on the right. She flashed her badge and was escorted to the administrator, Dr. William Butler, who turned out to be a courtly, bespectacled, white-haired man who rose when she entered, shook hands, and guided her by the elbow to some chairs arranged around a coffee table. She disliked being physically guided by men, but because he was from an older generation when such things had been expected, she gave him some slack. He was tall, over six feet, and had the soft hands and bedside manner of a physician.

"What can I do for you, detective?" he asked once they were seated.

"I understand that the body of a murder victim from Arlington was brought here recently. I'd like to know about its disposition."

"Well," he smiled, "there has been only one of those lately, and I understand it was a rather famous corpse."

"Judge Fernando Fernandez from Miami. He was shot it the head at the Crowne Plaza Hotel in Crystal City several weeks ago."

"And what is your specific interest?"

"I'm the investigating officer, and we seem to be missing a forensic report. Did you perform an autopsy?"

Dr. Butler frowned and cocked his head. "I'm afraid I don't understand. We were informed by the Arlington County Police that the case was closed and no autopsy would be required. Were we misinformed?"

"I'm afraid so, Doctor Butler. There have been two murders in Miami that may well be connected to the Fernandez case. It's possible that all the murders were committed by the same person. The Miami Dade police have requested a copy of the forensics report on the bullet that killed the judge."

Butler became uncomfortable. "Oh, dear. Then we certainly do have a problem. This is most troubling. The instructions your Arlington people gave us were quite specific. As you might imagine, we are incredibly busy here, covering as we do all of Northern Virginia. There was no doubt in this case as to the cause of death, so one less autopsy request can be a welcome thing, you understand."

She nodded, hoping there was still a way. None of this was good news, but there was a chance. The hell with what Jefferson and Hampton wanted.

"Is the body still here, Doctor Butler? Could you still perform an autopsy?"

Butler was genuinely distressed now, the blue eyes behind the glasses widened slightly. "I'm so sorry, detective, but the cadaver is no longer in our possession. We were informed that the individual had no next of kin and that there was no one willing to take charge of the body."

Krystal remembered Adele Fernandez saying that the judge must have had a will, but she could easily imagine the spurned ex-spouse caring little to nothing about the disposition of her ex-husband's body. Dread of what Butler would say next carved out a hollow in the pit of her stomach. "So, what happened to the body?"

"We sent it to Knoxville," he said.

She was confused for a moment before the significance dawned. Knoxville.

"You mean you sent it to the Body Farm?"

Encouraged that she understood what he was talking about, Dr. Butler nodded, the slight smile returning to his face. "Yes, to the Forensic Anthropology Center at the University of Tennessee Medical Center."

This could be good news. At least, she thought, there was still a body, or what was left of one. Her worst fear that the judge had been cremated had been avoided. The big question now was how she could gain access to the remains at the Body Farm, and then how to insure that the bullet evidence was preserved.

She thanked Dr. Butler for his help and asked him not to discuss her visit as it concerned an on-going investigation. She left him confused, but secured his agreement to keep mum.

She sat in her car for several minutes turning over the possibilities. It was clear that there had been a concerted effort to eliminate whatever evidence the bullet in Fernandez's brain might offer. This went much farther than simply declaring a case unsolved or closed. And it didn't allay her suspicions about Sara Hampton. This had her fingerprints all over it, perhaps literally.

She checked her watch. It was already after three in the afternoon. Probably too late to do any more today. But she would make a phone call to the one person who might get her into the Body Farm.

Chapter 40

Next morning Krystal skipped her usual stop at Starbucks, and drove directly to the office. She planned to clear up whatever paperwork awaited her. She had to get up to date on current cases, and she planned to re-start her usual morning briefing for with her subordinates the next day. She had only begun when Marty Jefferson's secretary rang with an order to see him right away.

She had an appointment at 10:30 AM downtown, and she hoped whatever Marty wanted would not take too long. With a sigh she trudged to the elevator and took it up to the Deputy Chief's floor.

The Deputy Chief's door was open, as usual. When she was inside, Jefferson said, "Close the door, Murphy." She closed the door behind her and stood in front of his desk.

"I've tried, Murphy, I've really tried, but you just can't bring yourself to cooperate, can you? I recommended you for promotion, but you show no gratitude. You are not a team player, and you are embarrassing this department."

"I don't know what you mean, Marty."

His palm slapped the desktop with a loud smack, his exasperation breaking through the carefully cultivated calm, suave manner. "Damn it! Don't lie to me, Murphy. You're ignoring your duties and still trying to stir up trouble. You visited Forensics yesterday and continued to ask questions about the Fernandez case ... the CLOSED Fernandez case. And then you left the office. Where did you go?"

That little red-haired shit, Headley, obviously had squealed on her. She wasn't about to tell Marty Jefferson about her visit to Manassas. "I just drove around," she said, not bothering to deny that she had visited the Forensics Unit. "I wanted to clear my head." If the excuse was good enough for Sara Hampton, it was good enough for her.

She wondered if Jefferson had contacted Dr. Butler, as well. Would Headley have had the guts to tell the Deputy Chief that he had spilled the beans about the disposition of the judge's remains? If he had, Jefferson would know she was lying.

The Deputy Chief gave her a look she couldn't interpret – equal parts disgust, anger, and something else. "Well, Murphy, you will then be pleased to learn that you'll have plenty of time for head clearing in the coming weeks. Give me your badge and your weapon. You are on indefinite suspension as of now. Frankly, you'll be lucky if you have a job to come back to."

This should not have been a surprise. What else had she expected? Intra office politics could be vicious. Marty Jefferson was a climber, and Sara Hampton must have brought some pressure to bear on the Department, maybe even through the Chief of Police. Marty was constitutionally incapable of resisting such pressure and would have bent like a reed in a strong wind. She bit back the words that sprang to her lips. Nothing she could say would change Jefferson's mind and secure his cooperation. Politics trumped everything.

She unclipped the pistol and badge from her belt and laid them in front of Jefferson.

"I'll take the keys to the police vehicle, as well," he said.

She laid the keys on the desk. "Is that all?"

"That's all." He gave her an unvarnished thousand mile ghetto stare.

Without another word she turned on her heel and marched out of his office. She didn't bother returning to her own office. Someone else could already be in there, and she had no desire to set foot in that den of resentment again. In fact, she might well never again be welcome in this building. She may well have thrown away the career it had taken a lifetime to build.

But she had another card to play, a powerful card that trumped the Arlington County Police and the Office of the Commonwealth Attorney.

Chapter 41

There was more than enough time to make the 10:30 appointment. *Thanks, Marty, for kicking me out so early in the morning.* She used her cell phone to summon a taxi to her apartment where she retrieved her venerable Toyota Corolla, a car she had acquired while still in college. If her father had taught her anything, it was vehicle maintenance. *Change the oil every 3,000 miles.* The engine came to life immediately, and she roared into the street.

What had led to today's drama? *Know the truth.* The phrase seeped unbidden into her thoughts and brought with it memories of that last conversation with Thomas Stewart about deception and truth. Thomas had been right. She would employ deception in her search for the truth.

She chose the 14th Street Bridge to enter DC, and miraculously found a parking spot on the Mall. She hoofed two blocks up 9th Street. The buff colored, multi-storied concrete bunker of the J. Edgar Hoover building stood before her across the broad expanse of Pennsylvania Avenue.

The building was not unfamiliar to her, and she had a very special acquaintance inside.

It was strange not presenting her badge and surrendering her weapon at the entrance. Fortunately, the status of the man with whom she had an appointment guaranteed she would have no problem getting through security. Deprived of her law enforcement credentials, an escort was required, and presently, a young man in a dark suit appeared to escort her to her destination on the third floor.

The plaque at the side of the door proclaimed the office beyond to be the territory of Executive Assistant Director Enoch Whitehall. The young man in the ubiquitous dark suit and tie that was the uniform of the FBI opened the door and presented her to Whitehall's secretary, a woman of indeterminate age who exuded an air that was equal parts efficiency and ferocity, the dragon protecting the entrance to the sorcerer's lair. The secretary dismissed the escort and asked Krystal to take a seat while she announced her arrival to her boss.

That proved unnecessary as the door to Whitehall's office opened and the cadaverous frame of

Michael R. Davidson

the man himself, the epitome of the fabled government "man in black" loomed in the doorway. Black was perhaps not the best descriptor for Enoch Whitehall. Gray to the point of blending into his surroundings to a point of near invisibility also was an applicable description. But when he turned his attention to you, the hatchet face with its blade of a nose and deep-set gray eyes, could be mesmerizing. Whitehall's full title was Executive Assistant Director of the Counterintelligence Division. Krystal was not completely convinced that he was in a position to help her, but she knew he would give her a fair hearing. Oddly enough, it had been Marty Jefferson who had placed her in contact with him a long time ago in connection with an especially complicated case.[4]

"Krystal," said Whitehall, "This is an unexpected pleasure. Please come in." He stood aside for her to enter his office and waited for her to be seated before resuming his place behind the desk.

"Director Whitehall," she began, "I have a problem."

She did not expect a "call me Enoch" from Whitehall. He was a man who naturally commanded formality, perhaps as a mechanism for avoiding personal entanglements. Once again, she was taken by the neutral nature of his office. There were no personal photographs, no "vanity wall," only a single framed photograph on the wall behind the desk of a tall young man, a much earlier version of Whitehall, shaking hands with former Director J. Edgar Hoover.

---

[4] "INCUBUS," Michael R. Davidson, 2012.

She wondered how old Whitehall really was. Other than the plaque on his desk that proclaimed his current title, there was no item that hinted at his identity.

"A problem you think I can help you with?"

"I don't think counter-intelligence is what I need, but I hoped you could pull some strings for me."

"I see that you required an escort today, and I don't see a badge. I find that troubling, given what I know about you. Are you in trouble?"

"Yes. I've been put on indefinite administrative leave."

Whitehall put his elbows on the desk and steepled long, bony fingers. The calm, gray eyes studied her from under graying, untrimmed brows. She wondered what he saw: a police officer under a cloud for some serious infraction, a rogue with too little self-control, or someone he had come to respect.

Without taking his eyes from her, he picked up the phone and pushed the intercom button that connected him to his secretary. "Jeanne," he said, "please hold my other appointments."

He replaced the receiver and said, "Tell me about it."

She told him everything, the discovery of Fernando Fernandez's body at the Crowne Plaza, the frenzy of the Dawn Tandy tragedy, the two subsequent murders in Miami, and the likelihood that the Fernandez and Cottrell murders were related. And she did not hesitate to voice her concerns about the suspicious actions of Sara Hampton, her strange appearance at the Cottrell residence, and her efforts to put an end to the investigation leading to her administrative leave. Finally, she told him about the shell game with the judge's body. Throughout her recitation Whitehall sat like a sphinx, sometimes with his eyes closed, as he absorbed the information.

"So you see," she concluded, "I'm now effectively barred from officially continuing the investigation."

He was silent for a few beats as he ordered his thoughts, then, "The evidence you cite is circumstantial but strongly suggests that the three murders are in some way connected. Most troubling is the puzzling attitude of your superiors in Arlington and the Commonwealth Attorney, not to mention her presence at one of the crime scenes. The absence of a discernable motive is a problem, the missing link that would connect the dots. Have I correctly summarized the situation?"

"Yes. And I think that one step toward identifying that connection would be to retrieve the bullet that killed Judge Fernandez. That would provide a definite, undeniable connection between the murder in Washington and those in Miami."

"Possibly. It's certainly material evidence that should already have been retrieved and analyzed. Your Sara Hampton has done an effective job in preventing this."

"Can you help?" There it was -- the real question. Everything hung on Whitehall's response. She thought she saw a way. "Three murders by the same person make the perpetrator a serial killer by definition. Doesn't that bring the FBI into the case?"

"Actually," he said, "the current definition of serial killing was developed several years ago by the National Center for the Analysis of Violent Crime. The correct definition is 'the unlawful killing of two or more victims by the same offender in separate events.' And the FBI does not automatically become involved. But this gives me an idea, although I don't see how it will help in your personal situation."

"Forget my personal situation. What's the idea?"

"You say there have been two murders in Miami that in all likelihood are related and that these murders occurred at separate places at separate times."

"Yes, but we're still waiting for confirmation that Cynthia Cottrell was killed by her husband's gun that was taken by his killer."

"The FBI has provided assistance to local law enforcement in such cases for decades, but only if it is requested by the appropriate law enforcement agency. In this case, that would be the Miami Dade Police Department."

The feeble flame of hope that had waned upon her return to Arlington now waxed brighter. At least, she could count on the cooperation of the MDPD, especially that of a certain homicide detective.

"How about the bullet?" she asked.

"There are a couple of ways that could be handled. The FBI has a good relationship with the people in Knoxville. The best alternative would be for Miami-Dade law enforcement to request that the bullet be recovered to assist in their investigation. The FBI would almost certainly support that request, although it probably would not be necessary. The less preferable alternative would be for us to make an informal request, insofar as any request from the FBI can be informal."

"I think we can count on the MDPD," she said with mounting confidence.

"They should know how to contact the Critical Response Group. If you can confirm that the MDPD intends to make the request, I'll give Quantico a heads up."

"Thank you, Director Whitehall. This means a lot."

"Krystal, given your current situation, your role in this must be passive."

It was a word she did not fully understand.

There was a parking ticket on the Corolla's windshield. But it didn't bother her. Whitehall had given her much more of his time than she had expected. Lost in thought she didn't notice the figure that shadowed her back to her car, just as she had not noticed the car that had followed her from her apartment earlier that morning.

Chapter 42

From across North Barton Street, the driver watched Murphy park and enter the apartment building. Given her actions since returning to Arlington, it was likely that the disgraced detective did not plan to abandon the Fernandez case. Steps would have to be taken, and quickly. It may already be too late. The visit to FBI Headquarters was puzzling and troublesome. She had friends there. Whatever she had been up to, she was dangerous, and however it all ended, Krystal Murphy would not be around to see it.

Krystal picked up the phone as soon as she entered the apartment, but just as quickly replaced it in its cradle and sat down to think. Should she mention her suspicion to Velazquez? There was no particular reason not to do so, but she didn't want to be cut out of the case for bureaucratic reasons. This deception stuff was getting easier.

When Velazquez answered she got right down to business. "Do you have the ballistics on the bullet that killed Cottrell?"

"Yes, we do, but without a comparison it's not of much use."

Before she could tell him her plan, he continued, "There is something else, however. You were right about the shell casings we found at Cynthia's. Brian Cottrell's fingerprint was on them."

Enthusiasm returned to its formerly achieved level. "So that established a link between the two murders."

He was intrigued by what she had discovered about the disposition of Fernandez's body and her conversation with Enoch Whitehall.

"So, you see," she concluded, her words tumbling over one another, "the two murders in Miami meet the new definition of a serial killing all by themselves. You can call on the FBI for support, and we can retrieve the bullet that killed the judge. That's a legitimate line of investigation."

"I can try to convince the powers that be down here to contact the Bureau," he said with much less conviction that she might have wished.

"You think there'll be opposition to the idea?"

"No more than usual when there's a possibility of the FBI butting into a local case."

"But there aren't really jurisdictional problems. I've worked them before, and they were nothing but helpful. The idea is to provide assistance, not take over cases."

"You have no idea of the turf problems we have in Miami with the DEA, FBI, ATF, the whole alphabet. There's a lot going on down here besides this case."

"Will you try?" It sounded so pathetic. "You could limit the request to securing the bullet from Fernandez's body."

"Well," he said, "it wouldn't hurt. Like I said yesterday, we're chasing our tails down here, and I think the answers are up there in Virginia. I'll get right on it."

"Ray," this was the tricky part, "can you make sure this stays between just you and me? I mean, no one from the MDPD should mention this to Arlington County."

He snorted. "I guess not! Not with your prosecutor being the number one suspect and all."

"Ray," it was only fair to tell him, "I've been suspended. This is my last shot."

"There's no one you can appeal to?"

"Not in Arlington County, not with Sara Hampton sitting where she is."

"I'll keep you in the loop, Krystal. Without you, we wouldn't have come even this far. I won't mention your situation to my people, either."

She felt intense gratitude and allowed herself to admit that she was really beginning to like Ray Velazquez.

The problem was not killing Murphy. Killing was easy. Bang, bang, you're dead! No, the problem was how to take advantage of it. Of course, it must be done, and the sooner the better. The obnoxious detective's death would eliminate yet another threat, but there was the problem of how to explain it in such a way that the authorities would be thrown completely off the trail.

An accident would be convenient, but arranging "accidents" was really quite difficult. Murphy could slip in the shower, her car could crash, or her apartment could burn down. But the death had to serve the purpose of distancing Sara Hampton from suspicion. An idea was forming, nebulous at first as inspiration often insinuates itself, but the outlines were becoming clearer.

Chapter 43

Thursday passed with agonizing slowness. Krystal did not leave the apartment fearing to miss a call from Velazquez. But none came. The adage that no news is good news did not apply to the current situation and led to all sorts of unhealthy speculation. Had Velazquez failed to convince his bosses? Had he not called because he did not want to disappoint her? By six P.M. she could restrain herself no longer and punched in his number on her phone. It took her directly to voicemail, but she didn't bother to leave a message.

Michael R. Davidson

There was nothing she could do – nothing! And it grated on her. She did not like having to depend on others. But she was virtually powerless without her badge. She had begun to curse Velazquez for his lack of communications skills, and the fresh bottle of Laphroaig on the kitchen counter was beckoning when her phone rang. She lunged across the couch and grabbed it like a drowning man after a life preserver.

The caller i.d. showed Ray Velazquez's number, and the evil thoughts of a moment ago were forgotten. "Ray?" She knew she sounded breathless.

"Where do you live?"

"What?"

"Where do you live?"

"Why?"

"I just checked into the Key Bridge Marriott, and I want to see you. We need to talk."

He was here in Arlington? Hell, yes, she wanted to talk to him! A quick survey of the apartment found it wanting considerable attention before it would be fit for the eyes of others.

"Why don't I come over there? It'll only take a few minutes. Wait for me in the bar on the top floor."

She dashed to the bathroom and took a look at herself in the mirror. The strain of the past couple of days showed all too clearly on her face, and she definitely needed to shower and wash her hair. Repairs were in order. Velazquez would have to wait a little longer. She didn't stop to wonder why improving her appearance was so important for a meeting with a professional colleague.

Forty minutes later she emerged from her apartment building in a black, sleeveless dress with a light sweater around her shoulders against the evening dip in temperature. She cursed the seldom worn high heels that hurt her feet. Why had she bothered? Belatedly she realized this was the same outfit she had worn the last time she'd seen Thomas Stewart. She wasn't sure how she felt about that.

Out of habit she'd placed the S&W .380 in her small purse. She didn't have a concealed carry permit because cops didn't need them, and without a badge she was in violation of the law. But she felt naked without a weapon at hand. Fifteen minutes later she parked at the hotel just across the Key Bridge from Georgetown.

The view over Washington from the top floor of the Marriott was spectacular and even more so at night when the city's alabaster monuments and architecture were illuminated. Velazquez had claimed a table for two near the window, and she studied him before he noticed her arrival. He looked handsomer than ever in a pair of gray slacks and dark blazer. The white shirt with no tie emphasized his tan. He stood when he spotted her and pulled out a chair for her, that infectious Latin lover grin lighting his face.

"Sorry it took a little longer to get here than I thought," she said.

He gave her a frankly appraising leer. "That's OK. It's certainly worth the wait."

She covered her embarrassment at the surge of pleasure his remark caused. "You rat. I've been waiting since yesterday to hear from you. What are you doing up here?"

"Not one for small talk, are you? One of these day's we're going to talk about something besides bloody murder."

"Maybe, but not today. What's going on?"

He shook his head, but the smile lingered. "OK, here's the deal. I explained everything to the boss, including our suspicions about the Hampton woman. We also called the FBI, and the Behavioral Analysis Unit will lend us a hand if we need it. We made a direct request to Knoxville for assistance, as well. And here's the kicker, I'm up here 'unofficially,' which really means undercover."

"So no one from Arlington knows you're here?"

"You got it. Wanna go with me to Knoxville tomorrow?"

It occurred to her that he would not have had to come to Arlington at all but could have travelled directly to Knoxville. Velazquez had gone hundreds of miles out of his way to include her, probably without his boss's permission. "You came all the way up here just so I could go with you, didn't you?"

He might have blushed under his tan, but she wasn't sure. "Well, it started out as your case. I figured we might as well keep it that way. It wouldn't seem fair otherwise."

"Does your department know you came here instead of directly to Knoxville?"

"For the time being, what they don't know won't hurt them."

It was possible that she sat there with her mouth open for several minutes, at least long enough for him to frown and ask, "Krystal, are you all right? You do want to do this, don't you?"

The frustration that had mounted inside her since the Tandy family tragedy burst like a soap bubble that had expanded to its limit. The guilt she felt, whether deserved or not, was a burden she had carried alone, but Velazquez had proven by word and deed that she was not alone, after all. Why hadn't she realized this before?

The release of tension left her struggling for control over unexpected emotions that were triggering certain hormonal responses with specific physiological consequences.

"Of course." Her throat had constricted, and the words came out thick and throaty. *Why was she so bad at this?*

"Great!" he said, "We'll take off first thing in the morning."

"Great," she repeated, "Erm, can we go to your room right now?"

The words escaped from her unexpectedly, taking her, as well as him by surprise, but he was a smart Cuban boy.

Chapter 44

She had made the "walk of shame" more than a couple of times in college, and so it was not an unknown experience to wake up naked in a man's bed. The splash of water reached her through the bathroom door, and she resisted the temptation to join him in the shower. It was not that she regretted spending the night with him nor that their lovemaking had been unsatisfactory. Quite the opposite. The previous evening had been a perfect conjunction of events and emotion that had dissipated her dark mood and given her renewed hope.

They had proceeded without another word to his room, and once inside had shed their clothes and following a passionate embrace had fallen into bed from which they had not ventured the entire night. She had reveled in their lovemaking with a total lack of inhibition.

Her hesitation now was not due to second thoughts, but she did wonder how the added dimension to their relationship would affect their ability to work together. Until last night they had been professional colleagues, two cops working to bring a complicated case to resolution – two equals. Would Velazquez now see her in a different light, treat her differently? Of course, he would. That was inevitable, and the emotional entanglement could get in the way. She knew the stereotype of the *macho* Latin male.

The lines from the classic song by the Shirelles resounded in her head for an instant: "...but will you still love me tomorrow." She was shocked by the involuntary evocation of love, a concept that had eluded her, or more precisely that she had heretofore evaded. But she could not deny that this had felt like more than just a roll in the hay. Was she worried about how Velazquez felt? She berated herself. *This is ridiculous!* She hadn't felt like this since high school. The armor she had worn for years as the tradeoff for building a career had been breached, and the unfamiliar state of confusion left her feeling more than just physically naked.

The sound of running water from the bathroom ceased, and she leapt from the bed to grab a robe, covering herself just in time as Velazquez stepped out of the bathroom. He'd wrapped a towel around his waist and was using another to dry his hair.

He smiled broadly when he saw her and said, "Hey."

"Hey," she said back and felt herself blushing as an unaccustomed heat consumed her body. "Erm, I'm going to take a quick shower, and then we'd better get on our way."

He crossed the room to embrace her, but she turned her head away when he bent to kiss her, struggling to resist the urge to let her robe drop to the floor and press her breasts against his bare chest. "Not now, Ray. We need to go."

Seeing the confusion and disappointment in his face, she quickly added, "I'm sorry, but if we got started again we might never leave this room, and Knoxville is a long way."

He recaptured his smile, stepped back and swept his arm toward the open bathroom door. "All yours," he said, "I'll get dressed."

He's acting like a gentleman, she thought, *I wonder what he's really thinking.*

He followed her in his rental car to her apartment and waited while she changed into her habitual jeans, a cotton polo and sensible shoes. She reached for her pistol and badge before remembering she no longer had them, and then scrounged in a drawer for an inside the belt holster for her S&W. It was still early in the morning, and with luck the roomy Ford Velazquez had rented would take them along the hypotenuse of Virginia's western state line to Knoxville in a little over seven hours. That would put them at the Body Farm around 4:00 PM. As they escaped the suburbs speeding westward on Interstate 66 Krystal could not avoid the memory of the last time she had driven this way to interview a defiant Dawn Tandy.

The highway finally merged onto truck-clotted Interstate 81, taking them south at last through the Shenandoah Valley, spectacular with spring foliage. As Velazquez settled into a maniacally aggressive battle with the 18-wheelers, Krystal sat back and closed her eyes. So they would at long last possess the bullet that had killed Fernie Fernandez. She had no doubt it would match the projectile that had taken Brian Cottrell's life. But so what? By itself the fact that the same gun had been used in the first two murders and that Cottrell's fingerprints on the shell casing from Cynthia's house showed only that all three murders had been committed by the same person. They already had been certain of that. There would be chain of evidence, but it would bring them no closer to proving Sara Hampton's guilt.

It was a piece of evidence they should have had from the very beginning. And the fact that Sara Hampton had engineered the hide-and-seek game they had been playing with Fernandez's corpse added to the circumstantial evidence they were building against her. Regardless, it would be next to impossible to make the case unless the Commonwealth Attorney made another mistake. The video recording of her at Cynthia Cottrell's gate was the strongest evidence they had, and that had been Sara's first mistake. Would she make another? The woman was smart and tough, and she had powerful allies. Krystal and Ray were holding weak cards against a strong hand.

The poker analogy led to another thought. Could Sara be bluffed? So long as the MDPD did not inform Arlington, there was no way for Sara to know what they were doing.

Loosing a steady stream of Hispanic curses at the traffic, Velazquez veered into the right-hand lane and ripped past an 18-wheeler that had been hogging the passing lane. Eighty miles an hour was the norm on I-81 South, but the Cuban was pushing the Ford closer to ninety.

"You'll get a ticket," she said. "This highway is lousy with State cops."

"There should be a law that 18-wheelers can't be in the passing lane. I think I'll propose that to my Senator."

"If we get pulled over, it'll delay our arrival even more."

Reluctantly, he eased his foot off the accelerator, and they fell into the rhythm of the heavy traffic. "You've been pretty quiet other than criticizing my superb driving skills."

"I'm just not sure how all this is going to get us any closer to Sara Hampton." She chewed her lower lip. "I'm thinking she might need prodding."

"Well, at the very least we'll confirm that the judge's murder is connected to the two in Miami."

"But it'll still be circumstantial and won't incriminate Sara. It'll be a good thing to confirm what we've suspected, but without a solid link to her, we'll be right back where we started."

"I think we've progressed way beyond where we started."

Agh! Her post-coital fears were raising their sweaty little heads already! "Keep your eyes on the road and your mind on the case, Ray."

Suitably chastened, he asked, "So, what are you thinking? What kind of 'prodding?'"

"We have to force Sara to make another mistake. This is going to sound crazy to you, but ..." And she outlined what she had been thinking.

When she had finished, he said, "*Puta madre!* You're insane. That could be dangerous in several ways, and it all hinges on the cooperation of someone whose cooperation we can't count on, if I know the type. If it doesn't work you can kiss your job good-bye for sure. Even if it does work, you might be out of a job."

"Yeah, I know," she said glumly, sinking her chin into her chest and crossing her arms. "I know."

Chapter 45

They continued to dissect and re-assemble the idea as Interstate 81 merged into Interstate 40 near Virginia's pointy southwestern tip, and carried them westward into Tennessee toward Knoxville and their destination, the University of Tennessee's William M. Bass Forensic Anthropology Center. The center was housed in a new, red brick building adjoining the campus of the university's medical center overlooking the city of Knoxville on the other side of the Tennessee River.

The Forensic Center was well away from the main medical center complex, near the river's edge and surrounded by several acres of wooded land that Velazquez identified as the area where the bodies were placed for study. Krystal imagined she caught a whiff of decomposition on the afternoon breeze and shuddered. What must it be like when the wind blew in the wrong direction? They parked in a large, almost deserted lot near the Center and walked around to the building entrance.

Velazquez seemed to know his way around and led her directly to the office of the Director, who turned out to be a middle-aged woman named Deanne Springfield dressed in khaki slacks and a checked, flannel shirt. They had phoned ahead to alert her of their arrival, and she greeted them with an enthusiastic, bright smile. "Ray," she said when they entered her office, "it's good to see you again."

He explained, "I was here last year for a course at the National Forensic Academy. It's a training program for cops."

He's just full of surprises! She was irked that he had not explained this before. This was the reason he had won such easy access to the Body Farm.

The formalities concluded, Dr. Springfield invited them to sit while she opened a file folder on her desk. "You're interested in corpse number 2213," she said, and for Krystal's benefit added, "It's our numbering system. It means this is the 22nd corpse inducted this year."

She studied the file for a moment. "I know what you're after, and you're in luck, or maybe we are. The procedure won't interfere with the study of this particular corpse." She looked up at Velazquez.

"Angie Morgan is in charge of this one. I'll call her now to let her know you're here."

"Angie?" For the briefest of moments a look of discomfort crossed Velazquez's face as he shot a wary glance at Krystal.

"Yes, she's studying the differences in decomposition rates between clothed and unclothed corpses."

At that moment there was a light rap on the door and a young woman dressed in olive green one piece coveralls and running shoes entered the office. Her dark hair was pulled back in a ponytail, and the olive green coveralls did nothing to conceal the figure beneath. Her face lit up when she saw Velazquez who had risen at her entrance, "Ray," she exclaimed, "it's great to see you again."

As Dr. Springfield explained, "Angie is one of our brighter grad students. She'll complete her training here in June," the researcher advanced with a welcoming smile, and Velazquez awkwardly accepted her light embrace and peck on the cheek, but his eyes fixed on Krystal.

Non-verbal signals can transmit an incredible amount of information in an instant. *Omigod,* she thought, *they've slept together! I knew this guy was a horndog.* For the first time since they'd met Ray Velazquez was embarrassed.

Oblivious to the little drama that was being played out before her, Dr. Springfield continued, "Angie, would you take over for me now? You know what's needed."

"Sure," said Angie. She addressed Krystal and Velazquez, "Would you like to come with me to 2213's plot?"

Velazquez raised his eyebrows at Krystal, who replied rather too quickly than she would have liked, "Erm, no thanks."

"How about you, Ray?" Angie asked. "It's been a while since you were here."

"No thanks, Angie. I'll wait here with Krystal."

Angie looked appraisingly from one of them to the other, and her mouth turned up at one corner in a mischievous tilt that suggested her intuition was every bit as sharp as Krystal's. "OK," she said, unruffled, "I'll be back in a jiffy."

They retreated to the foyer while Angie headed for the wooded area that hosted the corpses.

"Erm, Angie was one of the instructors for the course I took," said Velazquez.

"I'll be you learned a lot from her."

Krystal's amusement grew in direct proportion to his discomfort.

In a short time Angie was back carrying a large plastic bag that contained a rounded object the size of a human head.

"Got it," announced Angie, holding the bag up as if it were a hunting trophy. Krystal could see bits of hair and the shape of a nose pressing out against the plastic. "I'll take this to the lab. Shouldn't take long. Anyone want to watch?"

No one did.

While they waited Velazquez showed her around the facility. There were classrooms and labs and more people than Krystal expected. She did not miss the fact that the vast majority of students were female. *Velazquez must have been in his element in this place.* And suddenly she was less amused.

The Cuban regained his habitual good nature and manner, but Krystal was a firm believer in gut feelings and suspected that he knew that she knew and vice versa. *But why should I care? I didn't even know him before a couple of weeks ago.*

After a half-hour Angie found them still wandering through the building. She handed a small plastic evidence bag containing a .22 caliber bullet to Velazquez. "Here you are, Ray. I hope this helps."

She led them to the foyer where they signed the appropriate evidence transfer documents and then accompanied them to the door. "Don't hesitate to call if you need anything else, Ray," she said as she gave him a peck on the cheek.

Krystal imagined Angie laughing hysterically as they walked back to the car. Velazquez didn't look at her all the way to the parking lot. She didn't know whether to be angry or amused. She decided on amused. They needed to get on with the case.

They settled into the car, and Velazquez asked, "What now?"

Krystal could not determine whether it was real or imagined, but the sharp tang of decomposition seemed to have found its way into her nostrils and found a place to hide somewhere deep in her sinuses. She couldn't wait to get away from the body farm, this homage to death. "You have to get that bullet back to Miami ASAP. Let's drop the rental at the airport here.

You fly back to Miami, and I'll catch a flight to Washington.

"We could spend the night here and fly out in the morning." It was more a question heavy with hope than a statement.

"Yes, we could do that, but we don't have the luxury of time. Every minute that goes by our hope of bringing this thing to an end gets farther away. The case comes first, Ray."

The hope leaked out of him like air from a punctured balloon and his shoulders slumped in defeat. Krystal could almost feel sorry for him.

"Listen, Krystal ..." he began.

She interrupted, "Ray, come on. What happened last night just ... happened. We've got to keep our heads in the game now."

She could almost see his hormone level dropping as his face arranged itself into a pattern that suggested he was trying to figure her out. He started the car and said, "The airport is only about ten minutes from here."

They dropped the rental at Enterprise and rode the shuttle to the terminal. Delta proved to have a flight leaving at 6:40 that would get Velazquez into Miami at 9:45, and there was an earlier, non-stop flight to Reagan National that would get Krystal back into Washington at 7:30. The trouble was that the $525 one-way ticket would almost deplete her bank account.

"Ray, I'm going to rent another car and drive back tonight. It'll give me time to round out our plan to flush out Sara."

He didn't argue. He promised to call her as soon as the ballistics test was complete, and she left him in the ticket line to catch the shuttle back to the Enterprise lot. They embraced before she left, but with only chaste kisses on the cheek.

Krystal pulled into her apartment parking lot at 1:00 AM Saturday morning. Long solo drives at night are conducive to thought, but do not necessarily produce somnolence at journey's end. She did not sleep well, finally giving up at five in the morning and brewing a pot of coffee. She munched on a piece of toast as she mentally assessed the plan she had disassembled and then reconstructed several times during the drive. In fact, looking at it in the cold light of dawn, she realized it had not changed very much since she had first explained it to Velazquez. The concept had poked through her consciousness like the first crocuses of spring and grown seemingly of its own accord to full maturity. She assumed that her subconscious had gathered the pieces, assessed the possibilities, and drawn the only possible conclusions. Maybe this was what instinct or intuition really was.

Chapter 46

Velazquez called late Saturday afternoon with the forensics results. He'd had the lab working overtime.

"You were right, Krystal. The two slugs match."

"Good. So now we can confirm that this all started up here and not in Florida."

"There's still the possibility that Brian Cottrell hired the killer in Washington."

"I don't think so. It just doesn't make sense, given what happened to Cottrell at the hands of the same person. Anyway, it's too late to chase that goose. I'm going to set things in motion up here."

Concern colored his voice. "The plan? Krystal, that's very dangerous. You can't do this all alone. If you do this, I'm coming up there."

"That's a good idea, but there's something else I need you to do first, something we always intended to follow up on, but never got the chance."

"I'm listening." The alarm was replaced with resignation.

"Can you still check up on the Daddy's Girls angle?"

"Why now? Don't you think things have progressed beyond that? You're stirring up a hornets' nest up there all by yourself."

"I just have a feeling," she said. "Cynthia Cottrell was a Daddy's Girl, and she and Sara Hampton were in school together. Maybe Sara did the same thing. Cynthia had nothing to lose by admitting the association, but Sara's political hopes would be dashed if it were revealed that she was a former semi-prostitute."

"The missing motive," he breathed.

"Bingo."

"I'll get on it right away, but you slow things down up there. "I'll catch a flight and be there Monday."

"I'll set it up for Monday evening."

As soon as he closed the connection she dug out the business card with Tim Reiner's cell phone written on the back. She would call the Washington

Post reporter tomorrow, and she would have to choose her words carefully.

Ray replaced the receiver and checked his watch. It was just after four P.M. It was 70 miles north on I-95 to Palm Beach, and week-end traffic shouldn't slow him down. Krystal's insistence on moving ahead with her plan left him no choice other than to check out her supposition as quickly as possible. He had no idea whether Daddy's Girls even maintained accurate records. He suspected that once girls went off the payroll, their records would be destroyed. This could well be a dead-end.

As he wove the red Porsche in and out of traffic, he wished they had followed up on the Daddy's Girls lead sooner, before Krystal had been called back to Arlington, and he berated himself for the lapse. If her hunch was correct, if a connection were established with Sara Hampton, the case against her would be stronger, and the dangerous tact Krystal now had embarked upon would have been unnecessary. If he dug something up now, he would definitely call Krystal off.

The Porsche hit over a hundred miles per hour whenever he found a stretch of open road ahead.

Annie McGuinness, a former Miami prostitute, was the proprietor of Daddy's Girls. Decades earlier she had discovered the advantages of a perfectly lawful "introduction service" over illegal prostitution. She collected a hefty five-figure up-front "registration fee" from the usually well-to-do men who availed themselves of her services and nothing at all from the girls who derived their own benefits from the relationships. It was a win-win business from which Annie earned a handsome income for her Sub-chapter 'S' Corp, which she reported dutifully to the IRS and paid the appropriate taxes.

The Daddy's Girls "headquarters" turned out to be a modest house in the Westgate sub-division of Palm Beach. The first thing Velazquez noticed was the overflowing mailbox by the door. He rang the bell and rapped loudly but elicited no response. A peek in one of the windows revealed only a darkened interior. Velazquez's scalp prickled with a cop's instinct that something was amiss.

He made a circuit of the house that revealed nothing and returned to the front door. On a hunch, he tried the knob, and the door swung open. His scalp prickled even more, and he drew his weapon and went inside, sweeping to the left and right, but he was greeted by silence and an unpleasant odor that he recognized instantly.

Keeping his gun drawn, he proceeded from room to room through the darkened interior until he found one of the bedrooms that had been converted into an office. On the floor lay the source of the bad odor, a white-haired woman well on in years who had quite obviously been bludgeoned to death. The pool of blood around the corpse was black. Annie McGuinness had obviously been dead for several days.

The office had been ransacked, and the computer was smashed, its hard drive missing. Velazquez released a string of Cuban epithets into the death-laden atmosphere of the room.

Chapter 47

At two o'clock Monday afternoon Dustin Smiley burst into Sara Hampton's office, his face pink and his eyes round with something bordering on terror. Such unannounced interruptions of the Commonwealth Attorney were rare, and she met the arrival with annoyance.

"Whatever this is about, it'd better be important, Dustin," she addressed the interloping head of Media Relations who practically skidded to a stop in front of her desk. She did not invite him to sit.

"Sara," he said this with an inward take of breath that made her name sound like the last gasp of a dying man. She gave him a sharp look as she belatedly realized the man was in a state of high agitation.

He gulped in some more air and continued. "I just received a call from Tim Reiner at the Post. You need to hear this."

"Sit down, Dustin, catch your breath. I'm listening." A hollowness began to carve a space in her chest. Whatever it was, Smiley's demeanor signaled nothing good. "What did Reiner want?"

"That's the thing," said Smiley, his words tumbling over one another. "He didn't want anything from us. He actually was doing us a favor, alerting us to trouble. The relations we have with the press are two-way. We give them information, and they reciprocate when it's really important. I work hard to maintain that kind of relationship."

He paused, expecting praise.

"Get to the point, Dustin."

"You're not going to like it, Sara. Everyone knows about Krystal Murphy's situation, how she's gotten herself in bad odor with everyone in the department, what a self-centered trouble maker she is ..."

The mention of Murphy's name set Sara on edge. The hollowness in her chest began to fill with cold dread. *What had that bitch done now?*

"What did Reiner want?" She repeated the question.

"It's crazy. Reiner said Murphy called him this morning and asked to meet with him, said she had information that should be made public, information about you, Sara!"

Sara almost rose from her chair, but willed herself to remain calm, clenching her fists so hard her nails bit into her palm. "What did she say about me?" she demanded.

"She told him she didn't want to go into detail on the phone. That's why she wanted a meeting. Reiner wanted to check with me to see if I had any idea what Murphy was talking about. He said she had hinted that she had information about you that would make the front page. Reporters like Reiner can't resist leads like that, but he's a cautious sort who tries to double check everything, and he'd already heard over the grapevine that Murphy had been put on administrative leave. He was sniffing around to see if something was brewing here that concerned you, whether she was on a tear to hurt you."

"And what did you say?"

"I told him Murphy has a lot of black marks against her and is in real trouble with the department, and confirmed that she's been put on indefinite suspension for insubordination. I know I shouldn't have told him so much about internal affairs, but I didn't want him to think Murphy was in any way reliable, especially now."

"Have they met yet?"

"No. Reiner agreed to a meeting tonight at her apartment. He wanted some time to do some background before seeing her. He was very grateful for what I told him about Murphy."

Sara drummed her fingers on the desktop. "You did well, Dustin. I won't forget this. Murphy may well be slightly unbalanced. She's haunted by what happened to the Tandy family while she was in Miami, despite the undeniable likelihood that it was Dawn Tandy who murdered Judge Fernandez. She's displayed signs of instability for some time now, and the department is planning to recommend she receive psychiatric counseling. She apparently sees me as the cause of her troubles."

"But what can we do about Reiner?"

"Leave that to me for now, Dustin. And be sure to let me know if you hear from Reiner again."

"Of course, Sara. I'm so sorry about this. I'll be sure to keep you informed." In response to the Commonwealth Attorney's calm reaction to the news, Smiley had regained his composure. Sara Hampton was a person on the way up, and her gratitude was valuable. She would need loyal people on her staff in the future. Dustin Smiley would be an excellent press aide to a congresswoman or senator.

As soon as Smiley left the office, Sara picked up the phone. Krystal Murphy could not possibly have any proof of Sara's guilt, but even a hint of scandal in the press could spoil her political ambitions forever. Her call was answered, and she said, "Come see me right now. We have a problem."

Chapter 48

By late Monday afternoon, Velazquez still hadn't shown up, and Krystal was beginning to regret that she had no more effective weapon at hand than the S&W .380. It was a nice little automatic, especially for back-up, easily concealed and quite accurate. But the .380, even with hollow point rounds, lacked the knock-down stopping power of a .45 or even a 9mm. But such guns were expensive, and she had made do with the service Beretta PX4 Storm that Captain Jefferson had confiscated. She missed its weight on her belt.

One reason for her concern about firepower was that Velazquez had been delayed; the other was the dark-colored car parked across from her building's entrance. She had set up her observation post by her front window and had camped out there in an over-stuffed chair for most of the afternoon. The car made its first appearance around five P.M. cruising slowly southward on North Barton towards 10th St, and then again ten minutes later as it circled the block. It was now parked across the street in front of Barton Park and had not moved for the last hour. No one had gotten out of the car, and its tinted windows prevented her from seeing inside.

The remainder of the afternoon stretched toward evening like a dark path through a dark forest to an uncertain destination. And this was the second reason for concern. Velazquez finally called to warn her that dealing with the situation in Palm Beach had taken most of the morning, and he was having trouble getting on a flight to Washington.

He had called Saturday night to inform her of what he had found in Palm Beach and then again on Sunday to fill her in on forensic details. She should not have been surprised. If all the suspicion she had piled onto Sara Hampton was correct, the Commonwealth Attorney was a clever and ruthless killer and a formidable opponent, but when had she had time to murder Annie McGuinness? According to Velazquez, the woman had been dead for at least three days, meaning she had died the same day as their visit to the Body Farm, and Krystal was fairly certain that Sara had been in Arlington at the time. In any event, it stretched credulity that Sara would have risked another lightning trip to Florida. The murder of the Daddy's Girls founder, the fact that the woman had been bludgeoned to death, was inconsistent with the manner in which Fernandez and the others had died and raised legitimate doubt.   Pimping by whatever name was a dangerous business, after all. But if her conjecture about Sara Hampton was correct, and she was confident it was, the coincidence was just too neat to discard.

The knock on the door could come at any time and her confidence was shrinking with every second that hurtled toward whatever was going to happen tonight. Without Velazquez her plan was fraught with uncertainty and danger, but things already were in motion.

Would Sara come for her alone or wait until Tim Reiner showed up at the apartment this evening? She hated the idea of putting Reiner in such a situation. She'd insisted that they meet in her apartment because it was a venue she controlled where Velazquez could remain hidden until the critical moment. She should call Reiner and warn him off.

The uncertainty about Sara's reaction to the line she had cast in her direction with the call to Tim Reiner added to her mounting tension. It was quite possible that nothing would come of her plan at all. Despite watching Krystal's apartment, Sara might decide not to take the bait. The woman was wily. And she was an experienced attorney and prosecutor. She knew what it took to make a case and had been successful to date in concealing her guilt.   The question was how far would she go to prevent even an unprovable, but very public blemish on her record?

It was an old saw that criminals always return to the scene of their crime. Krystal's experience had taught her that every criminal fears making a mistake that will lead to arrest and incarceration, and Sara Hampton would be no different. If she were guilty Sara would be unable to ignore the possibility, however unlikely, that Krystal had uncovered new evidence. And that curiosity would be her undoing ... hopefully.

Lost in a kaleidoscope of doubts, she was startled by a knock at the door. She looked at her watch. Tim Reiner had arrived for the scheduled meeting at 6:00 PM. It was long past the time to call the whole thing off.

The reporter looked the same as when she had last seen him, except that today Mick Jagger's tongue showed redly through his open blazer from the Rolling Stones logo on the front of his T-shirt.

"Hi, Krystal," he said, as though he had known her all his life, and slouched through the door. She closed it behind him and ushered him to the sofa.

She had no idea how long they would have to wait, so she began to repeat what she had told him the day before on the phone, a recitation no reporter worth his salt could resist, but she also emphasized the risk, especially without the back-up she had been counting on from Velazquez. "You do understand how dangerous this will be?"

He wasn't pleased by the news. "It's too late now, anyway. After my call to Smiley, we're in this together, whether I like it or not." He spread one arm across the back of the sofa. "You have anything to drink?"

"Erm, sure. Scotch ok?"

"A girl after my own heart." He attempted a devil-may-care smile.

She retrieved the bottle of Laphroaig from under the sink and grabbed a couple of short glasses. Drinks in hand, they both settled back on the sofa. Reiner raised his glass toward her, and they clinked, before sipping the amber liquid. Krystal allowed only a drop to pass her lips. Her reactions would have to be sharp today.

He saluted her with his glass. "This is good stuff, the sign of an educated palate."

They were interrupted by a firm knock at the door, and Krystal nearly dropped her glass. Sara had waited for Reiner to arrive and now wasn't wasting any time. It began.

She shot a cautionary glance at the reporter and stepped toward the door. The hairs on the back of her neck stood at attention as an involuntary shiver coursed down her spine. Now was not the time for second thoughts, but they crowded in on her nonetheless. What if she had not thought of everything? She envisioned Sara Hampton on the other side of the door with Brian Cottrell's big .45 aimed directly at it. A few pulls on the trigger and the big slugs could rip through the door and tear her in two. She suddenly wished she had her S&W in hand, but it was too late now. Everything depended on getting Sara to talk before she tried anything deadly.

The Commonwealth Attorney would be curious, would want to know what new evidence she might be up against. The plan hinged on this.

Sarah stood to one side of the door and said, "Who is it?"

The voice that answered was a surprise. "It's Captain Jefferson, Krystal. Open the door."

She rolled a calf's eye at Reiner, still on the sofa, who raised a quizzical eyebrow, but looked relieved.

What the hell? Jefferson would spoil everything. That rat Smiley must have talked to him. She resigned herself to an unpleasant confrontation with her boss and a failed plan.

Jefferson was standing in the hallway tapping his foot when she swung the door open. He saw Reiner over her shoulder and shook his head in disgust. "What the hell is going on here?"

Striding past her into the room, Jefferson confronted the reporter. "What has she been saying, Reiner?

The reported took a calm sip of the scotch before replying. "There appears to be important new evidence in the Fernandez case that points to a person we would least expect to be a murderer. Lieutenant Murphy thinks it should be made public, and I'm just the guy to do it."

Jefferson pivoted to face Krystal. "What's he talking about? What new evidence? You are officially on suspension, you know. Now, tell me what's going on here. Are you trying to get even by lying to the press?"

"I can't say, Marty. I really can't. I can't trust you to do the right thing anymore." As angry as he appeared, she might be able to convince Jefferson to leave. The possibility that Sara would appear was dimming.

Jefferson turned again to Reiner. "What did she tell you? What new evidence? Think about who you're talking to. This woman has some sort of personal vendetta against the Commonwealth Attorney, and I intend to put a stop to this foolishness right now."

Reiner sipped the scotch again, then smacked his lips, and gave Jefferson a lopsided grin. Standing up to officialdom was how he buttered his bread. "I said nothing about Sara Hampton, Captain, and I'm not about to tell you what my source told me in confidence. That's the way it works."

Krystal was impressed by the reporter's *sang froid.*

"Oh, I think you'll tell me," growled Jefferson as he stepped a few paces away from Krystal. "I think you'll both tell me."

He reached into his jacket and withdrew a pistol. Pointing it at Krystal, he instructed her to sit next to Reiner on the sofa.

She was startled. "Marty, what the hell ..."

Reiner sat up straight and would have risen to his feet had not Jefferson swung the gun in his direction. "Just stay where you are. I'm not playing games, Reiner. You're going to tell me what I want to know, both of you."

"Or what?" asked Krystal as she settled onto the sofa next to Reiner.

"Or I'll shoot one of you and make the other talk."

Her astonishment must have been evident because Jefferson barked a laugh that had nothing to do with the soft-spoken, ambitious police officer she had known. She would never have imagined Marty Jefferson acting this way. But here he was with a weapon trained on her and the reporter.

"What's going on here, Marty?"

"I'll ask the questions, Krystal, if you don't mind."

It crashed into place - Sara was playing a wild card that Krystal had not, could not have anticipated, a joker in the deck. Sara had a confederate. She could now guess who had killed the woman in Palm Beach.

"You're working with her, aren't you?"

A small smile twitched one corner of his mouth. "Politics make for strange bedfellows, don't they?"

"Politics?" Krystal was momentarily confused.

Jefferson's lips mirthlessly twitched again, but his eyes remained deadly serious and the gun did not waver. "And bedfellows," he said with another strange, barking laugh.

"You and Sara have been sleeping together!?" Thinking back to the days before the Fernandez murder, Krystal could not believe that Sara, the wife and mother of two, could have been carrying on an affair.

"For several months now."

So there it was. Jefferson had been working with Sara from the beginning, helping her sweep the

Fernandez case under the rug. Probably leaking the video cassettes to Reiner. Trying to make the body disappear. Insisting that she drop the case ... and committing murder himself. The man had nothing to lose now.

Jefferson evidently was beginning to enjoy himself, intoxicated by the ambrosia of power, and some of his old, casual swagger returned. Lifting the mask was invigorating, liberating him from the burden of lies he had had to maintain. "Oh, I'm no romantic fool. I know she'll never leave her husband, and I don't really care. But Sara is an ambitious woman, and she knows how to use men to advance her career. She always has, after all. When she's elected, I'll become her chief of staff, and it's onward and upward from there." He abruptly caught himself and the murderous gleam returned to his eyes.

"But enough about me. Now, you're going to tell me all about this new evidence."

"So you can quash it," breathed Krystal.

"That's right."

"And what about us?" she asked.

"Oh, I have that all worked out. You see this gun in my hand? It's your own service weapon, Krystal, the one I made you turn in. Before I leave tonight you will have killed Mr. Reiner here and then committed suicide." He switched his gaze to the reporter. "You'll get your front page story, Reiner, but not the one you were planning."

Keeping the gun trained on the reporter, he continued, "I can make it quick and painless or slow and painful, Reiner. Murphy here has to die with a single bullet to the brain, a murder-suicide. She has every reason to kill you – that story about Dawn Tandy you wrote. You can thank me, by the way, for dropping those discs over the transom. But I can take more time with you, if I have to. Talk and die quickly, or I'll start with your knees, and in the end you'll talk anyway."

The antagonist was not the one she had expected, but the scene was developing just as Krystal had envisioned it -- Jefferson would not kill anyone until he had learned what the "new evidence" was, how much it threatened him and Sara. Without the guarantee of an armed Velazquez lurking in the bedroom, she decided things had gone far enough. With Jefferson's attention focused on Reiner, she slipped her hand between the cushions of the sofa and wrapped her fingers around the reassuring solidity of the S&W she had pre-positioned there.

As she withdrew the pistol the movement caught Jefferson's eye and he swung in her direction, but she already had her weapon trained on him. Years of practice, both in the military and the police made her action automatic and deadly. Normally she would have aimed center mass, but the large pistol in Jefferson's hand and her lack of full confidence that the .380 would knock him down forced her to concentrate on a different target. She fired twice in quick succession, and the hollow point Hornady Critical Defense rounds slammed into Jefferson's shoulder at a thousand feet per second.

The gun fell from Jefferson's hand as his arm flopped uselessly to his side, his shoulder shredded by the especially destructive rounds that had impacted within centimeters of one another and expanded in his flesh and bone. Krystal had been correct – the .380 slugs had not knocked him down. For the first time in the years she had known him, surprise and confusion marked his face. As the roar of the reports reverberated off the walls, he stood there swaying for a moment, still not understanding what had happened. He looked down uncomprehendingly at his useless arm, the sleeve of his jacket now drenched in blood, and then with a muffled cry dropped to his knees to scramble frantically with his good hand for the pistol he had dropped.

As Reiner looked on with something between horror and relief, Krystal leapt to her feet and kicked the pistol away from the wounded man who then crumpled to the floor grasping his shoulder. To the reporter she said, "Call 911. We need an ambulance over here right away. He's losing a lot of blood. Tell them to notify police, too. Then get a towel from the bathroom and get over here to put pressure on the wound."

When Reiner did not move immediately, she repeated the order more loudly, and the man finally responded, going through the motions of the phone call like an automaton. Despite her having warned him beforehand of what could happen, he was in almost as much shock as Jefferson.

While Reiner was retrieving the towels, someone began banging thunderously at the door. Krystal grabbed the Beretta Jefferson had dropped from the floor and faced the door. "Who is it?"

Chapter 49

She opened the door to a grim-visaged Ray Velazquez, pistol drawn, and tensed for action. "I heard the shots," he said, "What the hell happened?"

He looked past Krystal to see Tim Reiner with an already crimson soaked towel doing his best to staunch the flow of blood from the prone body on the floor. "Don't you think I'd better come in so we can close the door?" Velazquez holstered his weapon.

Reiner looked up from his task. "This must be your cop friend from Miami. You're a little late, aren't you?"

"Ray," said Krystal, "this is Tim Reiner, the reporter who's been helping us." She waved vaguely in the direction of Jefferson and the stain he was leaking onto the carpet. "And this is Captain Marty Jefferson of the Arlington County Police – my boss."

Velazquez had finally caught a flight and driven frantically from the airport and raced into the apartment building, knowing how late he was. Unfazed by Reiner's criticism, he knelt for a closer examination of Jefferson. "I thought we were expecting a woman."

"She sent her boyfriend instead," said Krystal, "and I'm pretty sure he's your Daddy's Girls killer."

At this, Jefferson raised his head and said through teeth gritted in pain, "There's no way you can prove that."

The shock had worn off, and Jefferson was feeling the pain from his wounds. Krystal knelt beside him so she could be certain he heard every word.

"Maybe, maybe not, Marty. You don't mind if I call you Marty now, do you? But Reiner and I can both press charges of attempted murder against you, and you did admit to working with Sara Hampton while you were holding a gun on us. All of that should add up to a nice long prison sentence or perhaps even the death penalty."

She pointed to Velazquez. "This is Detective Ray Velazquez from the Miami-Dade Police. His investigation of the Daddy's Girls murder scene turned up some interesting evidence," she lied.

Picking up on Krystal's tack, Velazquez said, "She's right, Jefferson. There's no way out for you. And we have the death penalty in Florida, too."

Experience had taught Krystal that the very nature of committing an illegal act creates a sense of guilt, and guilt begets doubt, and doubt begets fear of discovery. There are hardened criminals who appear to have no conscience, but science says otherwise. She'd recently read an article by some British researchers who discovered a region of the brain called the "lateral frontal pole" that they claimed imparts a sense of right and wrong to everyone. Only humans possess this Brussels sprout sized organ that supposedly connects our brains to morality. So everyone knows very clearly when they have done wrong. Some held to the belief that criminals subconsciously want to be punished, but Krystal thought that was taking a theory too far.

Captain Marty Jefferson had this capacity in abundance, and given the extent to which he had screwed up today, it was not difficult for him to believe he had screwed up in Florida, as well. As a cop, he'd seen such scenarios played out many times. "Can we make a deal?" he asked.

Chapter 50

The wail of a siren outside signaled the arrival of the ambulance Reiner had called.

Krystal wanted to squeeze all the information she could out of Jefferson before he was taken away and had a chance to think and lawyer up. She especially wanted Tim Reiner to hear it.

The reporter from the *Washington Post* had been a willing accomplice to the plan to entrap Sara. Her proposal was as surprising as it had been intriguing. Krystal had sought his help out of desperation borne of a lack of other allies. Going for broke, she left nothing out when she described to him the way the

Fernandez murder investigation had developed and what she and Ray Velazquez had concluded. Her allegations regarding the Commonwealth Attorney strained credulity, but Reiner could not help but agree that the suspended detective had grounds for her suspicions.

There was little for him to lose, really. If the entrapment scheme did not produce proof of Hampton's guilt, Reiner would lose nothing while gaining some fascinating background on what was happening inside the Arlington County Police Department. If, on the other hand, the Commonwealth Attorney were to be exposed as a cold-blooded killer, he would serve as a witness against her and at the same time win exclusive rights to a story that could well bring him a Pulitzer. It was worth taking a risk on a spring evening.

Reiner had not expected to come so close to death, but as he explained to Krystal, he'd spent two tours in Afghanistan embedded with the troops, and guns were not foreign to his experience. Krystal gained a new respect for members of the press, at least where Reiner was concerned.

Still kneeling beside Jefferson while the reporter pressed a towel to the wounded man's shoulder, Krystal nodded up to Velazquez. "Can you go out to the curb and guide the paramedics up here? And take your time. I want a couple more words here."

Velazquez shrugged. Krystal deserved the chance to drag more information out of Jefferson.. There was always the possibility that the s.o.b. would change his mind once he was patched up and in hospital. "Sure." He raised his voice so as not to leave the wounded man in doubt about his ultimate fate. "I can't wait to get him to Florida."

He stepped out into the corridor that had been brightly lit when he came in but now was dark. "Hey," he started, but before he could finish the sentence there was a flash and the report of a pistol from the darkness. With a moan, the Miami detective slumped against the doorframe and slid to the floor, downed by the impact of the large caliber bullet in his chest.

Her combat training kicked in, and Krystal reacted immediately. The Beretta was still in her hand. She mentally kicked herself for letting her guard down. Jefferson had not come alone.

Sara Hampton emerged wild eyed from the darkness and stood framed in the doorway, a very large automatic pistol held with both hands before her. Her face was white and so contorted with rage and fear that she was almost unrecognizable as she swung the pistol around searching for a target.

From the floor Jefferson screamed, "Shoot her, shoot her now!" and pointed toward Krystal with his good arm.

Sara swung the pistol, bug-eyed in her direction, and Krystal raised the Beretta and pulled the trigger twice. This time she did not divert her aim from center mass, and the .45 caliber rounds slammed into Sara's chest with devastating force, knocking the slightly built woman completely off her feet. She landed on top of Velazquez's legs, and lay still.

Chapter 51

It was like being under water. Time had become somehow distorted as she went through the motions of shooting Sara Hampton, seeing every detail with preternatural clarity, like a sidereal slideshow. As the double booms of the pistol's reports faded, Tim Reiner remained frozen where he knelt beside Jefferson. Things had happened so fast that he had not had time to react, and now he stared in disbelief at the two bodies sprawled in the open doorway.

Real time reasserted itself, and the present crashed into her with the force of a freight train. She remembered to breathe. With a cry, Krystal leapt to the doorway, where she roughly rolled the woman's inert body off of Velazquez. His chest was covered in blood. Frantic, she ripped his shirt open to reveal the wound.

He was breathing, taking in air in shallow gasps, alive but fading. His eyes were open, and she wasn't sure he was seeing anything until she realized his eyes were focused on her. A quick examination of his chest revealed the entry wound from which frothy blood was issuing.

The frothy appearance of the blood was the classic sign of a sucking chest wound. The bullet had penetrated his lung, and without immediate treatment he could die, drowned in his own blood. Krystal applied pressure to the wound with one hand while waving at Reiner with the other.

She didn't even notice the doors to other apartments opening and the heads of her neighbors poking timidly around doorframes.

"Reiner!"

When he didn't react, she screamed at him. "Reiner! Snap out of it." .

The reporter finally recognized that she was shouting at him.

"Reiner, go to the kitchen and look in the drawer to the right of the sink. Bring me the Saran wrap!"

Reiner hesitated with a glance down at where he still held the towel over Jefferson's shattered shoulder. Krystal screamed at him again. "Forget that sonuvabitch, and get me the damned Saran wrap!"

When Reiner finally headed for the kitchen, Jefferson tried to rise. Krystal picked up her pistol from the floor beside Velazquez and pointed it at her former boss. "Move again, Marty, just a little, and I'll blow your fucking head off!"

Reiner hurried out from the kitchen with the red box of plastic wrap, and Krystal instructed him to tear off a square. He handed the thin plastic sheet to her, and she placed it over the wound in Velazquez's chest, holding it tightly down around the edges to create an airtight seal that was made imperfect by the slippery blood.

Only seconds had passed, but time had become a precious commodity that could not be wasted. The ambulance they had summoned for Jefferson was downstairs, she knew, and she ordered Reiner to fetch the EMT's as fast as he could. Keeping the pressure on Velazquez's chest, she rolled him onto his side, so the side of his chest with the wound was closest to the floor. This would prevent his good lung from filling with blood.

Thanks to the airtight seal, Velazquez's breathing eased. On the floor beside him lay Sara Hampton's body. The look frozen on her face was one of terminal surprise. In death her eyes remained open and staring, perhaps at a future now lost in an eternity where political ambition counted for little.

Velazquez's eyes focused on the body. "She shot me?" Even through the pain his voice was disbelieving.

Elated that he was talking, albeit with difficulty, Krystal replied, "Yes, she did."

"And you shot her?"

"Yes, I did."

"Is she dead?"

"Yes, she is."

"Good."

"Am I going to die?"

"If you do, I'll never forgive you."

There was the briefest of a flash of those white teeth that hovered undecided between a smile and a grimace. "I'll do my best not to disappoint you," he said.

There was a distant ding from the elevator at the end of the corridor followed by the tramp of a lot of feet in a lot of hurry as the EMT's and several police with guns drawn rushed toward them.

As soon as he spotted the Arlington County cops, Jefferson yelled, "Arrest that woman! She just killed the Commonwealth Attorney!"

Chapter 52

The cops were momentarily bewildered as they took in the mayhem that lay before them, trying to make sense of what they saw. Then, recognizing the corpse of the Commonwealth Attorney, plus the figure of the wounded police captain on the floor of the apartment, they did what cops do, what Krystal herself would have done, and ordered her to raise her arms above her head.

"I've got a sucking chest wound here," she shouted over her shoulder, "and it needs pressure."

The cops also recognized Krystal, but in response to Jefferson's persistent bellowing, two of them grabbed her roughly, twisting her arms behind her back and yanking her to her feet despite her protests.

Casting a desperate eye toward the EMT's, she yelled, "Take care of him, for Heaven's sake!"

She didn't resist as the cops dragged her away from the bodies on the floor, retrieved the two pistols, and gave the EMT's the all clear signal to move in. One of them looked up from Velazquez and said, "Good work with the plastic wrap," before bending to back to work.

Another medic was examining Jefferson who was spouting orders to take Krystal away and to arrest Tim Reiner, who had ceded his place at Jefferson's side. He stood, still holding the bloody towel, trying to make sense of what was happening. The reporter might not have lightning reactions to being shot at, but he was no slouch when it came to assessing a situation and coming up with the right words to describe it.

When a cop closed in on him, handcuffs in hand, Reiner said, "Jefferson's a goddamn liar. He was going to kill us, and Murphy shot Hampton in self-defense after Hampton shot the man they're treating out there. Hampton barged in here waving a humongous gun."

The cop paused, confused, and Jefferson tried to raise himself again but was easily restrained by the EMT who had taken Reiner's place. He did manage to repeat his order to arrest Reiner and the cop resumed his advance, instructing Reiner to turn around and extend his arms behind his back.

While this was going on Krystal, whose hands already had been cuffed, was arguing her case in an entirely unladylike manner with the cops in the hallway while Velazquez, struggling to recover his strength, supported her story in a weak voice.

"I'm Detective Velazquez of the Miami-Dade P.D., and I've been working this case with Detective Murphy here. Listen to her. You guys are going to look like a bunch of first class assholes if you don't. Your Commonwealth Attorney here was goddamned serial killer!"

"And I can prove it," Reiner's voice cut through the confusion. By now he too had been cuffed. To the policeman who was gripping his arm he said, "If you reach into my inside jacket pocket you'll find a digital recorder. If you listen to the recording, you'll see we're telling the truth."

In the end, the cops decided to leave the cuffs on Krystal and Reiner while they took them to headquarters where things could be sorted out under calmer conditions. Velazquez and Jefferson shared an uncomfortable ride together in the back of the ambulance. The nearest hospital was at Georgetown University, just across the river from Arlington.

Chapter 53

The violent death of the Commonwealth Attorney and the wounding of a police Captain added up to sufficient motivation for the Arlington County Police officer on duty to notify Chief of Police Everett Fogerty, who decided it would be prudent to get to police headquarters as soon as possible. The Chief was in no doubt that his department would soon be embroiled in a public relations shit storm of gargantuan proportions. When he learned that the shooter was Krystal Murphy, Fogerty was doubly enraged. Sara Hampton had warned him days earlier that the young, female detective was fixated on the

Fernandez case to the point of becoming seriously unbalanced. He had agreed with her and Captain Jefferson's recommendations that Murphy should be put on indefinite administrative leave and ordered to undergo a psychiatric examination.

When he arrived at the Department he found Murphy, *Washington Post* reporter Tim Reiner, and a tall, African-American man in an expensive suit waiting at the table in the interrogation room. Fuming, he slammed the door behind him and glared at Murphy. "What the hell have you done, Murphy?"

Before she could answer, the man in the suit interjected, "Chief Fogerty, before we go any farther, I think you should listen to a recording made earlier this evening at Detective Murphy's apartment."

"Who the hell are you?"

"My name is Lawrence Fisherman. I'm an attorney for the *Post*. For the purposes of this matter, Detective Murphy has agreed to allow me to represent her interests, as well." Fisherman placed Reiner's pocket recorder in the middle of the table. "Until you've listened to this, I've instructed my clients not to say a word."

Stymied, Fogerty sank heavily into one of the chairs at the table. The attorney pushed a button on the recorder.

Ten minutes later, Fogerty sat white faced and at an abnormal loss for words. The attorney quietly said, "Chief Fogerty, tomorrow morning Mr. Reiner here will have all of this on the front page. Undoubtedly, it will go national immediately, and we expect extensive television coverage, as well. There is no doubt that this is a "60 Minutes" kind of story. The way your department handles things will be a big part of that story. Mr. Reiner's testimony, substantiated by the recording, leaves no doubt that Detective Murphy acted purely in self-defense. May I suggest that the handcuffs be removed from my clients without delay?"

Fogerty's brows collided in thought as he considered his options. He was a careful man who always thought before he spoke. "I'll order them released immediately after they've provided written statements. The *Post* may count upon the Department's full cooperation, as well as my own. Your clients will not be treated as suspects in any way." He took a deep breath and loosened his collar. "As a matter of fact, I was becoming suspicious of the vendetta that Commonwealth Attorney Hampton and Captain Jefferson seemed to be waging against Detective Murphy. I only wish there had been time to have Internal Affairs look into it before all of this happened."

Krystal started to say something, but Fogerty cut her off, his voice smooth as glass. "You are to be commended, Detective, for your perseverance and bravery in the face of deadly force. I won't forget." He pronounced the last three words with special emphasis.

For once, Krystal was speechless.

As soon as they were released, she headed across Key Bridge to the Georgetown University Hospital. Velazquez was out of surgery and recuperating in the intensive care unit. They wouldn't let her into the unit, but she exacted a promise from the supervising nurse to let her know the moment he woke up ... if he woke up. Chest wounds could be tricky, but the nurse said the surgery had gone well, in large part thanks to someone having sealed the wound with Saran Wrap.

She wondered who had coined the phrase, "waiting room." Such places are for those who must wait on outcomes they cannot control. "Waiting" connotes a category of helplessness and complete dependence on strangers for the lives of their loved ones. Would the temporary inhabitants feel any better if it were called a 'lounge' instead? No, that would be disrespectful.

Tonight the place was empty except for an older couple in one corner with stricken looks on their faces holding hands. Occasionally, they would put their heads together and pray, placing their hopes beyond the hands of the surgeons and technology.

Krystal was engulfed by a sense of *déjà vu*. The last time she had been in a hospital was to visit Thomas Stewart when they brought him back. While the doctors' attention had been focused on the head injury, death's accomplice, a tiny, undetected piece of shrapnel half the size of a fingernail, had stopped Thomas's heart forever. And now Ray Velazquez had a hole in his chest from a .45 caliber bullet that had torn into him at supersonic velocity to tear flesh, break

Michael R. Davidson

bones, and shred organs. All the confusion and emotion that Velazquez had aroused in her washed over her like storm waves against a rocky shore, crashing against her, eroding the wall she had built around herself and carrying huge chunks of it out to sea. All of this for a Miami cop she had known only for days.

Marty Jefferson was in the same hospital chained to a bed with an around-the-clock guard. Marty's connivance with Sara had been a surprise, but looking back, she couldn't believe that her instinct had failed her in his case, and she heaped more guilt upon herself.

Faced with the finality of Sara's death, aware of Reiner's recording, and fearful of Florida justice, Jefferson had made a deal, accepting prison over death, and confessed the entire affair. Using alias documents he had from an undercover operation, he flew to Palm Beach and murdered Annie McGuinness. Sara had feared that some record of her past as a Daddy's Girl might still exist, and in any case, Annie knew her. Sara had insisted on eliminating anyone who might remember.

That she had been right about Sara Hampton, even that she had put the murderess down, was anti-climactic now, as she waited. The guilty deserve punishment, but the innocents who perish by their hand do not get "justice." Justice might matter to "society," but the victims don't really give a damn. They're dead forever. Wasn't it the very nature of homicide investigations that the finality of death was a prerequisite, the beginning rather than the end, leaving them to look backwards rather than forward?

Dawn Tandy would never finish college, never play on an Olympic soccer team, never escape the squalor and despair into which her family had fallen and that in the end had killed them all. "Justice" was a relative term.

If there were any real justice in the world, Ray Velazquez would walk out of the hospital alive and whole. That was what she hoped for more than anything. It would be a sort of redemption, something positive left over from the pain.

End

Afterword

I really like Krystal Murphy. She first appeared in her role as a stubborn Arlington County cop in my second book, "Incubus," and figured even more prominently in "The Incubus Vendetta," where she had to battle a vicious serial killer. I thought she deserved her own book, and here it is. Krystal may have a few more stories in her.

Special thanks are due to my good friends Ray Velazquez, Bob Hammond, and Enrique Perez for allowing me to use their names in Krystal's story.

Gratitude also goes out to my wife, Alma, for her patience as I spent hours at the keyboard, and to Thomas Davidson, Clabe Taylor, and David Edgerton Gates for the kindness of reading early drafts and providing invaluable advice.

All authors crave feed-back and live or die by word of mouth. Hopefully you enjoyed this story, and if you did, it would be an act of kindness and very much appreciated if you were to leave a customer review at Amazon.com, even if only a couple of lines.

Stay in touch and up-to-date at

www.michaelrdavidson.com

The Author

Michael R. Davidson was raised in the Mid-West. Heeding President Kennedy's call for more young Americans to learn Russian he studied the language, and military service took him to the White House where he served as translator for the Moscow-Washington "Hotline." His language abilities attracted the attention of the Central Intelligence Agency, and following his military service Mr. Davidson spent the next 28 years as a Clandestine Services officer. Seventeen of those years were spent abroad in a variety of sensitive posts working against the Soviet Union and the Warsaw Pact. In the private sector he worked as a business owner and security and economic development consultant before devoting full time to his writing.

Also by Michael R. Davidson

Did the Cold War end or did the KGB find a way to retain its power and dominate the new Russian Federation? "Harry's Rules" is an espionage thriller set against the backdrop of post-Soviet Russia in the early 1990's.

Who killed President John F. Kennedy? A long buried secret that could change the course of history draws murder to a quiet Washington suburb. Only an exiled CIA officer can solve a mystery that both the White House and the Kremlin will protect at all costs.

Revenge is said to be a dish best served cold. A suicide bomber and a serial killer are the instruments chosen by a deposed Russian president.

But his targets are anything but helpless.

Find them all at: www.michaelrdavidson.com
All books also available at Amazon.com

THE CALIPHATE SERIES

THE INQUISITOR AND THE MAIDEN - Disillusioned by Spain's falling fortunes in the 30-Years-War, Eduardo Macías returns home. His reputation as a valorous soldier wins him the position of Captain of the Santa Hermandad, a Spanish force charged with protecting the people and maintaining the law. He is forced to accept a mission by officials of the Holy Inquisition to investigate a charge of heresy against a nobleman with royal ties. What he discovers places Eduardo at odds with the Inquisition, and he must decide between honor and excommunication.

RETRIBUTION – The saga that began in 1492 continues into the turbulent present. An ancient enemy threatens the world with nuclear terror, and CIA officer Robert Strachey and his friend Spanish Police inspector Alberto Macías find themselves in a race against time to avert a holocaust.

Find them all at: www.michaelrdavidson.com
All books also available at Amazon.com